# The Ex-Factor

# The Ex-Factor

## Andrea Semple

KENSINGTON BOOKS

http://www.kensingtonbooks.com

KENSINGTON BOOKS are published by

Kensington Publishing Corp.
850 Third Avenue
New York, NY 10022

ISBN 0-7582-0644-5

First Kensington Trade Paperback Printing: October 2004
10  9  8  7  6  5  4  3  2  1

Printed in the United States of America

*To Matt*

# Acknowledgments

Huge thanks to:
Emma, Gillian, and everyone at Piatkus, for their hard work and enthusiasm.
Paul and all at the Marsh Agency, for believing in this novel from the start.
Lisa Jewell and Yasmin Boland, for their advice and encouragement when I needed it most.
Mum and Dad, for letting me do what I want in life, and for being the strongest people I know. I love you both and am so proud of your courage in recent times.
All my other family and friends, for their continued love and support. Especially Dave, Katherine, Harvey, Mary, Richard, Phoebe, and Clive.

# *Chapter*

# 1

I don't know what to do.

This is worse than it sounds, believe me.

You see, the thing is, knowing what to do is, well, it's what I do. It is my job, my *raison d'être*, my *thing*. I'm Martha "Relationship Guru" Seymore. Yes, *the* Martha Seymore, as in the Martha Seymore who fits between "Real Sex" and "Your Stars" on page sixty-nine of *Gloss* magazine. The same one you can chat with live on-line every Thursday evening at JustAskMartha.com. That's me, the girl who gets paid to lend an ear to the cheated and jilted, the undersexed and over-attached.

And the advice fountain never runs dry. I have an answer to every question, and believe me I get some good ones:

Dear Martha,

Is faking an orgasm deceitful?

Dear Martha,

Should I lose weight for my lover?

Dear Martha,

My boyfriend doesn't want sex until our wedding night, should I wait for him?

Dear Martha,

My partner wants us to engage in a threesome with a farmyard animal, what should I do?

And, never one for false modesty, I am qualified, too. A degree in Psychology and a Master's in the Clinical Characteristics of Love Relations are the crown jewels of my glittering CV. But here I am, a bewildered fresher on her first day at the University of Life: clueless and without a timetable.

I suppose it would have been easier if I hadn't been naked. If Luke hadn't decided to tell me when we were mid-foreplay I would have been able to walk out straight away, head held high, leaving all the inevitable questions happily unanswered.

But no.

I was in bed with him, enjoying one of our Saturday-afternoon romps. There I was on top of the sheets, welcoming his kisses as they charted their way up inside my leg when, with no warning, he stopped.

"I can't . . ."

Confused at this abstract reluctance, I asked him what was the matter.

He lifted himself up off the bed, flashed a quick look at himself in the mirror, and then his face adopted a contorted expression, as if he was trying to pull a piece of glass from his foot.

"Martha, I've got to tell you something."

I watched as his cantilevered cock started to sag.

"It's about last night . . ."

Last night. Luke's monthly bender with the geek squad from *Internet Planet* magazine. I'd spent the night at Fiona's.

"What about it?" I asked, tugging the sheet back over my body.

He stared straight into my eyes, then paused, as if making some sort of calculation. "I slept with someone."

The sentence seemed to be over almost before it had begun. Too quick to take in. It was like I'd been stabbed. There was total shock, confusion, then nothing, then the pain set in. My face must have looked blank as the words took time to form their full meaning.

*Two hours before.*

*The city had been alive with traffic and noise. Luke and I were on New Bond Street, window-shopping with mock-intent and taking pleasure in the late spring sunshine. Although he'd been quieter than usual, and had seemed less willing to humor me with his normal brand of arch-miserabilism, I had attributed this to the hangover his pink eyes were exhibiting.*

*Aside from his limited conversation, everything had seemed normal. In DKNY he sat and patiently flicked through the communal copies of* Wallpaper *and* i-D *while I tried on the entire second floor. In Prada he had nudged me discreetly to point out a C-list celebrity contemplating an overpriced pair of slip-ons. And in Calvin Klein, when we were out of view of everyone except the CCTV, he'd whispered some horny ramblings into my ear while casually parking his hand on my bum.*

*Outside as we had weaved through the Saturday crowds we were a Couple in Love, soaking up the rays of the sun and the jealous eye-darts of the single. I didn't detect any of the textbook hallmarks of infidelity: no elaborate cover stories, no perplexed forehead-scrunching, no forced good humor, no sense of nostalgic longing for something which had been lost or thrown away.*

"I slept with someone."

It's funny, however many words it takes to build a relationship, it always only takes four to knock it to the ground.

The shock had more force than any I'd yet experienced because unlikely as it may sound, this was completely unexpected. There'd been no warning signs, no fault line identified. Luke was faithful. He may have believed in nothing else but he *believed* in our relationship. So this excursion, this breach of faith, was an impossibility. The thought that he could search for pleasure elsewhere had never passed through my mind. Now that it was there as a physical reality, I felt sick.

There was an emerging trace of anger, but this was initially overshadowed by a strange feeling of shame. I was naked in front of a stranger. A stranger I had shared a bed with for two years of my life, but a stranger nonetheless. I looked for my knickers but couldn't remember which direction I'd thrown them in. While I searched, Luke set about answering my unspoken questions.

"I was drunk . . . I can hardly remember it . . . it was a mistake . . . a really bad mistake . . . I shared a taxi because we were going the same way home . . . I hate myself . . . I had to tell you . . . you have to believe me . . . I love you . . ."

When I have pointed out, as I have on a number of occasions in my "Do the Right Thing" column, that the key to maintaining a successful relationship is to learn something new about your partner every day, this was not what I'd had in mind.

I looked up at him in disbelief, then down at his cock which was now the size and shape of a button mushroom. I located my knickers and bra and put them on awkwardly, trying all the while not to let my eyes give anything away. I moved across the room to the chair where my jeans and top were and finished dressing. Luke remained motionless, his bare arse and back bathed in gold light from the window behind him.

Fully clothed, a more complete sense of anger emerged. I looked for something to throw at him, something sharp enough to cause permanent damage. My shoes. The gray Fendoluccis with the lethal heels. One of them should do the job.

"You've got to believe it . . . it meant nothing . . . *nothing* . . ." He was animated now, and could see the venom in my eyes. "Well, say *something* . . ."

But I wasn't saying anything. He reached for his boxer

shorts and held them over his groin, like a fig leaf. I grabbed the shoe and flung it at him at full velocity. His reflexes were ninja-sharp—he moved quickly out of its path and the shoe hurtled on through the window.

Smash.

*Fuck.*

Picking up the other shoe I made my way out of the apartment.

"Martha, wait!"

I turned as I opened the door and broke my silence. "Did you think of me?"

"What?"

"When you were fucking this girl did you think of me?"

"Why are you doing this to yourself?" I couldn't believe it. It was as if I'd brought this situation on myself.

"Just answer the question, Luke. Was I in your head?"

He looks at me, exasperated. "Yes, of course you were. You were in there the whole time."

It felt weird the way he was saying this, as if I'd been an accomplice, or at least a witness to the whole thing. However, the fact that I'd been there, within his conscious thoughts, did make it easier to walk out without hesitation. The idea that he could have been thinking of me while touching and kissing and fucking this nameless girl was somehow worse than if he'd blanked me out. It made the infidelity more extreme, more brutal.

"It's over, Luke. I just hope she was worth it." My voice sounded strange, detached. As if prerecorded.

Once outside I navigated my way around the shards of broken glass and recovered my shoe. Luke was left standing naked at the top of the communal stairway calling my name. The fucker.

There was an old couple on the pavement across the street staring at me as if I'd just escaped from somewhere. In a way I suppose I had. Although it didn't feel like that—not yet anyway.

"Martha, please, Martha—"

His voice was now vaporizing into nothingness as I walked down the street towards Notting Hill Gate Tube, dazed and distraught.

# *Chapter*

# 2

Heading east on the Central Line to Bow, crammed between the armpit of a Saturday worker and the backpack of a German tourist, I try my best to gain some sense of perspective. I am, after all, armed with the relevant knowledge for exactly these situations.

This is no big thing, I reason. It happens all the time. Of course it does. Every second of every hour of every day, in every corner of London. Relationships end: some with a bang, some with a whimper; it's a fact of life.

I try to remember times where I might have felt worse. But this is always going to be a self-defeating strategy, as effective as chopping off an arm to divert attention away from your headache.

I think of the only major personal tragedy of the last decade: when my gran died four years ago. Perversely, I want to recall the emotional turmoil I must have felt. However, all I remember is an overriding sense of guilt. Not the kind which makes you feel in some way responsible, but that which is brought on by an absence of pain. That which poses the question: why isn't this bothering me? No. Nothing compares to the pure, unadulterated, irrational grief I'm experiencing right now.

Then, for the first time in the last twenty minutes, a pragmatic thought enters my head. *I am homeless.* The only punishment I have inflicted on Luke has been to kick myself out of his apartment. All I am left with are the contents of my Anya Hindmarch handbag (purse, Marlboro Lights, lip gloss, mobile phone, echinacea capsules, used tissues) and the clothes on my back. Well done, Martha. *That* will teach him. Of course, I know I will have to return for my belongings at some future stage, but not today. That is impossible.

Almost instinctively, I have decided to head for Fiona's. Fee is my best friend, a part of me as I am a part of her. Her best-friend credentials are easy to identify: she cares, but she doesn't judge. Despite the fact that she is half German (on her mother's side), she is bemused by the whole concept of *schadenfreude.* If I'm feeling really shitty, there is no evident shade of triumph with Fiona, no smug sympathy. There is never an "I told you so" or an "I thought this might happen" with her, even when she has. Now that's a rare quality, especially with friends. She is also the one person in my life whose history most mirrors mine. We were at university together and played hookey from the same cognitive psychology lectures together. We laughed, cried, and fought together, got out of our heads in Ibiza together, and then, as soon as we had graduated from Leeds three years ago, we moved to London together.

During our first year in the big city we had lived in the same flat and shared the same riotous vodka-fueled adventures. Then, within the same month, she'd met Carl the Fashion Photographer and I'd met Luke the Lying Cheating Bastard (formerly known as the Sexiest Journalist on the Planet). Although we inevitably saw a bit less of each other, the symmetry was left intact. Until now, of course. All of a sudden everything is looking decidedly lopsided.

When I arrive at the apartment complex I pause for a moment to compose myself before buzzing the intercom.

"Hello."

"Fee, it's me."

"Oh, hi, I'll buzz you in."

I let myself in when the door sounds and walk down the hallway to her apartment. She's standing there waiting for me, a slender silhouette against the door. As I get closer she reads my face.

"What's the matter? You look dreadful."

I stand there in front of her, resisting eye contact. "I'm, uh, it's—"

There's a part of me that doesn't want to tell her. Not because she won't know how to handle it. She will. In true PR-girl fashion she can always find the silver lining. It's just that, in her head right now, Luke and I are still together and have no reason to separate. Breaking that illusion can only make me feel worse. Somehow I force the words out.

"It's over with me and Luke."

Her face crinkles and tilts sympathetically to one side. She stretches out her arms to beckon me for a hug. "Oh darling, *come here.*"

My head nestles into her shoulder, the tears break through, accompanied by what must sound like a whining and self-pitying splutter. This lasts for about two minutes while Fee strokes the back of my head affectionately.

"I'm sorry," I whimper when my eyes have emptied.

"Whatever for?"

I lift my head up and rub my eyes. "I've got snot on your T-shirt."

We go inside. Carl is not there. He is away in France, working on a fashion shoot.

"So what happened?" she asks, handing me a cigarette. I tell her the situation in between deep and desperate drags. When I explain exactly *when* Luke told me, her response makes me smile. "What a titwad."

I should point out that Fiona has always had an eccentric way of swearing. Other examples of her fruity vocabulary include "big hairy bollocks," "flying fuckety fuck," and, my favorite, "galloping gonads." It's as if she's acting out a script cowritten by Quentin Tarantino and Enid Blyton. (I suppose this is as you would expect for the person who has watched the video of *Grease* while out of her mind on Ecstasy.)

But Fiona is a good listener. She knows when and how the supportive "mmms" and "ahhhs" are required. She doesn't overplay it and she acts genuinely concerned. Even her outfit helps: fluffy slippers, sweatpants, and pink T-shirt. Her hair tied back in a neat, comforting, symmetrical ponytail. She looks how you would imagine a cup of cocoa would look if it had a fashion sense.

"Well, I suppose you've got to give him something; he had the balls to tell you."

But this to me means nothing. It was inevitable he would tell me because secrets were never possible between us. From our first night we were open with each other, exposing our souls in a way quite new to me, at least within the confines of a boy-girl framework. Truth is one of Luke's big things. And he's always on the lookout for it. Sneering at any attempt to cover it up. On a personal level this was always what had attracted me to him. OK, he was a cynic. But he was an interested one. It had felt good, having someone who was not only concerned with the hard facts of your biography, but also in the softer stuff: your opinions, how you think about things, and grand life-and-death things, at that.

Unraveling each other, getting as close to the truth as words allow is, however, a dangerous game. It's about ownership, not only of each other's pasts, but thoughts as well. There are no longer any places for secrets to hide, no uncomfortable truths to be glossed over. Everything is suddenly up for grabs.

Which, in this instance, must have made it difficult for Luke. I mean, he must have tried to cancel it out, to keep it to himself, but it was no good. As he had once proudly concluded in one of his articles for *Internet Planet*, "Information wants to be free, and that is its natural inclination." And so it proved.

But then, I don't know.

My mind goes off on one. Perhaps the fact that Luke told

me *is* significant, although not in the way Fee imagines. Perhaps Luke, at a subconscious level, wanted it to be over. Perhaps having meaningless sex with a stranger was so exciting that he had realized what he'd been missing. Then my mind really starts to torment me. What if the sex hadn't been meaningless? And what if it wasn't a stranger? Maybe Luke knew this girl. Maybe he's been having an affair. It's mathematically possible: although we're together sixty percent of the time, that still leaves forty percent unaccounted for . . . Cheating on a relationship expert would certainly satisfy his dark sense of humor . . .

Then Fee's voice punctures my train of thought. "You're welcome to stay here as long as you like."

Although I appreciate the offer, I am only too aware that this is a short-term solution. Carl is due back from France in a few days and may not be as keen on the idea as Fiona seems to be. And, to be honest, the prospect of sharing the same living space as Carl is none too appealing. I mean, sure, he might look like Josh Hartnett's older, longer-haired brother, but he falls somewhere between Mariah Carey and Ozzy Osbourne on the mental stability scale. Fee says he's a changed man and that he's now more interested in her than in snorting half of Colombia up his nostrils. She's certainly put the work in trying to "help him through his difficult patch," as she likes to euphemize (the period during which his nose journeyed where no nose had gone before, snorting cocaine straight from heaped teaspoons—rolled banknotes were either too tedious or, given the cost of his habit, too hard to come by).

But even so, I'm entitled to remain suspicious about a man who prefers to look at me from behind a camera and who has spoken a sum total of ten words to me in his entire life. ("She's out," "She's not here," and "Are you wearing a wig?") Anyway, aside from the Carl issue, more than a week on that sofabed and I'll be having to make an appointment with the chiropractor.

I will need to find my own place, however scary it might

first appear. All my life I have always been a part of other people's living arrangements—Luke's, Fiona's, my parents'—and the prospect of finding a place of my own is indeed terrifying.

"And tonight," Fiona tells me, rubbing her hands, "we'll get some videos, get absolutely sloshed, and make a voodoo doll of That Complete Loser."

I laugh despite myself. "That sounds good." And it does, although not anything like as good as the thought of having an early night with Luke, or at least with the Luke of my former imagination, the one who was faithful, who only had eyes for me, who wasn't willing to throw it all away in the backseat of a taxi with a girl whose name he didn't know, or care to.

"What about your stuff?"

"My stuff?"

"Yeah, you know, all your worldly possessions."

"Oh shit, yeah. I don't know."

Then Fiona sets out the itinerary. Tomorrow we will go around together at about one o'clock, a likely time for Luke to be in the pub. We'll take her car, pack all my stuff, then bring it back and store it here until I find a place to live. From the way she is talking, you would think she was planning a high-risk military operation. I nod a lethargic approval, then pour myself a glass of wine.

Before I can take a sip my mobile phone goes off, and I can tell that it is Luke without even checking the display. Instead of answering it I wait to hear if he has left me a message on the voicemail.

He has: "Martha, hopefully when you get this message you'll be feeling a bit more rational and more willing to listen to what I've got to say. Please call me, we really do need to talk. I know I was wrong, which is why I had to tell you, but this doesn't have to be the end. Surely you of all people understand that? I just think you've made a rash decision."

*Surely me of all people?*

"This," I tell Fiona, "is a cheap trick." He's using my job

against me, trying to bring my status as a patch-up merchant into the argument. Fiona mumbles in supportive, but unconvincing, agreement. What is especially irritating is that this stance is coming from a man whose own choice of career reflects his real personal strengths in the same way that Dr. Jekyll resembles Mr. Hyde. I mean, this is the IT journalist who can't even add an attachment to an e-mail message without asking for help.

"And as for *me* making a rash decision. Ha! Well, that is rich. I mean of course it's me. Of course it is. Of course I *made* him go off last night with some sex-starved nymphobloodymaniac. Bastard." I switch the phone off and wait for my head to explode.

"Are you OK, Martha?" Fiona asks, once I have voiced my feelings.

"Yeah," I say with forced casualness, before taking another gulp of Merlot. "I'm fine."

But my head is a mess. And as a psychologist, I can provide a neurological explanation. So get ready, here comes the science part.

The natural brain stimulants dopamine, norepinephrine, and phenylethylamine—the chemicals of love—are now in free fall. The happy feelings they have managed to generate over the two years since Luke and I have been together are now being reversed, and are turning into their diametrical opposites.

You see, Bryan Ferry was right. Love *is* a drug. More specifically, it is what the 1982 Conference on Love and Attraction famously described as "a cognitive affective state characterized by intrusive and obsessive fantasizing concerning reciprocity of amorant feelings by the object of the amorance." (Well, it's famous if, like me, you are one of the twenty-seven people in the world to have done a master's degree in the subject.)

You'll know when it happens, they tell you. And I did. One moment you are a normal, rational human being, able to discriminate between all that is good and bad in the modern world, and the next you act as if you've been lobotomized and you've just been given the brain of one of those happy-clappy daytime TV presenters.

All of a sudden you'll find yourself with a copy of *OK!* and realize you are no longer reading it ironically. You'll start laughing at the "funny" bits in *The King of Queens* and find yourself saying things like "I know Celine Dion's crap but she's got a powerful singing voice."

But now it's cold turkey. Never mind "Heroin Screws You Up." Love, that's the real killer. Luke may not have come with a government health warning, but he's causing me damage. It's the phenylethylamine, that's the real problem. Trust me. That's real heavy shit. Acting like speed, it's that stuff which has the power to keep you up all night talking "a mile a minute" with each other and then indulge in an acrobatic sex session at six in the morning. And when you hit a rock, it's that same chemical which can tear you apart.

Being able to break down your feelings scientifically does not, however, always make them easier to deal with. Alcohol, on the other hand, can work wonders. With this thought in mind I quietly resolve to spend the rest of the evening getting completely and utterly shitfaced.

# Chapter

## 3

A breakup is not a once-only event. You have to relive it, reenact it, remix it, and then repackage it for each particular audience. Your friends get one version, your family gets another, while the truth floats somewhere in between.

This breakup is a particularly hard one to present to people. While I'm OK with the words—"it was a mutual decision," "it's best for both of us," "we work better as friends"— they are belied by my tone of voice.

Fiona was easy. The others, however, may present more of a challenge. None more so than my mom, whose supernatural talent for telephoning me at the worst times possible is confirmed at eight o'clock on Sunday morning when my mobile rings.

"You sound *dreadful*," she tells me. "Where are you?"

"I'm at Fiona's," I croak wearily.

"I tried Luke's but there was no answer." She says this with a high inflection at the end, as if it was a question.

"Oh, yeah, um, I stopped the night at Fiona's. It was her birthday," I say unconvincingly, wondering whether to tell her the truth. "How's Dad?" I ask, in a play for time.

"Daddy's *fine*." In the "fine" I detect the subtle hint of innuendo. "We're having one of our special lie-ins," she giggles.

You see, although my parents spent the first eighteen years of my life sheltering me from even the idea of sex, they now seem hell-bent on making me aware that sexual activity doesn't have to stop when you turn fifty. Whether it's my mom's Pilates classes or my dad's previously postponed midlife crisis which has brought about this new lease of lust, I am not sure. All I know is that the idea of my parents "getting it on" makes me want to vomit.

I then ask her about work because I know that as soon as she is on the subject she will ramble on for at least twenty minutes, giving me the latest on her doctorly traumas. And I'm right. She goes off into a monologue about problem patients, gormless GPs, staff politics, and the never-ending saga of Rachel the receptionist (aka "the laziest woman alive").

All the time she is talking I take deep, silent breaths, trying to steel myself. When she reaches a full stop, I decide to come out with it in one go: "Luke and I have broken up."

There is a silence.

When my parents first met Luke last year he charmed the socks off them. Little did they know I had briefed him beforehand: "Feign an interest in classical music and alternative medicine and you'll be laughing," I'd told him. After a Pizza-Express lunch and walk along the South Bank my mom pulled me to one side and said with flushed enthusiasm, "Oh, Martha, Luke's wonderful . . . I think he'll be good for you."

"What, what, what do you mean?" she eventually asks, with a trace of aggression.

"It's over, we've split, that's it . . ." I go on to give her the "mutual decision" spiel, mixed with some classic Martha Seymore trick-cyclist bullshit about relationships running their course. To my surprise, she swallows it.

"Oh, I'm so sorry."

"Mom, seriously, it's the best for both of us." I then make an excuse about Fiona having just made me breakfast and conclude the conversation. Thankfully, my dad has gone to the gym, so it will be left up to Mom to break the news.

\* \* \*

Starting badly, the day gets worse.

When Fiona gets up, she drives me round to Luke's to collect my stuff. The bedroom window is now patched up with a flimsy piece of chipboard, making the apartment look derelict.

I use my set of keys to let us in and, as we enter, I run through the possibilities of what we might find:

1. Luke curled up in a fetal ball, crying my name over and over again.
2. Luke lying dead on the bathroom floor after taking five boxes of Nurofen and writing me a heart-wrenching suicide note.

Or, worst-case scenario:

3. Luke getting his freak on with the mystery Miss X in a state of such unbridled ecstasy that he is oblivious to our entrance.

As it turns out, he's not there. Clearly he's not so devastated as to miss his Sunday lunchtime piss-up at the Blue Bar.

Part relieved, part disappointed, I go with Fiona into the bedroom and set about packing. The room suddenly has an immense power. Luke is everywhere. In my head I run through a "Bastard" mantra to keep back the emotion. *Fucking Bastard. Cheating Bastard. Fucking Cheating Bastard.* And so on.

Realizing that I can't stay here long I bundle all my clothes and shoes into *bin liners* and grab my laptop. All the mutual stuff I leave (much to Fee's bemusement). The books, the kitsch movie posters, the CDs, the Art Deco ashtray—these are no longer just objects any more, these are souvenirs of something I don't want to remember.

I go into the kitchen to write Luke a good-bye note. Everything seems charged with a negative energy. The kettle, the knife rack, the silver oven, even the toaster: all seem like objects of hate, like subtle and secret weapons in an invisible war.

The note I leave is simple and to the point:

Dear Luke,
This was *your* decision.
Martha

I underline the "your" twice for dual emphasis.

Within twenty minutes of having entered we are out of there and driving back. As we move down past Great Portland Street, I realize for the first time that I may never see him again.

I try and make conversation with a reluctant Fiona, for whom every car journey is a rerun of her driving test, but it's no good and, despite my best efforts, I am too weak to stop thinking. Or rather, what I am thinking about is too strong to let go of, as if my own cognitive processes are now beyond control. Needless to say, my thoughts are of Luke. I am not missing him, but rather anticipating what I *will* miss about him, which may or may not amount to the same thing.

I will miss tickling him into reluctant laughter each time he gets one of his twisty faces.

I will miss watching him wince as I squeeze his blackheads.

I will miss our friendly banter during our weekly shop. Like last Wednesday:

(In Boots)

ME: Why don't we get that shower gel?

LUKE: Which one?

ME: The aromatherapy one.

LUKE: 'Cos it's a load of bollocks, isn't it?

ME: No it's not, it's proven to work.

LUKE: So was witch-burning. And leeches.

ME: Well OK, you can go and find some nice exfoliating leeches to wash yourself with, but I'm going to settle for a lavender body scrub, OK?

LUKE: I was just saying.

\*   \*   \*

(In Waitrose)

LUKE: Mart, why do you always go for the organic stuff?

ME: Because it's healthier.

LUKE: (Holding up a robust, genetically modified carrot next to its puny, organic cousin) But it's half the size and it's twice as expensive. It's a load of bollocks.

ME: Size isn't everything Luke, you should know that.

LUKE: What was that supposed to mean?

ME: Nothing. I was just saying.

Perhaps most of all I will miss sleeping with him. And I mean just that. *Sleeping* with him. You see, to my mind, it is the sleeping, not the sex, that defines a successful relationship. After all, you can have fantastic, bed-breaking sex with someone you hardly know, or even with someone you don't like. Sleeping together, on the other hand, is much more difficult to get right. The openness required for a sexual partnership to work counts for nothing when compared to that needed in order to nod off with someone. With Luke, however, it was the most natural thing in the world. In bed he would cast all his daytime cynicism aside and relax. He would cuddle into my back, lift his knees up and, as if to shield me, rest his arm on the outside of my leg.

And this was how we fell asleep, night after night, for nearly two years.

I already know that the nostalgia for those deep, dreamless nights will become overwhelming. I will miss everything. The warmth of his body, the feel of his legs under mine, even his stale morning taste. *Oh Luke, you bastard, I miss you already.*

When we get back to Fiona's she tells me that she has got a lot of work to do for tomorrow so, if I don't mind, she'll have to leave me to it. I try and arrange my belongings as neatly as possible, which is quite difficult in a flat not much bigger than a shoebox. Especially when you consider that Fiona has converted it into a shrine to anal retention.

And then I feel guilty: for bringing my chaos into Fiona's ordered world. I resolve to find a place of my own as soon as possible.

In a desperate desire to fill the void of Sunday afternoon I charge up my laptop and check my e-mails. There are 111. Admittedly around fifty of these are instant deletables—dubious invitations to get a new home loan, buy Viagra, win a holiday in Las Vegas, participate in hot teen action and enlarge my penis by three inches (guaranteed). But in between the false promises of a better life there are the subject lines of a more desperate reality:

I'm scared of losing him
My boyfriend is impotent
I love his best friend
He doesn't know I'm pregnant
He wants me to dress up as his mother

I click on a message headlined "Single Forever?" And read:

*Dear Martha,*
*I'm an outgoing person with an active social life, but find it hard to meet attractive, single men. When I do meet someone I really fancy, they're either attached or not interested in a relationship. What should I do?*
*Eve Bloom, 23, Retail Assistant, Edinburgh*

Surprisingly, I find it easy to provide a reply:

*First you need to ask yourself why you feel you should be in a relationship. Is it for you or the people around you? Do you want a monogamous relationship or is it something you feel pressurised to enter into? At a certain age, after a certain number of partners or a certain length of time, there is undeniable pressure to be in a "grown-up" relationship. But it is possible that you, without real-izing it, are acting in a way that puts single men off and sends out the wrong signals.*

*The other possibility is that you do want a relationship, but are going about it the wrong way. Every time you are attracted to a single man you may automatically expect it to lead to a dead end. This inevitably means that it does lead to a dead end. If you change your frame of mind to reflect what you really want, rather than what you think you should have in order to fit in, you'll end up being more successful.*

I am impressed by the authority of my own advice, despite the fact that I realize I am not giving the whole picture.

# *Chapter*

# 4

Of course, the main problem about being a single, twenty-something female is the fact that the quickest route back to coupledom tends to be found by forming an attachment with a single, twenty-something male. The men I know, unattached and in their twenties, are unattached for good reasons.

Take three not-so-random examples:

Name: Stuart Price
Age: Twenty-six
Occupation: Web programmer
Interests: Computers, John Woo movies, Domino's pizzas, piss-artistry, breast jokes, playing with his software

Stuart is Fiona's older brother and, I have to admit, he's very committed to his brotherly duties. You know, piss-taking, shit-stirring, ego-sapping, and all the other hallmarks of sibling affection. I see him quite a lot; he's round at Fiona's every other night for a free meal and some female company, even if it is his sister's.

On the looks front he's not the star prize, but he's not hideous either. I mean, he doesn't have a mustache or anything and he's in pretty good shape considering his diet of takeaway food and his excessive alcohol consumption.

However, aside from the fact that he is my friend's brother, there are a number of other factors which act as successful deterrents. While he is no longer a boy (the generous bulge in his combats testifies to that), it would be stretching a point to call him an adult. It's almost as if he is trapped in some state of pubescent purgatory, unable to pass through to manhood.

This immaturity is manifest in the way he expresses himself. Or rather doesn't. True to the computer-geek cliché, Stu is not someone who strikes you as well in tune with his feelings. This probably accounts for his permanently confused expression.

His immaturity is also evident in his living quarters, which Stuart shares with a bunch of fellow cybernerds in a glorified shed in Whitechapel. I've only been in his bedroom once, when I was borrowing a CD-ROM off him to help me work on my website, but it made a lasting impression.

His duvet was on the floor, along with a selection of unwashed socks, pizza boxes, club flyers and lad mags. In terms of furniture, there was a wardrobe, a scary-looking bedside chest of drawers and a few precarious shelves with computer games and videos. There was a single bed against the wall and, above, a cluttered assortment of *FHM* posters stuck together in a haphazard fashion. The smell is what I remember most, however, a dank and fusty amalgam of sweat, stale cigarettes, takeaway pizza, spilt beer and crusty bedsheets. When he referred to the room as his "love den" I didn't know whether to laugh or cry. The idea that any woman of legal age could be aroused in such an environment was ridiculous, almost perverse.

I'm probably being a bit hard. I mean he's quite sweet in a Basset Hound sort of way, and his heart's in the right place, I'm sure. It's just that regarding relationships with the opposite sex he's his own worst enemy. After all, any bloke who refers to a woman's breasts as "bazookas" is destined for a long, lonely stay in the Land of the Single.

Anyway, you'll meet him soon, so you can judge for yourself.

Name: Guy Longhurst
Age: Twenty-eight
Occupation: Features Editor, *Gloss* magazine
Interests: Italian food, the House of Gucci, body fascism, serial seduction, mirrors (and any other reflective surfaces)

Guy is the best-looking man you have ever seen in your life. Times two. Multiply George Clooney to the power of Brad Pitt and you're getting close. He's equipped with that kind of dangerous man-beauty which you know could really hurt if you got on the wrong side of it. You could fall for him in an instant, get lost in those dark chocolate eyes and never be able to find a way out.

Until he opened his mouth, that is.

As with so many beautiful men, Guy's looks come at a price. The price of being a bit of a wanker. He's the type who thinks that everyone and everything around him is put on the planet for his own amusement. I suppose that this condition is born out of the fact that he is the only male in an office of "nubile, young überbabes" as he likes to collectively call us.

Of course, Guy isn't single because he's an arsehole (my faith in womankind isn't *that* strong), Guy is single because he wants to be, or maybe even needs to be. Commitment is suicide as far as he's concerned because his whole reason for living is to spread his seed as far and wide as possible. It's as if he can only confirm his sense of self-identity by hearing the sound of a new woman calling his name while in the throes of passion.

He's tried it on with every girl in the office and, I would say, has had a forty percent success rate so far. Indeed, according to office legend he only got the job in the first place after implementing an aggressive seduction strategy on Sally Marsden, the group publisher.

Although he has, occasionally, indicated that he would be willing to "service my affections" (his favorite euphemism), he's generally kept his distance. Of course, this may have been to do with the fact that I was with Luke or that I'm simply not his type (although Guy doesn't seem to narrow himself down to "types"), but I believe it has more to do with my status as a Relationship Expert. After all, this provides quite an impenetrable and intimidatory force field for someone who thinks that monogamy is something you make dining tables out of, and whose idea of "going the distance" is doing it three times in one night.

Perhaps this is why he's been trying (and failing) to colonize page sixty-nine with competition features and glorified advertorials for beauty products no one wants to buy. Anyway, trust me on this one. Bit of a wanker.

Name: Siraj Nair
Age: Twenty-five
Occupation: Graphic Designer
Interests: Lying in bed, talking high art, watching low TV, getting stoned

Siraj is my closest male friend, although he used to be more than that.

An art-college graduate who was waiting for the world to catch up with the Neo-Dada Revival he had unleashed from his bedroom studio, he was a good guy, still is, and right for me at the time. Having just arrived in London we were both still very young and in student mode. We both lived in cheap, cheerless shared accommodation in Camberwell—me with Fee in a second-floor flat on Haig Road, Siraj with a raggy collection of his art-college mates in the middle of a decrepit Edwardian terrace near the Tube station.

The first time I met him he was slouched on the floor at the house party of a mutual friend of a friend. There were, I suppose, two principal reasons why I strategically parked my bum next to him on that fag- and beer- (and God knows what else) stained carpet:

1. He was cute, in that unhealthy, undernourished, never-done-any-physical-exercise-in-his-life sort of way—dressed in a Che Guevara T-shirt and a battered pair of jeans. What struck me, though, as I looked through my vodka-goggles, were his eyes, dark and dopey, and his tousled, woke-up-in-a-hedge haircut. I can remember marking him down with an IFR (Instant Fuckability Rating) of eight out of a possible ten.
2. He was in the process of constructing an unfeasibly large, nine-Rizla, white carrot of a joint.

Cocooned inside a cloud of marijuana smoke, we slowly got to know each other better.

An hour in and the conversation and laughter became punctuated by interludes of clumsy kissing. Two hours in and we moved our smoke cloud into one of the empty bedrooms, and began to engage in some rather lethargic foreplay. Ten minutes later, with sex seeming like too high a mountain to climb, we fell asleep in each other's arms. When we woke we somehow made arrangements to see each other again.

And that was that. It just happened. We fell into a relationship. A classic TV romance. No, not like Scott and Charlene or Ross and Rachel or even Richard and Judy. What I mean is that our relationship developed and diminished in front of the small screen. The TV would be on continuously, even when we were asleep. It was the only distraction either of us could afford once we had spent all our money on rent, Tube fares, super noodles, cheap wine, condoms, and cigarettes.

We spent more time at Siraj's house because he had a TV in his bedroom and could get a clear reception for Channel 5.

When we weren't working we would laze in his bed for such lengthy periods that even John and Yoko would have been itching to get out of their pajamas.

Virtually every milestone in the course of our thirteen-month relationship occurred while watching the box. The first time we had sex was during *Question Time* (he later confessed that he'd managed to avoid premature ejaculation by concentrating on a head-to-head between Margaret Beckett and Ann Widdecombe). And our first row took place in front of *Who Wants to Be a Millionaire?* with Chris Tarrant acting as referee and counting down our lifelines. Our most serious row—a drunken exchange of jealous accusations—was acted out in front of the classic Ricki Lake episode, "We May Be Identical Twins . . . But I Hate Your Guts!"

Perhaps the most significant scene in the history of our bizarre love triangle (me, Siraj, TV) was The One Where We Spontaneously Exchanged Our First I Love Yous While Nursing Sunday-Morning Comedowns in Front of *Friends*.

Although this exchange was heartfelt, it marked the beginning of the end for our relationship. Before the "I love yous" it had been easy. We'd got to that comfortable stage where we didn't feel we had to impress each other. The point at which awkward silences stopped being awkward.

After the "I love yous" things were different.

There was pressure. The heavy weight of commitment was starting to be felt. We knew it wouldn't be long until we had to make a Big Decision.

I had always known Siraj wasn't The One. We weren't a perfect fit. He was always more like a mate with added sex interest. I was only twenty-two, for God's sake. So was he. Slowly but surely, we unwrapped ourselves from our cosy routine. I'd spend more time with Fee and fewer nights at Siraj's.

In fact, if I remember rightly, there was never one moment when we actually broke up. We just slipped out of it, the same way we'd slipped into it.

No tears, no insomnia, no loss of appetite. With Siraj, the

ex-factor has never been an issue. The emotional GBH I am experiencing now never kicked in. It was as simple as switching channels. We had loved each other, I really believe that, but it was the sort of love which is caring rather than obsessive, never fully coming into focus. Soft, affectionate—more Glenn Miller than Glenn Close.

Anyway, the point is that since we split Siraj has remained single, out of choice, and has evolved into the classic commitment-phobe, preferring to have platonic relations with the girls he cares about and sexual ones with the ones he doesn't.

This triumvirate may or may not be representative of contemporary single manhood, I no longer feel in a position to tell. All I know is that I can't be bothered to find out. The idea of going out and playing the dating game (as grown-ups call it) is about as attractive to me as attaching cowbells to my nipples and rollerblading naked down Oxford Street on a Saturday afternoon.

# Chapter
# 5

I've been putting it off. I've been trying to get on with a bit of work when really I should be on the phone, making the call I know I have to make if I am going to save face. If I am to stop her, my oldest friend (and I mean friend in the full Shakespearean sense of the word) from finding out of her own accord. You see, telling Fee is one thing—Desdemona is an entirely different fish-kettle. (No offense if you know her.)

She might already know. Fuck. I'm going to have to call her.

Six months ago, Portobello Road.

"Martha, that woman's looking at you." Luke's voice, ventriloquized.

"What woman?"

"Other side of the street."

"Oh my God," I mumbled. And then the identity was confirmed by the sound of the voice, a voice which sent me back to forgotten sleep-overs and school discos.

"Martha, is that you?"

"Oh my God," I repeated, only more audibly, "Desdemona!"

"Martha!"

It's funny, isn't it? No matter how many times you think the past is over, that you've beaten it, it always comes back, calling your name.

We gave each other a pantomime hug in the middle of the street.

"It's been a long time," I suggested eventually.

"Seven years," she said, without deliberation.

"Christ! Has it been that long?"

Seven years! Seven years since we left Durham and went our separate student ways (her to Bristol, me to Leeds) and lost contact. Although I could not vouch for her, in my case this loss of contact had been deliberate. For instance, when my parents moved house I had made no effort to inform her of their new address.

"You look fantastic," I told her with reluctant sincerity. Although Desdemona's face had been well preserved, there were differences in her appearance. Her makeup, for instance, had a subtlety to it that wasn't evident seven years ago, complementing rather than contradicting her ice-blue eyes and strict blond hair. Her dress sense, as you would probably expect, had also evolved. In fact, it had undergone a radical Sloanification. Her angular body was now vacuum-packed in tight, Chelsea denim garnished with a Burberry cap and Blahnik booties. Altogether, it was a look which said many things, most of them beginning with F.

"Thanks," she said without even the suggestion that she could return the compliment.

"This is Luke, by the way."

"Hi," Luke's arm flipped up as if greeting a fellow Apache.

"Wow, Martha, haven't you done well," enthused Desdemona, with a girlish flutter.

"What about you?" I asked, angling for bad news. "Found the love of your life yet?"

"Well yes, I have, believe it or not. Someone you will probably remember, actually. Alex, *Alex Norton*—you know, from school. Met up with him again a year ago, in Durham. Both of us were back visiting parents. He's a chef now, at the Galgarry . . ."

That will teach me, I thought, as I felt the color drain from my face.

*Alex* Norton.

Alex *Norton*.

Alex *fucking* Norton.

The name didn't just ring a bell, it set off a bloody fire alarm. You see, Alex Norton hadn't just been my old school-mate, he'd also been my old school *mate*. My first time. My five-second rollercoaster ride. My cherry-popper. The first one to say, "I love you."

Observing my ghostly expression, Desdemona broke off to ask, "Are you all right, Martha?"

"Ab-so-lute-ly fine." But then I snapped out of it. "It's just, well, what a surprise. How amazing. I mean that's really fantastic. I'm so pleased for you."

The way she smiled at me was strange, as if intended for Luke's benefit as much as my own.

"So you both live around here?" I asked.

"Just off Ladbroke Grove. What about you?"

"Jameson Street, with Luke. Just over there." I pointed vaguely behind me. "What sort of work are you doing?"

"I'm a headhunter."

For a delirious second, I thought I was hallucinating. An image of Desdemona garbed in Amazonian tribal wear with a poisoned dart under her arm flashed into my mind. I was about to die.

"A headhunter?"

"Yes. A corporate headhunter, it's my job to look for the best new media talent in the country."

"Oh yes, of course. That's, that's fantastic."

"Mm, that's really interesting," interjected Luke. "So, do you work for dotcoms or bricks-and-mortar clients mainly?" It was rare that he got to air his geek-speak in public, and I could see he was relishing the opportunity.

"Both really. Although most of the VC funding has dried up in the dotcom sector, the traditional blue chips are the ones really after the best tech players."

This was all too much. The last time I had seen Desdemona she had been talking about getting a summer job at the local bakery. Unable to compete with this shiny new vocabulary she had acquired, I resigned myself to the sidelines and offered the odd "That's fantastic" every now and then.

". . . anyway we must all get together and catch up properly," Desdemona said eventually. "I bet you're just dying to see Alex again, aren't you, Martha?"

"Yes. Dying."

We exchanged numbers and parted.

As I walked back to Luke's I hardly said a word. My mind was in turmoil as it traveled back in time.

I remembered how she had been, officially, the Most Attractive Girl at school, and also (completely unrelated, of course) the one girl in our year with identifiable breasts. To be fair, however, Desdemona offered more than just a womanly chest. Her skin was blemish-free and radiated a constant healthy glow while her blond glossy hair and cobalt-blue eyes seemed cruel in their perfection. Small wonder, then, that when it came to the other sex, Desdemona was always two steps (and three bases) ahead of me.

The boys couldn't cope and Desdemona knew it, exploiting the fact at every opportunity. If I remember correctly her favorite target was a gangly, curly-headed creature whose body appeared beyond his own control. Paul Hobb, that was his name. Not only was he shooting up in height with such speed that we were sure we could actually see him elongating in front of our eyes, but also he had a penis that would pendulum between hard and soft at the slightest provocation. Aware of this, Desdemona would look at him from the raised side platform our class inhabited during the thrice-weekly morning assembly. The minute she sat down she would stare and stare until she had his attention, which was initially signalled by a crimson blotching across his face. Even without making eye contact, Paul could sense the threat of her newborn sexuality from across the hall.

The challenge Desdemona set herself was to make him hard by the time we had to all rise for Mr. Banton, our totalitarian head teacher. We were able to tell whether this had been achieved, not so much by the awkward protrusion in Paul's Farah trousers but by the fact that he would lever forward awkwardly, left hand in pocket and face in full blaze, as if someone had just massaged Deep Heat over his testicles.

I can remember on one occasion he had to stay like this for ten minutes while Mr. Banton, having being provoked by the fat-tie posse into taking a hardline stance on school uniform, reiterated the three founding precepts of Banton's LAW (Look right, Act right, Work right).

As the nods and nudges spread infectiously through the hall, Des turned to me and flashed a look of triumph. She had won, and Paul Hobb (or Hobb Knob as he was known henceforth) had been destroyed.

"That was cruel," I told her after assembly.

"Oh Martha, lighten up," she returned. "It was only a bit of fun. And anyway, I can't help it if I have such an effect on boys, can I?"

And, as she grew older, it wasn't just her fellow pupils she was having this effect on. She had somehow pulled off the Herculean task of being equally liked and admired by both pupils *and* teachers. By the time she was fourteen every male teacher (band of gold or not) fell under her Lolitan spell. Just ask Mr. Knight, our roving-eyed French teacher ("*Pour aller à la bibliothèque?*" Desdemona would pout, as if auditioning for the lead role in *Betty Blue*). In fact, her sex appeal helped so much that when she entered the poky examination room for her GCSE oral, Mr. Knight held back on the record button to ask if she had a problem with any of the words on her role-play sheet. This chivalrous gesture not only saved her the embarrassment of having to refer to her penpal as "*un ami de stylo*," but it also helped her to sail through to a Grade A.

This sort of favoritism, you might reasonably imagine, must have made her unpopular among her peers. But no. On the contrary. Desdemona had made damn sure that she would never be on the wrong side of the schoolyard apartheid. She would never be branded with the village kids, the musicians, or any of the other untouchables. For one thing, she had been smoking since thirteen. Not, I should add, that she derived any enjoyment from it.

Anyway, must get back to the point. The point being that at school, for all our differences, Desdemona and I had been inseparable. I'd found her fascinating. All her posh little idiosyncrasies and petty cruelties. The way she could reduce boys to dust with the blink of an eye. I hated her and loved her at the same time, in the way that only school friends can. It just seemed she had so much to *teach* me.

But it wasn't my decision, our friendship. It was hers. She'd been the one with the power to decide, and who was I to refuse? This is probably why the myth that you can't choose your family but you can pick your friends has never washed with me. Although I eventually settled into the arrangement quite well, I wouldn't have been able to change it even if I had felt otherwise. Resistance was futile.

Why she, the most popular girl in school, chose me as her best friend was something I regarded as a mystery. True, I could offer her help with her homework. True, I always looked old enough to buy cigarettes (and, from fourteen, bottles of Thunderbird). True, we both thought "Rhythm Is a Dancer" by Snap was a work of sublime artistic genius. But that, as far as I could tell, was about it.

However, with hindsight it makes more sense. The fact that my teenage self had been a complete nonentity was, in all likelihood, my unique selling point. My nondescript pubescent face, framed as it was by drab, dark hair, must have served to accentuate her sunny good looks. And the morbid view of the teenage darklands I inhabited made her relentless lust for life even more visible and attractive to those around her. So I suppose we worked as a contrast of light and shade, a "friendship born out of chiaroscuro" as Siraj might put it.

It was only at university, when I met Fiona, that I fully under-stood that friendships could follow a different pattern. That they could be mutually beneficial to both parties, and allow you to shine together. This realization probably explains why the break from Desdemona had been so complete. It probably also ex-plains why, when I heard her voice at the end of the phone two days after seeing her on the Portobello Road, my heart sank.

As I didn't have a good enough excuse at hand, we arranged to meet, with boyfriends, at the Three Floors bar in town. Although it was an unnerving experience to meet my first true love in the company of my present one, the evening passed quite smoothly. Desdemona was surprisingly tactful and Luke and Alex appeared to hit it off. I suppose what made it easier was the fact that Alex bore absolutely no resemblance to the gawky teenager I lost my virginity to. At the end of the night, sandwiched on the back seat of a minicab, I felt guilty. Perhaps I'd got it wrong about Desdemona after all.

To compensate, it was I who decided to initiate the next meeting. The next of many, as it turned out. During the last six months I have seen or spoken to her on an almost weekly basis. On days when I've been in work I sometimes call her to arrange an after-work drink.

It's easier than it ever used to be, now we've found our-selves; but that's not to say I don't still have my reservations. I mean, it's nothing like with Fiona. I still sense competition. In the conversations about work, about London, about our social lives, or our men. Especially our men. It is still there lurking in the background, waiting for a time like this.

Reluctant as I am to do so, I have decided to call her. Right now, from Fiona's apartment. If I do not, it will only be a mat-ter of time before she phones Luke or goes round to hear his side of the story. Oh fuck it. I pick up the receiver, I dial, I tell her. And as I tell her, there is absolute silence at her end of the line. None of the supportive noises I am used to with Fiona. It is a test of strength, but I continue regardless, until I reach my final full stop.

"Oh Martha, poor little you. I don't know what to say," are her eventual choice of words.

"You don't have to say anything. I just thought I should tell you."

"Weil, who was she, this girl?"

"I haven't a clue. According to Luke, he hadn't either."

"What did he say?"

"Oh, you know, what you'd expect. That it meant nothing. That it was a stupid mistake . . ."

"And do you believe him?" she asks, almost rhetorically, as if she already assumed that I couldn't.

"Well, I don't know if that's the point. The bottom line is that he slept with someone, and I don't know if I can forgive him."

"I suppose it's weird, the shoe being on the other foot."

"What do you mean?"

"Well, with your job and everything."

There it is again. That old "isn't it ironic?" chestnut. This is probably a mistake after all.

"Hmm. Des, you know, thanks for listening, but I'd better go."

"OK, sweetie. Look after yourself. You know I'm there if you need me."

Well no, actually, I don't, but I tell her I appreciate the support.

# *Chapter*

# 6

It's Monday morning and I am waking up to discover Fiona's living room is upside down. Oh no, maybe it's not. The shooting pain in my neck is telling me that it's my head which is upside down, hanging off the edge of Fee's sofabed. Despite the pain, I have a vague feeling that I have to be somewhere.

And then I remember.

Work.

Within the last month I have signed up for another year's worth of relationship consultancy with *Gloss*, and had my role extended to encompass certain editorial duties. What this means, aside from a swollen paycheck, is that my freelance days are over. Veronica, the arch-editor, now wants me on an exclusive basis. She wants me where she can keep an eye on me. In the office, in an editorial meeting, in, in . . . fuck, in forty-five minutes.

It takes me all of five seconds to realize that there is no way on the planet that I can face going into work today. I climb out of bed and decide to phone Veronica and tell the truth.

As I dial, however, an extract from a Do the Right Thing column I submitted a few weeks ago slips into my consciousness. Someone had written in after being dumped by their fiancé. This someone, this girl, was devastated and wanted advice on how to cope in this new boyfriendless world. She didn't feel like she could function properly. She wanted me to tell her to take a break. I didn't. Instead, and I can remember this word for word, I told her that "you must not let things fall apart. Every routine aspect of your life outside your relationship must be confirmed, however hard it may feel now. Throw yourself into work and get on with your social life. Now, more than ever, is the time to be busy." Well done, Martha Seymore.

The phone is picked up before it has time to ring.

"Veronica Knight," she clips.

"Hi, it's Martha," I say in a deep voice while holding my nose with my free hand.

"You sound terrible."

"I feel it. Summer flu I think. I was feeling all right yesterday so I thought I'd be fine, but I don't think I'll be able to come in."

"Well don't worry, don't come in until you feel better," she says with such sympathy that I feel a twinge of guilt (alongside a degree of surprise—Veronica is not renowned for her sympathetic qualities). Better than looking like a hypocrite, I suppose.

"Thanks," I mumble, a little too healthily.

"But remember we're having an extra editorial meeting on Wednesday," she says, reverting to her normal tone. "And it is quite important that you are there."

"OK, I'll do my best."

"In the meantime, I'll phone if there's anything urgent."

She signs off and I put the phone down.

Fiona is up, dressed and immaculate, munching on a triangle of toast and Marmite.

"Morning, camper," she chirps.

"Morning," I respond wearily.

"I've put some toast on for you. And there's some muesli in the cupboard if you want it." She really will make an excellent mother one day.

"Thanks," I say as the toast jumps to attention. "I'm not going in today," I add.

"I know. I heard. It's probably best. At least until you get your head in order."

I nod in mute agreement while looking for something unhealthy to spread on my toast.

"I'm going to tidy up all the mess I've made," I say, when I find the peanut butter.

"Oh, don't worry about it. How do I look?" she asks me with a hint of urgency. Today, I remember, is a Big Day for Fiona. For the first time since working at Hope and Glory PR, she is accompanying her boss on a major pitch. I turn away from the kitchen unit, knife in hand, and look at her properly, head to toe. Her hair is divided by an impossibly straight and symmetrical part, her make-up is perfectly invisible, and her charcoal trouser suit has been ironed with such diligence that it looks like it could stand up of its own accord. A fashion alchemist, Fiona is the only person I can think of who successfully knows how to master the equation, Hennes plus Top Shop equals Prada. Altogether she is infinitely more than the sum of her high-street parts.

If it wasn't for her innocent, brown-owl eyes she could almost look intimidating.

"You look . . . fantastic. You'll knock them dead."

"Oooh I hope so," she says, before finishing off a glass of pink grapefruit juice. "I'm completely *shitting* it."

She then switches into fast-forward and puts her plate and glass in the sink, grabs her coat, checks one last time in the mirror, gives me a hug, and walks out the door, all within the space of thirty seconds.

Left alone, in slow motion, I contemplate with dread the gaping, wide-open space which is the rest of the day. What do single people do with all that *time*? There's just so much of it all of a sudden.

First off, I do in fact tidy up. I don't quite know how I've done it, but over the past, what is it now, forty hours, Fiona's minimalist flat has been transformed into the set of *Withnail and I*. Despite the mess, the limited size of the place means it isn't long before I have Sheened and Swiffed it back to order.

Next up, I do some shopping. I pretend to myself that I am doing this for Fiona's benefit. So that I don't munch my way through any more of her supplies. The reality, however, is that I need comfort food and—as I am not Peter Rabbit—the edible contents of Fiona's kitchen (sugar-free Alpen, steamy bags of watercress, a loaf of Hovis multigrain, raw carrots) are not up to the job.

I step outside into a grey East End morning and head off on foot for the Whitechapel branch of Sainsbury's. Halfway there, I am accosted by a candyfloss-haired old woman who must have lost the plot at around the time Britain went metric.

"My fudgie's got a lumpy bungle," she tells me.

"Excuse me?" But I'd heard correctly the first time. "Oh, that's terrible," I say sympathetically.

She then grabs hold of my arm and looks at me through her milky eyes as if I am the last person in the world capable of saving her fudgie.

"Can you help me?" she asks, as the tears start to curdle. "Please girl, can you *help* me?" Her hands clamp tight on my arm.

As we become swallowed up by the crowd of misfits spilling out from Stepney Green Tube station, I am thinking: Why me? And why, surrounded as I am by a swarm of people, can't I just shake her off and run for cover?

Then a wave of guilt hits me.

I notice her clothes.

She's wearing a scraggy, matted cardigan which comes down nearly as far as her ankles, underneath which is a faded T-shirt, whispering the slogan "Live life to the max." An old Pepsi freebie, I hazard. Her face is marked with dirt and, if it wasn't for the absence of teeth, her breath would suggest that she has been living for the last year on a strict diet of raw onions.

Bewildered, I put my hand in the pocket of my jeans and pull out a pound coin. She flinches and moves her free hand up across her face, the way Superman might if you showed him your kryptonite collection.

"No!" she shouts, to the amusement of three gangly youths standing nearby. "My fudgie—"

"I'm sorry. I don't understand. I've got to go." My arm twists free. "I can't help you." And then one more time, just so she understands: "I. Can't. Help. You." The tone of sympathy is barely detectable now.

She looks at me, disorientated. And in the corners of her mouth I detect the memory of another, younger woman. Of a woman who had lived and loved, and lost.

Like we all do.

"I'm sorry," I say helplessly, turning and walking away. My pace quickens as I hear the old woman's gruff howl mingle with teenage laughter in the wet morning air.

I don't know how Fiona does it. Living here, in the East, surrounded by all of life's comedies and tragedies. There's just too much reality going on for my liking.

But what about Hoxton and Shoreditch, she always argues. "They've got the same creative buzz about them that Notting Hill had fifteen years ago," she will say, paraphrasing *Time Out*. "Och," I will scoff. "It's just journalists wanting something new to write about."

Cultural appropriation, that's what Siraj called it in one of his more *South Bank Show* moments. "It's about borrowing from authentic cultural signifiers until they are denied authenticity. It's like Robin Hood in reverse. The rich robbing the poor for a bit of street cred." (He never applied the same high-minded logic to his collection of Che Guevara T-shirts however.)

But Fiona doesn't see it. Nothing bursts her mockney bubble. Guy Ritchie's number one fan, that girl. Give me West End glitz any day of the week. At least you know where you stand with it.

Back two hours from Sainsbury's I am sitting in front of Fiona's TV, devouring my second tube of sour-cream Pringles, and watching adverts telling me to spoil myself "because I'm worth it."

I feel wretched. And it's not just from lumpy bungle lady, either. There's an empty feeling in my stomach which won't be filled however many Pringles I decide to pop. It's Luke. Or, more accurately, the absence of Luke that is causing this feeling. Every atom in my body is urging me to pick up the phone and dial the number I have given out as my own for the last eighteen months. Somehow, I resist. It's Monday, I tell myself, by way of consolation. *No one* has casual sex on a Monday, so if Luke's enjoying himself right now it's with his own company.

But what *is* he doing? I *need* to know. It's too much.

To be forced to become one person again, after an intense experience of being two, is among the most psychologically demanding tasks of life, and I don't know if I'm up to it. Even aside from the mental challenges, there are other problems. As the textbooks tell you, feelings of despair may be converted into physical symptoms, proliferating in headaches, ulcers, fatigue, nausea, dizzy bouts, palpitations, and all manner of debilitating general ailments. I tell you, I'm starting to realize there is such a thing as too much information.

The phone rings. I have a completely irrational but overwhelming feeling that it is Luke. No. I *know* it is Luke. Even the phone itself appears to be telling me that this is the case. *Luke, Luke* it bleats. *Luke, Luke. Luke, Luke. Luke, Luke. Luke.*

"Hello," I answer, my heart bursting with expectation.

"Marts, it's me." I cannot remember a time when I have been less happy to hear Siraj's voice.

"How did you know I was here?" I ask him, making no effort at all to mask my disappointment.

"I spoke to Luke."

My heart picks up again. "What did he say?"

"He said you walked out on him," he says, in a matter-of-fact tone.

"Did he tell you why?"

"He told me it was none of my fucking business." This rings true. Luke has always hated Siraj, and has never been able to understand the concept that I am able to talk with an ex-boyfriend without accidentally dropping my knickers.

"He, um, he, um—"

"Slept with someone?" God. Is it that obvious? Am I that boring in bed?

"Yes," I confirm, deflated.

"The wanker."

"I know."

"Do you know who it was?" Excuse me? What sort of question is that?

"No. I don't. And I really don't want to talk about it."

"I'm sorry, Mart, I just don't know how he could." His voice is warm and smooth.

"Do you mean that?"

"Yes. Course I do."

"OK. Sorry I snapped. I'm just not myself."

"You're not likely to be."

Sometimes I regret ever breaking up with Siraj. He may be a lethargic pothead with intellectual pretensions, but he has an almost feminine capacity for empathy which is so useful at times like these. Mind you, now I come to think of it, it's a capacity which has only really been evident *since* we broke up.

We carry on chatting for a while, Siraj's slow-moving voice serving as therapy, before he asks me if I want to go to this new Magritte exhibition. I agree for some reason, although I may decide to cancel at the last minute.

Seconds after I have put the phone down, Fee arrives back from her Big Day somehow looking as immaculate as when she left. Although she is telling me that the pitch was heavy going, her voice is light and her tone optimistic. She also adds that her boss was very pleased with her performance in the meeting.

"That's fantastic," I say with forced enthusiasm.

"But enough about that. How was your day?"

"Not so bad," I lie. "I've done a bit of work, got some shopping in, tidied up a bit."

"And are you feeling a bit better—in yourself?" Her eyes are wide and sentimental. Like a Disney rabbit's.

"Why, yes, I'm fine. Hardly given him a second thought to be honest." I say the sentence in one breath, to get it over with.

"Good, good." Fiona is now in the kitchen inspecting the fridge and food cupboards, which must be considerably more cluttered and calorific than she is used to.

"Wow, you got a lot of stuff, didn't you?"

"You know me," I say. "I could binge for England."

I remind myself yet again that this is only a temporary solution, that I must tomorrow look for somewhere to live. Fiona would never say anything out loud but I know what she's thinking. Carl will be back and it will be awkward, what with my bed doubling as their living-room sofa. Fiona goes into the bedroom and changes out of her work wear into something "a little more comfortable," as she always puts it (in her piss-takey gigolo voice).

I sit and think about my action plan for Finding a New Place to Live. Or at least, I try to. I just seem to come up with deterrents. Five to be precise:

1. I'm finding it hard enough to make myself breakfast at the moment, let alone handle a pushy estate agent.
2. Although I bring in a regular, and quite healthy, stream of money, I have one of the worst credit scores in the Western world. This makes even renting difficult, and rules out the possibility of getting a mortgage until I am about 107.
3. The cost of renting a studio apartment in central London

for six months is significantly higher than the annual gross domestic product of most developing countries.

4. People who advertise the fact that they have a room to let or a flat to share fall into two, equally off-putting categories. They are either mad old ladies with five budgies and twenty-five diarrhea-infected Siamese cats or they are serial killers. Or both. This is fact.

5. The fear of flat-sharing with a psychopathic, budgie- and cat-loving pensioner fades into nothing when compared to living, cooking, and watching TV on my own. Day after day. Night after night. Forever and ever. Amen.

It's just turned eight when the door buzzes. My heart stops while Fee heads for the intercom. For a second I think it's going to be Luke, armed with an apologetic bouquet of flowers. It's not. It's Stuart, armed with a completely indifferent Oddbins carrier bag full of cigarettes and alcohol.

As he lumbers into the room, I can tell that he knows about me and Luke. I feel awkward for him, and decide to put him out of his misery. "I suppose Fee told you about Luke."

"Uh, yeah. That's why I brought these round," he says, clearly improvising as he lifts a six-pack of Red Stripe from the carrier.

"Martha doesn't like lager," informs Fiona.

"Well, I got a bottle of wine too," he tells her.

"Stu, it's *Monday*," she reprimands.

He grunts and then crash-lands on the sofa, sneaking a crafty cock-flick as he descends. The archetypal omega male, away from the natural surroundings of his wankpit.

"Stu, it's a lovely gesture," I tell him. "Really it is." He responds to my words with an awkward smile, although it should be pointed out that *all* his smiles are of the awkward variety (at least when he's sober).

The rest of the evening is spent listening to Stuart talk about all the interesting websites he has been visiting recently. Although we are pleased to hear that he is at last branching away from sites with domains such as BigMelons.com and OralPleasure.co.uk, we could still do without a full run-down of the site contents for AmazingMovieFacts.net.

Did we know that, contrary to popular belief, Alfred Hitchcock did not appear in all his movies and that the little-known *Lifeboat* is the exception?

Did we know that Cinderella has been made into a movie fifty-eight times or that Tom Hanks is related to Abraham Lincoln or that Kevin Spacey's surname is a made-up contraction of the name of his favorite actor, Spencer Tracy?

Did we know that the Jedi's teachings are officially recognized as a religion in Australia owing to the fact that over ten thousand *Star Wars* fans listed the film's ideology as their chosen faith on census forms?

No, no, and no, but we do now, thank you very much.

# Chapter

# 7

Real estate agents have their own dictionary, don't they? I mean, the words are familiar but the definitions are completely different. A case in point. The area of London I'm in at the moment has been described as "up-and-coming" by the agent, although "got-up-and-left" would clearly be more accurate. Walking down this "quiet and idyllic tree-lined street" (translation: burglar's paradise), it seems that every other house is silently grumbling to itself about its sorry old state.

It's not as if I'm after much. Just a half-decent one-bedroom apartment. You know, like the one in that Renault ad on the box or that one featured in last month's *Vogue Décor*.

Fifty-one, fifty-three, fifty-five . . . ah, here it is, fifty-seven A.

Oh. Right. OK, very funny.

The ground-floor flat presents itself before me as a vision of flaky door paint, crumbling brickwork, and '70s curtainage. The 57A is painted in a shaky mucus-green on the brickwork next to the door. A shitheap, in other words. Oh well, first impressions aren't everything.

I sit on the steps and wait for the agent. He is five minutes late when he arrives, talking importantly into his mobile.

He raises his eyebrows to acknowledge my presence and

beckons me to follow him as he opens the door. Inside, the flat is even worse, and makes me realize that "bijou" must be French shorthand for "death by claustrophobia." The living room is smelly and slightly damp, equipped with swirly carpet and Habitat furnishings from a bygone era.

The agent clips his phone shut, slimes me a grin, then proceeds to tell me about the benefits of south-facing windows and original fireplaces to which I "hm" and "ah" in a noncommittal fashion. Next, he shows me a sink, shower, and toilet-equipped cupboard which he laughingly calls a "bathroom," and a kitchen so narrow that we have to turn ninety degrees and scissor-step our way inside.

"So what do you think?" he asks eventually.

Er, hello. I'm a sane, rational person who has the full capacity of sight and smell and, furthermore, who has grown quite attached to First-World living standards.

"I think I'll have to think about it," I say, and make my exit.

This unfortunate episode is repeated four more times today, in four different postal districts, as more desperate agents attempt to win me over with their own key-jangling brand of acrylic-tied, wet-look charm. In fact, I'm sure I recognized one of them from that *Estate Agents from Hell* program I saw last week.

But I have no other option than to put myself through this. You see, Fiona's Carl arrives back tomorrow night and, although he will make a show of being sorry about me and Luke, I sense that he will be less than happy about my encampment in his living room. And he's not the kind of person you'd want to end up in a confrontation with. I don't know what it is about him. It's hard to explain. He's always been, as far as I can tell, good enough to Fiona. It's just that he is always so guarded that you start to think he must have a reason to be like that. That he might have something to protect, or hide away.

Anyway, the point is that I have to find somewhere to live quick-sharpish, however impossible the task may seem. And, judging from today's ramshackle evidence, it really does seem impossible.

When the house-hunting is over exhaustion descends like a wet blanket. Which, as it happens, is exactly what Fiona calls me when I tell her, via my mobile, that I may not be able to attend the LiquidNRG launch party she has arranged for us to go to tonight as I have an editorial meeting tomorrow morning.

"It will help you take your mind off Luke," she suggests, with a charm so natural compared to the slime-mongers I've been dealing with today, I am easily sold.

"Oh OK, if you say so." After all, I do owe her one. Lots in fact.

Two hours later we are getting ready to go out. At university, aged eighteen, this would have meant making around twenty costume changes, singing along to crap music with a hairbrush microphone, and grimacing our way through a bottle of cheap vodka.

Now, aged twenty-five, this means making around twenty costume changes, singing along to crap music with a hairbrush microphone, and grimacing our way through a bottle of *expensive* vodka. Ah well, that's maturity for you.

Fiona is in particularly spectacular high spirits tonight, in an enthusiastic attempt to dry my blanket before hitting the party. Having undergone a radical Gaynorfication she is now on the bed, hairbrush in hand, singing a second-person remix of "I Will Survive" with all the camp confidence of a drag queen. In response to my nonplussed expression she then launches into a warbled version of Moby's "Why Does My Heart Feel So Bad?" followed by a madcap interpretation of "Survivor" by Destiny's Child, all part of one of our old tacky holiday tapes.

It sounds stupid but I always feel special when Fee's like this. That's because I am the only person who ever gets to see this side of her. The inner child normally buried under all that PR-girl armor.

The launch party for LiquidNRG is peopled by the usual collection of Soho somebodies and also-rans, diluted with a number of sober-suited brewery executives. Fiona has dragged me here, to the Baa Baa Rooms, early so I'm well and truly on my way, wired on this caffeine-guarana-vodka-tequila-infused green fizzy pop. Oh well, I am thinking, I might as well take the whole week off.

"I'm sorry," Fiona says once we have found somewhere to perch.

"What for?"

"For forcing you to come," she says, looking at me with her storybook eyes.

"You didn't. You just suggested it might be good for me. To take my mind off Luke. And it is."

"It is what?"

"Taking my mind off Luke."

"Are you sure?"

"Sure I'm sure."

Sure I'm sure I'm sure. But my mind is only *off* Luke because it's not actually *on* anything. Other than caffeine, guarana, vodka, and tequila of course.

Two feathered transvestites walk past handing out lollipops.

Fiona, even though she is on her fifth bottle of LiquidNRG, maintains her work ethic. She suggests that we go and talk to the editor of a dance-music website who has just appeared amid the throng.

"Is it OK if I just wait here?" I ask her.

"Course. I'll try not to be too long."

I sit back and try to blend myself into the furniture, a difficult task considering its fluorescence.

Oh shit, I've been spotted. That gimp over there, the one with the ironic sense of hairstyle, he's just caught my eye and won't let go. *No. Don't. I'm not interested. Really.* But it's no good. He starts to zero in, cutting a jagged path through the smoggy room.

Where *is* Fiona?

Then, for the first time in a week, something goes my way.

From out of nowhere, this woman loses her footing and free-falls down three steps before crash-landing by my feet. I stoop to haul her up.

"Are you *OK*?"

The woman straightens herself up and flicks hair from her face in a hilariously ostentatious manner. Although she is clearly out of her skull, it is difficult not to be impressed by her appearance. She looks fantastic. Unreal, even.

"I'm fine, sister," she hiccups. "The airbags cushioned the impact." She says this with a nod towards her buoyant chest.

Her red hair, full lips, and politically incorrect dimensions combine to form an intoxicating effect. Don't get me wrong, these are not the kind of good looks you get envious of or the kind that inspire hatred on a first viewing. No. This is the type of contagious beauty that makes you feel good about yourself, that somehow makes those within its proximity better-looking too.

Although the gimp has backed off, those other penis-equipped members of the party are now looking in our, or rather *her*, direction.

"Mind if I sit down?" she asks, extravagantly tilting her head.

I say not at all and she introduces herself. "Jacqui Falstaff."

"Martha Seymore."

We exchange CVs, and I discover that she puts on the Dollar Disco at the Zouk club, in Clerkenwell, which she crudely advertises as "the best place in town to claim your share of Very Important Penis."

When Fiona returns I can see she is taken aback by this flame-haired cyclone, although she soon gets whipped up by her Force Twelve personality.

Throughout the course of our conversation, we discover that Jacqui has had sexual encounters with approximately fifty percent of the men in the room. One of them, that Versaceclad pretty boy with flawless dentistry about five meters away, she has even had a relationship with.

"*Really?*" Fiona and I chime with a little too much surprise.

"Yes, really," she informs us, "although after three weeks it was clear it wasn't going to work out."

"How come?" I ask.

"He's a sexual primitive, completely unaware of a woman's basic needs," she answered thoughtfully. "I mean, he's the type of bloke who thinks cunnilingus is Ireland's national airline." She then laughs at her own punchline with such ferocity that it looks for a second as though she might fall over again. "Sorry," she apologizes. "Old joke."

It is quite comforting, really. To see someone so completely and genuinely uninhibited at an event like this, in deliberate contrast to the assembly of record execs, journalists, DJs, PRs, and other media freeloaders, all kissing air and arse in equal measure.

Although Jacqui Falstaff is clearly a card-holding member of the Beautiful People, she is different from the rest. For a start, she is beautiful. That is to say, if you took away the Gucci, the fake tan, and the high-maintenance haircut, she could still hold her own. Or rather, she could still get someone to hold her own for her.

I know I'm gushing. Always do when I'm sozzled. That's just me. But there's just something about her, something about those honest blue eyes, that makes me want to blurt my heart out as if I am in a confessional.

And that is what I do, to my own and Fiona's complete surprise. I blurt. Most of all, it will shock you not, I blurt about Luke. About how you can know someone and not know someone at the same time. About the unbearable paradox of being in love. About the fundamental difference between love-sex and lust-sex and how it may not be a difference at all. I drone on and on for what seems like seven hours, and assume that by the time I reach the end of my dreary monologue she will have slipped into a coma.

But she has not. In fact she is wide awake, sitting cocked on the brink of her seat. "You want to know my theory?" she asks, before blowing two thin trails of smoke out of her nose.

Fiona and I nod sincerely.

"A man is as faithful as his options."

I smile. This is a seductive statement. Although it goes against everything I have ever written regarding men and relationships, I can't help feeling right now that this could be the truth. Or more accurately, *a* truth. One of the many thousand love-truths out there we comfort or punish ourselves with.

I'm sorry. I think I need another drink.

# Chapter

# 8

Wednesday morning. Mortimer Publications.
Never the best place to nurse a hangover.

As I penguin my way through the slow, revolving doors of Glendower House, I start to feel the heavy weight of reality press down on me. In the background, there is the incessant growl of construction work—the sounds of the city reinventing itself, moving forward. Reminding me that, despite a vast amount of evidence to the contrary, life does in fact go on.

For the last few days, I have been acting as if this is impossible. That nothing goes on. But of course it does. Everything goes on, as oblivious to your concerns as these revolving doors. That said, it does feel weird, being back in this environment. The last time I was here, I was a different person. The last time I was here I had Luke, and all that went with him.

Now, deprived of my rose-tinted Fendi lunettes, it's as though I am looking at everything through fresh eyes. And boy, is it ugly.

Despite being home to such designer titles as *Gloss*, *Wardrobe*, *Sizzle*, and *Blasted*, Glendower House is quite possibly the worst-looking mid-rise office block in West London. No, make that the Western hemisphere.

The first time you enter it certainly confounds your expectations. The minimalist offices which shine from the pages of *Construct* (another Mortimer publication) are a far cry away from the dingy, low-ceilinged, high-fire-risk affairs here.

But it's not just the way it looks. It's where it sits.

You would not, for instance, expect *Gloss* magazine to be situated on the same floor as the award-winning trade title *Trout Farm International*. Or then again, if you're one of the many to have taken time out to giggle at Veronica's pompous mugshot on the Editor's Letter page, perhaps you would. But I'm hardly ever here, so it's not really my place to complain.

However, while I can, legitimately, work most of the time at home, these editorial meetings are what Veronica likes to refer to as "nonnegotiable." I don't really understand why. It is rare that any of my suggestions make it into print. Veronica says it is useful for me to attend, as it helps me to keep my contributions "in line with the whole *Gloss* ethos," whatever that is.

Anyway, I'm here. I've made it. In body if not in spirit. The sickly taste of LiquidNRG still at the back of my mouth. And Veronica, judging from her hypertense expression and cat's-arse pout, is not happy. She manages to condense the sentence "Oh, Martha, good to see you, hope you are feeling better" into one, awkward grunt, before getting down to the real business of ruining our day.

"This is not a good time," she commences, stating the obvious. "The May sales stats are about to come in and, to be brutally honest, every sign is that they will be fucking terrible." Her phone rings. "Yup . . . Yup . . . How much will it be? . . . No, just a ballpark . . . Yup . . . We've got to put it to bed by the end of next week . . . Yup . . . Yup . . ."

As she carries on yapping away I survey the room. Despite the fact that it is ten to nine everyone seems wide-eyed and bushy-tailed. Even Guy, who has no doubt spent last night playing hide the salami, is a mandarin vision of morning zest.

Veronica clunks the phone down. "Now, back to business. The stats . . . Sally is on my back about it, the sales team are getting shit from the priority advertisers, and we've got two rival launches happening this month."

Guy, who is sitting by her side, nods his head supportively, in the style of a deputy prime minister. The rest of us shift our buttocks nervously.

"And then there's every other fucking title going out with cover-wraps for their summer issues, which is impossible for us owing to Sally's tight-bloody-fisted budget for the next three months . . ." Veronica and Sally Marsden aren't what you would call bosom buddies, and not just because of their pancake chests.

Without any apparent provocation the printer behind Veronica suddenly wheezes into life. She pauses, before turning to pick up the printout.

Silence.

We watch her expression flit from cold steel to acrid dismay as she works her way through the sheet of paper.

"So there it is," she says ominously. "In black and white."

What is it? To look at her you would imagine it is a press release announcing the End of the World. She holds up the sheet for all to see and gives it a weighty backhand. It is a table with a list of numbers.

"Two hundred and fifty-seven thousand six hundred and eighty. Two. Five. Seven. Six. Eight. Zero."

For a brief moment I think I'm on *Countdown*. Two from the top and four from the bottom please, Carol.

"What this means," she says, close to collapse. "What this means . . ."

Guy charges to the rescue. "What this means," he says, "is that our circulation figures are now at their lowest point since Veronica came on board the good ship *Gloss* two years ago. And they're sinking fast."

But, unlike in Veronica's, there is no fear or frustration in Guy's tone. He is, as always, cucumber-cool, and his thoughts are transparent. You can almost hear the voice in his head at times like this. *I am fabulous*, it is saying. *I Am Fabulous. And everyone knows it. Who cares if my job is on the line? I am, and will always be . . . FABULOUS.* While Veronica remains standing, the whites of her knuckles now visible as she clenches the back of her chair, Guy's words roll on. "It also means that nothing can slip. It's survival of the fittest out there at the moment, so one sign of weakness and we'll be eaten alive . . ."

He goes on like this for another two minutes, evidently seduced by the sound of his own voice and his sub-Darwinian take on the world of magazine publishing, until Veronica has managed to gain some kind of relative composure.

"OK, so here's the bottom line," she says. "We've got three issues to get back above the three-hundred-thousand mark, before the ABC audit hits us. We've got to win back those stupid bitches who've decided to ditch us in favor of two hundred pages of advertorial and a free makeup bag. The only way we can do this is to go for fucking broke. A complete overhaul, that's what we need. Not the graphics, Kat, that's too risky . . ."

Kat, the art editor with the Henry Ford sense of fashion (any color so long as it's black), sits back in her chair with relief.

"But everything else, everything else must be reconsidered. That means we've got to ditch all those social-conscience pieces. You know. No more stories with titles like 'My Himalayan Hell' or 'Babies for Sale.'"

Zara, the staff writer and all-purpose vamp, who proposed both features, flinches with embarrassment.

"You see, I've started to realize that a few years ago these features were useful in attracting the sort of reader who wanted to *appear* like they were interested in reading about Third-World debt and female circumcision. Now they've given up the pretense. Frankly my dears, they don't give a damn. So let's leave all the po-faced change-the-world do-goody stuff for *Marie Claire* and the *Socialist* fucking *Worker* . . ."

As you can probably see for yourself, Veronica is now exhibiting a variety of characteristics commonly associated with the advent of a nervous breakdown.

"We're called *Gloss*, for chrissakes. That's what we've got to remember. Call it dumbing down if you like, I prefer to call it being realistic. There's only two things which sell a magazine: sex, beauty, and fashion, in that order . . ."

Although everyone has noticed, no one dares to correct her poor math. We wait as she lights a cigarette.

"Ultimately, it depends on the sex. We need to spice things up, that's what our market research tells us."

She then starts yammering on about focus groups and qualitative surveys and the spoon-fed opinions of the bright, young guinea pigs who took part.

"Fellatio techniques, blow job know-how—that came out on top . . ." While she is talking, I cannot help but notice that Guy is looking straight at me. What is it? Is there something my chin? No. It's not that kind of a look. It's almost as if he can sense I am single again, back on the market.

*Don't, whatever you do, make eye contact.*

*Resist, Martha, resist.*

*He's only playing a game, and if you look he's won.*

*Duh!*

*You idiot!*

And now to make things worse you're blushing. You sad, pathetic wench.

". . . everything, from 'Your Stars' to 'Fashion Police,' must now have a sex angle. And that means you too, Martha."

"Sorry?"

Veronica looks at me despairingly. "Sex. We need to sex you up."

Zara suffocates a giggle, while the corners of Guy's mouth take a smug downturn. I look down at what I am wearing. A beaten-up pair of Gap jeans and washed-out T-shirt. I may have been thinking urban casual, but I am probably saying urban flop-house.

"No, not *you*, Martha. Your *advice*."

"Oh, yes. Of course."

"Less of the My Boyfriend Left Me What Am I Going To Do sort of stuff, more of the My Boyfriend Can't Get It Up So I Left Him sort of stuff. Love doesn't sell. Not anymore. Not now we've passed from Generation X through Generation Y to Generation Why Bother."

And then embarrassment turns to anger. Hey, I don't have to put up with this. When Veronica decided to employ me, on the strength of *one* article, I'll have you know, she'd pretty much given me a free rein. A carte blanche. I had no practical experience. She understood that. She said it didn't matter. She had wanted a psychological perspective, and that had been my unique selling point. It made no difference that I was only twenty-four, or that the only piece of valuable relationship counseling I had ever given was to Wordsworth, my much-mourned basset hound, after he had the scissor treatment. But just recently I've started to feel that it *did* make a difference. OK, OK. She's been good to me. I grant you that. I mean, just look at the website. She could easily have just allotted me a page deep within the main *Gloss* setup. Instead, she gave me a separate site of my own with a fifty-fifty cut on the ad money. But still. A smidgen of *respect* wouldn't go amiss.

"No problem," I tell her. "Sex is my middle name."

At this, Zara makes a high-pitched squeaky noise. The rest of the room, excluding Veronica, breaks out into a fit of giggles. See, I'm a girl who serves many functions. While I am busying myself pretending to be a relationship expert, I double as a pretty good, if hung over, court jester.

# Chapter

# 9

"Do you think it's a good idea?" Fiona, bless her, is visibly concerned.

"Why wouldn't it be?"

"Well, for one thing, you don't know her. And for another, she just seems so, I don't know . . ." She searches for the suitable word. "*Dangerous.*"

I laugh out loud. I'm sorry, I can't help it.

"Dangerous? What do you mean? What's the worst she can do?"

"Well, I don't know, do I," she says, in a tone which suggests that she realizes she is being just a little irrational. "She might know *bad people*." The way she says the last two words is deliberately melodramatic. You know, like the precocious, basin-headed child in *The Sixth Sense* when he says to Bruce Willis, "I see dead people." And as Fee loved that film, I think it's a conscious reference. But underneath, I can see she is genuinely worried for me.

"Hold on. You just admitted yourself that we don't know her, so how can we judge how *dangerous* she is?"

"I don't know. She just seems the type."

If Fiona has a fatal flaw, and I'm not sure she has (at least not a fatal one anyway), it's that she makes snap, and often irrational, judgments about people, and sticks to them, regardless of how much evidence mounts up against her view. I suppose it's part of her need to order everything around her, to sort things into boxes and keep them there.

"Listen, Fee. I'm not pretending it's the perfect solution. But it's not like an arranged marriage or anything. I'm only going to be her flatmate."

Yes, that's right. Her flatmate. Well, what can I say? Seemed like a good idea at the time. She's got a spare room, I need a spare room. You could say it's the perfect solution.

"I know. It just seems a bit bollocky, doesn't it? I like you being here. That's all." She slides her hair behind both ears in one symmetrical gesture.

"Aw, hon, I like me being here too. But you know it's for the best."

We hug in true girly fashion and, as we do so, I get the strange feeling that I am letting her down, that she is deflating in my arms. She sighs over my shoulder, like a punctured tire.

Jacqui lives, ironically enough, in a church. That of St. Lawrence, proudly situated at the Holland Park end of Lansdowne Road. It was converted a few years back into six ambitious apartments. Quite tastefully done actually. Stainless steel ironmongery. Solid-core, cherry-veneered doors. Oiled oak strip timber hallway with as many of the original features left intact as possible, including the arched masonry, original woodwork, and a stained-glass window in the bathroom depicting the Sermon on the Mount. Of course, Jacqui has added some of her own signature touches. Japanese prints on the walls, a blood-red two-piece suite, Meccano bookcasing, wide-screen TV.

Despite the fact that Jacqui has a more, what should I say, *relaxed* approach to tidiness then Fiona, she's heavily into *feng shui*, or as she insists on pronouncing it, *fang shway*. Every piece of furniture, she tells me, is strategically positioned to ensure health and wealth and a regular diet of random shag-pieces. And who am I to be skeptical. It clearly seems to be working.

While most of the apartment is in reasonable order (although, as I've suggested, it comes nowhere near Fiona's standards), the coffee table in the center of the living area is a microcosm of chaos. An assortment of remote controls, magazines, empty wine bottles, brimming ashtrays, used tissues, melted candles, and hair curlers.

She directs me into the second bedroom, which is comparatively bare save for the two framed film posters (*Leaving Las Vegas* and *Wild at Heart*—Jacqui's got a bit of a thing for Nicolas Cage, or at least what she nostalgically refers to as "the pre-Mandolin version").

"Apparently this is where the altar used to be," she informs me.

"Do you ever find it weird living here?" I ask in return.

"What do you mean?"

"You know, in a church."

She looks at me with mock-heavy eyes. "Only on saints' days and religious festivals. Then it *really* gets to me. But I do find it more convenient for Communion on Sundays."

I smile and land my bag on the bed.

Within a couple of days I am almost acclimatized to this new environment. I say *almost* because I must admit that it is something of a culture shock, being surrounded by Jacqui and her constant conveyor belt of pumped-up pretty boys.

Not that I'd touch any of them. I wouldn't. I suppose in a way that's the problem. I mean, what is all that *about*? How does she do it? I'm sorry, but I've never really got to grips with casual sex. For one thing, it doesn't seem that casual. In fact, it seems like bloody hard work—all the bad lies, all that awkward minicab etiquette, and all those regretful morning-afters.

Take this morning. That hoover-headed creature who emerged from her bedroom with his hands gloved in his boxers. I mean, who *was* he?

All of a sudden, the sex I had with Luke seems like the most meaningful thing in the world. When I said that sleeping with Luke was great I wasn't referring to the shagging part, as you know. But right now I am starting to miss the sex just as much as the slumber.

Oh sure, it didn't just start out amazing. Our first time was not, as our American cousins like to put it, "all that." There were no fireworks. Or rather, there was one. A Catherine wheel which went round and round without getting anywhere for about thirty seconds before shooting off into the night sky.

But things got better.

We soon started to work to the same rhythm and, like the dutiful lovesmiths I imagined ourselves to be, made a conscious effort to find out what exactly turned each other on. In my case, this was pretty easy. As with most men, Luke only has one erogenous zone and it conveniently dangles between his legs. But he too achieved similar success, using his cool hands to venture into new territory and to indulge in his new-found pursuit—G-spotting.

It's always hard to pinpoint, isn't it? The precise moment when shagging becomes something more heroic. But in this instance it was easy, we both knew when the audition was over. When our eyes locked, and stayed that way, throughout the whole thing. My hands in his hair. His voice, more intense with each movement, repeating over and over, "I love you, I love you, I love you . . ."

Oh, OK, I might be romanticizing just a little bit. Guilty of looking back through my rose-tinted Fendi lunettes again. After all, I don't think we diverged that much from the national average, either in format or frequency. And I should stop trying to edit out the interludes of reality before, during, and after each flesh-on-flesh encounter. The fumbling and swearing and struggling as he rooted around in his sock drawer looking for a Fetherlite or the slight look of resentment as he unrolled it down over his cock. The precarious position changes and the whole sloppy ritual of the withdrawal. It certainly wasn't cinema sex; most of the time it wasn't even TV sex either (although I could swear I heard canned laughter on a couple of occasions).

And, of course, the road map of our bedtime adventures quickly became familiar to both of us. Within a very short space of time we knew where we could and couldn't go. We knew all the best short cuts and scenic routes, and when to take the high road or the low. Everything, even the new stuff, became a variation on a well-traveled theme.

But there can be no denying that, in its own honest way, it acquired a strange kind of beauty. We were partners in the act, and we became closer each time. Or at least that is how it felt. Yes, it was repetitive, but isn't that the point of sex?

True, the element of surprise evaporated early on, and we adopted a familiar framework. So what? Is novelty the only criterion for good sex? I know some people think so. The people who believe the principles for successful lovemaking are the same ones which apply for a fancy-dress party. But Luke and I never indulged in theme nights. There were never any vicar's tea parties or night-nurse patrols. And, call me old-fashioned, I never required Luke to dress up as Popeye and sing me a sea shanty in order to wet my whistle (whatever he might have told you).

The sex we had was, I suppose at least by some people's standards, fairly middle-of-the-road, away from the lay-bys of perversity. It didn't involve batteries, handcuffs, chocolate fondue, pasta-wrestling, party poppers, rose petals, third parties, readings from sacred texts, or donkeys. And most of the time it was confined to a bed. Yes, a *bed*, I know. Boring, boring.

But the familiarity of it all, the lack of experimentation, didn't matter. In fact, if truth be told, it helped. You see, before Luke, orgasms had been something I had studied but never experienced. The scientific manuals had told me only so much, and in rather unpoetic terms. *A complex sequence of processes occurring at the climax of sexual activity involving involuntary movements of the genital organs, voluntary movements of related muscle groups and neurophysiological responses keyed by spinal action that result in strong pleasurable sexual feelings culminating in an abrupt sense of relief of tension.*

That was as much as I knew and so I just always thought that an orgasm, like death by lightning or winning the lottery, was something that happened to other people. My numbers never came up. With Siraj, despite a couple of close-but-no-cigar near-misses, orgasms were off the map (for me, that is. For him they were always very close at hand, which I suppose was part of the problem).

I had managed to console myself that I was not alone. While researching my master's degree I discovered that female orgasms were a rarer occurrence than I had imagined. My favorite piece of bedtime reading became the edifying *Hite Report*, which produced the comforting statistic that out of a sample of over 3,000 women nearly two-thirds never, or very rarely, experienced orgasm in intercourse, and eleven percent never experienced it at all. I gobbled up the theories put forward by the beardy boffins that suggested that not having an orgasm was perfectly natural because "the clitoris is not precisely placed where it can respond to the thrusting of the male." At the same time, I cowered away from the belief that orgasm failure was a result of psychological damage inflicted by early experience.

Psychological damage? *Moi?* I don't think so.

Anyway, whether because of my biology or my psychology, the fact was that I had, like so many of us, resigned myself to a life of faking it. And in this I became an expert, sighing and moaning with such sincerity that I made Meg Ryan seem like an amateur.

However, with Luke I felt no need to fake it. I could be myself, work at my own pace, and let it all hang out. It was, if I remember correctly, on our fifth time together when it happened. My first Coca-Cola climax. The real thing. And boy, did I enjoy. I just arched my head back and gulped down the sugary pleasure as my body melted away into the promised land.

We'd been arguing actually. About what, I can't really remember. Something trivial. Or perhaps not. Oh yes, that was it, I remember now. Parents. Or more specifically, *his* parents, "the old sperm and egg." Brian and Margaret. They were coming down that weekend and I was going to meet them. Except I wasn't. "It might not be a good idea," he said obscurely. "They can be a bit hard work, and I don't think you're ready for it."

"You're embarrassed by me," I suggested. "You're scared they won't think I'm good enough."

"That's bollocks," he assured me. "It's just that they'll be planning the wedding within five minutes of shaking your hand. And besides, they're only coming down for an afternoon." It was a convincing thesis, and I was won over. Not straightaway, mind you, not before he declared his undying love and affection. Not before he told me I'd be seeing Brian and Margaret on their next visit, in a month's time. Not before he wrestled me to the bed with playful affection.

"I love you."

"I love you, too."

"No, I *really* love you."

"No, *I* really love *you*."

"Well prove it."

"How?"

"You know how."

"Oh"—kiss—"yes"—kiss—"I"—kiss—"believe"—kiss—"I"—kiss—"do"—kiss.

And he did know how. Or that is what I believed as I looked into the clear waters of his grey-green eyes, and waited as his touch turned my skin to gooseflesh. Indulge me just for the moment.

Everything was natural as he pulled his sweat-glossed body over mine and grew inside me. Our hands closed together in sweet unrest as we jostled for top position. And this time the fireworks were everywhere, writing our names in the black satin sky, complete with love heart and Cupid's arrow, in celebration of the fact that, at long last, love and sex existed together in the same universe.

What was it Woody Allen said? That sex is *only* dirty if it's done right? Pah! There was nothing dirty about this, boyo, I can assure you of that. This was the opposite of dirty. It was clean and transparent, and made everything Polaroid into focus. As innocent as strawberries, as that old poem puts it.

But now sex, or rather *good* sex, seems impossible again. The University of Life taught me that during orientation week. And this is all your fault, Luke, if you are listening.

All your fault.

# Chapter

# 10

Sex is, however, *always* possible for Jacqui. Which may in part explain why she is not really a morning person. In fact, to say that Jacqui is not really a morning person would be like saying that the Pope is *not really* a pro-abortion campaigner or that Miu Miu heels are *not really* suited to marathon running. The truth is that Jacqui and mornings hate each other's guts, which probably explains why they rarely come into contact. On those odd occasions when they do decide to meet up, like right now, things can get ugly. They can never peacefully co-exist.

I mean, just look at her.

There are badger's behinds exuding more grace at this present moment.

Oh, she is beautiful, sure, you can see that. Well, just about. Underneath the flame-red fright wig and smudged warpaint, there are traces of her natural self, but you have to squint to see them. To the untrained eye, observing her as she stands at the open fridge door glugging down a bottle of Evian, she could easily pass for one of the undead.

In my brief time staying with her in "the House of Sin," as she likes to call it, I have learned not to speak to her when she is like this. Not because she will snap back or be rude. She will not. It's just that she won't do anything at all.

But I don't need to ask her about last night; I can see she had a riot. Maybe even took part in one as well. She certainly had sex, and pretty phenomenal sex, too, judging from her John Wayne gait. Her pink eyes and droopy face-flesh testify to the levels of intoxication she managed to attain at wherever it was she went, and every other piece of her has its own knowing tale to tell. She sits down opposite me at the kitchen table as I open up my laptop.

I have been struggling, for the last few days, with this month's batch of readers' problems. Having once looked at the messages in my inbox with pity, I now feel envy for their senders. At least they have hope, at least they still believe. The trouble is, the person they believe in isn't themselves. It's me.

Before I split with Luke I'd just been starting to branch out. To do other stuff, aside from *Gloss*. I'd appeared a couple of times on a daytime call-in show for Sunshine FM, for instance. It had gone all right, actually. Came across like I knew what I was talking about in that either/or, sitting-on-the-fence sort of way I'd managed to perfect. But now that it is over, now that I have fallen off the fence, I am finding it too hard to climb back up.

That oblivious sort of detachment I used to wear like a badge has now disappeared. Possibly for good. It's all very well when you're acting as a correspondent, surveying the battle-ground from a position of neutrality, but what happens when you become stranded on the front line? When you are left in love's war zone to fend for yourself? How then can you regain that same objective position?

All of a sudden I am losing faith in myself. In my own advice. Everything I write, no matter how convincing it sounds, fails to inspire me with anything but self-doubt. It is all fiction. I might as well be writing a novel.

Every time I plead with a reader to forgive, or tell them that infidelity doesn't necessarily have to mean the end, what I really want to write is: "He's taken you for a ride. He doesn't care for you. He hates you, and he has expressed that hate by doing the one thing which will hurt you most. You must not, under any circumstances, forgive him. Love is not complicated. Love is easy. It is the easiest thing in the world. Which is why infidelity is the enemy of love. The enemy of us all. But there is hope. If we take no prisoners, we can still win this thing."

But I can't write that. It wouldn't get published. I'd lose my job. I don't even know if I believe it myself, now that I come to think about it. Truth being the first casualty, and whatever. I feel it, but that's something completely different altogether, isn't it? Then again, I'm finding it even harder to write the other stuff too. The sugar-and-spice stuff. The "there's an answer to everything" sort of stuff. Advice may be my stock-in-trade, but it's currently in short supply.

I have already put together a few responses for this month. Safe bets and easy options. Nothing heavy. My boyfriend has smelly feet. I fancy my boss. That sort of thing. But I know that won't be enough to get by.

I take another look over my laptop. Jacqui has fallen back asleep, her face crumpled and mouth open.

In an attempt to get back on track I decide to return to the beginning. Where this all started.

The first article I ever submitted to Veronica, the one which secured me the *Gloss* residency in the first place, was all about the giveaway signs of infidelity. "Lovewrecked: 10 ways to spot if your relationship is on the rocks." I bring it up in front of me now, in its original electronic format.

Although it wasn't really based on psychological theory, I had every faith in the authority of the piece. The whole premise—that if your boyfriend is cheating on you or losing interest, his behavior will give him away—seemed sound enough.

However, as I scan the screen, the advice again reads like a work of fiction. A string of paranoid questions addressed to an anonymous reader: *Does he talk to you less openly? Has his routine changed? Does he quickly get off the phone if you walk in unexpectedly? Is he paying more attention to his appearance without seeking approval from you? Is he less loving and affectionate?*

If I had asked myself these questions a month ago, I would have been able to say a confident "no" to each one without a second thought. But now, living in this new world of experience, it all seems hilariously simplistic. Of course we *want* to believe that there are warning signs and visible fault lines. Of course, we *want* to know what lies just around the corner. Of course we do.

And, I must confess, it all seems to make perfect sense. We know all this anyway, don't we? How to tell. What to look out for. We'll see it coming. It's imprinted on our brains, like an archetype. Ever since the Neanderthals, women have been telling each other how to find out what their partners are up to when they are beyond the cave. Looking at the shadows, trying to make sense of them all. Determined, steadfastly determined, to stop their battery boyfriends from turning free-range. Wanting to know exactly what rests behind their murky eyes.

We will never know. We can't.

As the world's oldest and truest cliché puts it, love is blind. And, white stick or no white stick, we will always be bumping into lampposts and stepping on dog turds.

But no, that's a cop-out. There must be an answer.

Leaving Jacqui unconscious on the kitchen table I walk across the room, pick up the phone, and call Luke.

The number, which is going to be lodged in my brain for eternity, has a strange effect on me as I dial. Every digit sends me back.

"Hello?"

"Luke, it's me."

"Martha!"

"Uh-huh."

"I've been trying to contact you. I phoned Fiona yesterday and she said you'd found somewhere to live although she didn't have a number. I've left a few messages on your mobile—it's always off."

As he speaks I am finding it hard to picture him. To piece his face together. Although I last saw him only a week ago, I can only see isolated features. His eyes. His mouth. The back of his shaven head. His nose. They won't fit together, but remain cut off, Picasso-style, the full memory file beyond recall.

It is only now that I realize why I've phoned.

"Luke."

"Yes."

"I need to see you," I say, with too much weight on the *need*. "I mean, we've still got a lot to sort out."

"My feelings exactly," Luke responds in a tone that makes me have immediate second thoughts. "When?"

"Tomorrow. I could come round to yours at about sixish."

"I don't know if that's such a good idea," he says ambiguously.

"Why not?"

"Well, you know, it might make it a bit difficult, a bit *charged*, being here."

"Well, where then?"

"What about Bar 52? Six o'clock, as you said."

"All right then, if that will make you feel more comfortable."

"OK. See you there."

"See you."

# Chapter

# 11

If you believed in color therapy you would not choose Bar 52 as the location to try and smooth things over with your ex-girlfriend. The tables are gray, the chairs are blue, and the bar itself is yellow. The walls, which alternate between screaming crimson and garish orange, were clearly painted by a color-blind psychotic with a bad sense of humor.

But Luke doesn't believe in color therapy. In fact, now I come to think of it, Luke doesn't believe in much at all. "It's a load of bollocks, isn't it?" is his stock response to any world-view or belief system which contradicts or even slightly questions his own. His own being that Everything is Bollocks (especially religious, political, and new-age theories). In the early stages of our relationship, before I fully understood the depths of this cynicism, I would occasionally say something along the lines of, "You can tell you're a Cancer," or "Keeping the toilet lid down is meant to be lucky." He would then look at me as if I was mad and say, "Don't come near me with those crystals, freaky witch lady," or something equally hilarious.

The wanker.

When Luke arrives I realize I am not ready. That I have not prepared myself. For his face. For his voice. For his whole physical presence. All of a sudden he is just *there* in front of me. The mass of atoms and broken promises who has caused me so much pain and self-doubt and free-floating anxiety over the past seven days.

And he just waltzes in, to a three-four rhythm, as if nothing has happened. As if we are old friends meeting for an amiable but indifferent catch-up session.

"You all right for a drink?" are his first words to me.

"I'm fine," I say, signaling my vodka-cranberry.

As he waits to get served at the bar I look for signs of distress. Any palm-itching or eye-shifting or brow-scratching. There is nothing. He smiles a thank-you to the barman and takes his beer.

"So. How's tricks?" he breezes on his return to the table.

*How's tricks?*

This whole situation is obviously a lot smaller than I had imagined, at least from where he is sitting. I decide to take the question in the spirit it is intended and ignore it altogether.

"Are we going to talk?" he asks after a minute. "Or are we just going to sit here?"

I look behind him as a crowd of bohemian-looking students enter the bar—goateed, and full of laughter.

"We are going to talk." My voice is matter-of-fact. I am starting to realize this is probably a big mistake. I know we need to talk, but what about exactly?

"So what have you been up to?" he asks.

"Nothing really. I've moved out of Fiona's. I'm living with a girl called Jacqui." I'll leave it up to him to fill in the gaps. "What about you?"

"I've been getting on with work, keeping my head down. You know. Been doing a lot of thinking as well, since you walked out . . ."

I raise a quizzical eyebrow.

"I mean, I reckon it was probably for the best. The way it all happened. Perhaps you were right to walk out."

My mouth opens and closes, guppy-style, but no words are there to come out. He gulps back on his beer and continues.

"I suppose if I'm being completely honest with myself I expected it. I mean, what else were you going to do? I'd left you with no other—"

He breaks off to make way for an explosion of goatee laughter two tables behind him.

"No other option. The other day when I got back to see your note I just kept looking at it and looking at it. Going over that same fucking line again and again. And then, *doof*, your words made sense. It was like a revelation. It was my decision. It was *my* fucking decision."

I sit staring at him, moon-eyed. This isn't how it was meant to be. The last time I saw him he was stark bollock naked calling my name from the top of the communal stairway. He had *needed* me. Now, sitting in front of me in full Diesel plumage, another picture presents itself. A portrait of independence. One which excludes rather than depends on the viewer. Even as he is talking to me, at this close, blackhead-squeezable distance, I am not here. There is no eye contact or acknowledgment of my physical being.

"Perhaps I'm just not ready. For wherever it was we were heading. I mean, perhaps I was scared, looking for a way out. Whatever. What you did last week—correction—what *we*, what *I*, did last week, it was for the best, for both of us."

He takes another swig and wipes his mouth. An indication that he has reached the end of his soliloquy.

I hadn't come to hear this. I had wanted pain, I had wanted suffering. I had wanted to see a bleeding heart. In truth, I'd wanted his head on a plate. Most of all, however, I had wanted to know that there were still possibilities. That when it had come to burning bridges I was the only one with the box of matches and can of petrol in my hands.

But yet again Luke is proving himself to be a master of surprise. For all the time I have known him he has been pretty much predictable. Not in a boring way, either. In fact, I have always believed predictability to be a severely underrated attribute. To know a person's mind to the extent that you can finish off their sentences and accurately guess their opinion on someone you have just met for the first time is one of the most wonderful things in the world.

To be shocked, to be jolted off course: there is nothing rewarding about that. Relationships, almost by their very definition, are essentially predictable. They need to be, to work. And that is why Luke was perfect. But now everything is uncertain.

Even the way he looks has changed.

Sure, the full-cushioned lips and suede chin remain intact, but there is something different and unsettling lurking under the surface of his grey-green eyes. Something elusive, slipping away from me.

"I'm glad," I say. "That things are so much clearer for you now."

I remember a conversation that occurred two months ago. Between me and Luke. We were naked in bed, his chest my post-coital pillow. The conversation was not particularly remarkable: just the typical exchange of love-confirming platitudes that occur after sex. The words that mean so much within the lovers' contracted world but seem futile beyond it. What stands out now, however, is a statement Luke made toward the end of our duvet talk.

"It couldn't get any better than this."

At the time these words had acted as central heating, warming me from the inside. Causing me to smile as my salty skin stuck to his. This was, as I had read it, a rejection of the world outside. I was master of his universe. Everything he had ever wanted was right there, lying on top of him. But now the words, and the tired tone in which they were delivered, are taking on an altogether different meaning.

"It couldn't get any better than this."

This wasn't an expression of belief in our relationship, but of its inadequacy. If this was the best he could get here, he wanted to be somewhere else. With someone else.

Which may explain why he is now exuding a Zenlike aura

of inner calm. Without a ripple of doubt passing across his normally troubled face.

We light cigarettes simultaneously, although with contrasting style. While his hands are steady, my fingers dance with the flame. What is happening to me? And then I realize. Confusion, that's what. The rulebook has been thrown, along with a Fendolucci shoe, completely out of the window.

My Luke, version 1.0, had been a singular creature. He was constant. He was faithful. He was a miserable bastard. (When it comes to men, I've never had a sweet tooth.) But now he has propagated himself and launched a thousand upgraded Lukes all at the same time. Too many to keep track of or store in my memory.

We drink up. We conclude. We part.

I go home, back to an empty church, and water my pillow.

# Chapter
# 12

I am asleep and dreaming.

It's a big-budget dreamwork: filmed on location, in Technicolor, with surround-sound. An unfamiliar dream, in an unfamiliar territory.

*We are in a Jeep. Fiona, Luke, and me—voyaging through a dense and dusty African landscape, being driven along by a nervy but benevolent park ranger. The air is filled with a rich cacophony of exotic sounds—the mating calls of the invisible birds which inhabit the trees around us.*

*The heat is heavy and causing the dry road we are traveling on to crease and ripple ahead of us. Fiona, wiping sweat from her brow, passes me a flask of water. I go to take a drink, and then at the point when the water touches my mouth, the Jeep is jolted from behind. The ranger struggles to keep us on the road as we turn round to see two rhinos, galloping at full speed, taking it in turns to butt the vehicle. Kerbam!*

*"Shiiiiiiiiit," squeals Luke, cocked on the brink of his seat. "We're going to die." Water is splashing all over my face from the open flask I am holding. Kerbam! Despite the fact that the ranger has his foot firmly on the accelerator, the rhino strikes are getting more frequent as their heavy gallop gains pace.*

*The ranger (who is, I now realize, being played by Nicholas Cage)* appears calm: "Hold tight, people," he suggests, as the Jeep careens to the left into the wood itself. "We can lose these beasts!"

But it's no good. The interludes between each "kerbam" are becoming shorter than ever as we whiplash from side to side.

"Oh no, this really doesn't look good," Cagey tells us as he observes that we are heading for a steep drop. Flanked, as we are, with a ten-ton rhino on either side of us, he is left with no choice but to stop and hope for the best.

But the rhinos haven't finished yet.

KERBAM!

As they push us closer to the edge, we can see the drop ahead. It will kill us, there is no doubt about that.

Me and Luke are now huddled together, each under Fiona's arm. We are doomed!

KERBAM! KERBAM! KERBAM!

The ranger is not a quitter, however. He's got to give the customers what they want—a happy ending.

Sweating under the pressure, he tries to reverse, away from the edge. But we are soon forced to realize that horsepower counts for nothing when put up against a pair of tank-sized, killer white rhinos.

The back of the Jeep now resembles a mangled tin can and, with each butt, the massive horns are inching closer to human flesh.

KERBAM! KERBAM! KERBAM!

The Jeep's front wheels are now over the edge, making the ranger's attempts to back out of the situation even more futile. Then, another sound.

Coming from the rhinos themselves. A high-pitched yelping accompanying each butt. Our vehicle is now a seesaw, teetering between two equally appalling fates.

One more butt will kill us. We know that.

"Well, I'll be damned," says Nicholas, after a few butt-free seconds. We turn and look to see one perissodactyl astride the other, engaged in weighty intercourse.

"We weren't lunch," concludes Luke, finally getting into his role. "We were foreplay." The Jeep lifts sharply, catapulting us into the air.

*"Whoaaaaaaaaaaaarghhhhhh!"*

*We are falling at five hundred miles an hour, while our arms and legs pedal in vain . . .*

I land awake in my new bed.

It takes me a few seconds to remember where I am, blinking a few times before the Nicholas Cage posters come into focus.

KERBAM!

Shit. The dream's not over.

I pinch myself. Guess it must be.

"YES! YES! YES!"

I look at my watch. It's five in the morning. Doesn't she ever stop?

KERBAM!

I thought church walls were meant to be thick.

KERBAM!

"Come on big boy, come on big boy, come *on* big boy!"

And, despite myself, I wind up thinking: was that what *she* sounded like? And worse, is that what she still does sound like? With Luke. Inside her, underneath her or behind her or on top, right now. Tonight. I torment myself with images of Luke and Her, the faceless, nameless girl, running through my head like a horror porno movie with a steamy soundtrack courtesy of Jacqui and the anonymous male in the next room.

"Harder!" Jacqui orders. "HARDER!"

Her bedfellow duly obliges and nearly demolishes the wall in the process. On second thought, there is absolutely no way Luke could keep up with this rhino guy, although he would have a lot of horn. What stamina! What rhythm! One, two, one, two, one, two, one, two, one, two . . . This isn't sexual intercourse, it's a bloody earthquake!

Jacqui lets out a roar so primal that there is no doubting her orgasm is the genuine article. And still Mr. Rhino keeps on pounding, gathering force and speed. He must have been going for ages. How long was I dreaming for?

I put my head under the pillow and try to blank out the noise. It's no good. The earthquake continues for another five minutes until rhino man makes a sound which signifies one of only two possibilities: he has either reached orgasm or he has died.

Either way it means that I can at last try and get some sleep before getting up for the editorial meeting.

Monday-morning editorial meetings are never fun at the best of times, and today definitely isn't the best of times. You see, after waking up to the sound of mating rhinos I lay there and saw my shitty situation for what it is. I am a relationship consultant who has absolutely no idea what makes up a successful relationship. Not a flaming clue.

Oh, I did know.

I knew it as well as I knew anything. It was as easy as reciting the days of the week. A successful relationship is based on . . .

Mutual Understanding
Sharing Your Problems
Trusting Your Partner
Being Open
Laying Down the Ground Rules
Loving One Another
Being Able to Commit

Ah yes, no surprises, are there? We all know it really, don't we? Well no, actually. I don't. Not any more. Every time I try and put an answer together I keep getting stuck, or coming unstuck. Whatever. Same difference.

And she will notice. Veronica will have realized that I am losing the plot. Although she says nothing during the meeting itself, I can see she is saving me for dessert.

"Martha. A word or two before you go."

See. Told you.

Veronica shuts the door and we are left alone. "Are you all right?" she asks me.

"Yes. I'm, um, fine. Why?"

"Are you absolutely sure?"

I nod.

"It's just that, looking over some of your recent replies, you seem a little, what's the word, *shaky*."

"Do I?"

She clicks her tongue and sighs hard. "Yes. You do." And then, slightly more sympathetically: "I hope you don't think I'm prying, but is everything all right, you know, *outside work*?"

Outside work. To be honest, I didn't think Veronica believed such a time or place existed.

"Um, er, what, what do you mean?"

"Your personal life, Martha, your personal life. You may think it's none of my business, but if it's infringing on your professional capability I have a right to know about it, don't I?"

"Yes. I, er, suppose you do."

"Well?"

"Well what?"

"Well, are you going to tell me what's up?"

"Up? Nothing's up."

"Love life?"

I resist the temptation to answer, "Yes, I do love life," and opt instead for "It's fine." (Translation: none of your bloody business.)

"You and that blokey of yours. Things going OK?"

Blokey? *Blokey?*

"Luke?"

"That's the one."

"Um—"

*Tell the truth, Martha. Do it. Don't dig a deeper hole for yourself.*

Nine times out of ten, honesty should be the policy of choice.

"Um, things are, things are—" Shit? Kaput? Over? Couldn't be worse? Apocalyptic? "Things are fine with Luke. Yeah. Things are fine."

"Fine?"

God, does she ever give up?

"Couldn't be better."

She examines me closely, the way a parent would a ten-year-old child after having heard bad reports from the baby-sitter. Only there is nothing maternal about that look in her eye. Or that chest. Or that Mussolini-inspired trouser suit. Or anything else about her for that matter.

The phone rings. "Veronica . . . yup . . . yup . . . yup . . ."

While she yups away, I look around her office with my bleary eyes. Normally, it is as neat and ordered as Fiona's kitchen. Today, however, it is a white box of paper chaos. Press releases, freelance contracts, junk faxes, anonymous printouts, advertiser reports, photo calls, death warrants. The whole place is covered. Only the walls, with their shining gallery of *Gloss* covers, remain as they always are.

I switch back to Veronica, who is now in McEnroe mode as she blares down the receiver.

"You cannot be *fucking* serious . . . we *need* that exclusive . . . this just couldn't be worse timing . . . no, no, no, it's OK . . . we'll survive . . . don't worry about it . . . yup . . . bye."

She slams the phone down and reaches in her bag for a pill which she washes down with the dregs of her by-now near-cold coffee. "Fucking bastard buggery fucking shitty *bastard*."

"Should I—?" I gesture towards the door.

"Yes. I think you'd better."

# Chapter

# 13

Fiona has only met Desdemona on one occasion. At my birthday, two months ago. There were quite a few of us actually. Me, Fee, Des, Alex, Luke, Siraj, Stu, Carl, even a few from *Gloss*. Perhaps not the most harmonious combination, with hindsight. Which probably explains why the night had been a complete write-off. Siraj and Luke airbrushed each other out of every conversation, Fee nearly had a panic attack after losing her purse at the Voodoo Lounge, Luke and Des ended up getting lost among the heaving throng of Fabric's dance floor, and a tequila-tanked Stu decided that the best chance of negotiating our way into the Laguna bar involved showing the door staff the contents of his stomach.

Afterwards, I had asked Fee for her verdict on Desdemona. "Well, it was a bit difficult to tell," had been her diplomatic response. But, I suppose, it *is* difficult to tell with Desdemona, isn't it? It's becoming more and more so.

Oh yes, of course, there's all that stuff at school. And all her subtle put-downs. All those early attempts to hair-flick me out of existence. But she's not all bad, is she? I mean, do you think someone like Alex would fall in love with a Grade-A bitch? Yes, she's hard. Yes, she can step on people to get what she wants. But she had it tough, you know, growing up. After all, she'd played the part of the rope in the tug-of-war that was her parents' divorce. And so the time between when she was eleven and thirteen had been one long sleepless night for her. No wonder she feels the need to reinvent herself more often than Madonna.

And in this e-mail she sent, she is making it even harder to tell:

> *Martha*
> *Tried to call. No answer, so thought I'd send this to your Hotmail account.*
> *To cut to the chase. I'm worried about you. What Luke did was horrible and you deserve better. You must come round sometime. Let me know . . .*
> *Ciao for now,*
> *Des*
> *xxxx*

Now I know e-mail is an impersonal medium and can leave messages open to myriad interpretations, but there did seem to be some sort of uncharacteristic warmth radiating from the computer screen when I read her invitation. I think it was the "you deserve better" which did it. Or maybe it was the "I'm worried about you" bit. Desdemona? Worry? About me? And then I check my phone. She's left a text: *Come round on Friday (8ish) and Alex will cook us something special Des xxxx*

Just for once, I decide to give her the benefit.

But when I arrive at Desdemona's I realize I have been mistaken. It really isn't difficult to tell.

You see, not to put too fine a point on it, the meal is a disaster.

No, I don't mean that. The meal is in fact fantastic. Garlic-baked tomatoes to start, tagliatelle with hazelnut pesto for main course, and something called Chocolate Oblivion for dessert. All cooked by Alex and each course equally sublime.

So, no. The food is perfect. The disaster part is served up by Desdemona. From the moment I get there she is pressing all the wrong buttons.

"Oh Martha, you're early," she tells me when I arrive. "I was going to change . . ." She looks me up and down. "But on second thought I don't think I'll bother."

When I hand her the bottle of wine on the way in, she says: "Oh Merlot, right, OK," as if it wasn't OK at all. As if I'd just handed her a hand grenade instead of a mid-priced, perfectly acceptable, tried-and-tested bottle of red wine.

And she just carries on the whole time, putting me down, killing me softly.

But to be honest, I could just about cope if it wasn't for Alex. He's just been so goddamn *nice* all evening. Not to mention gorgeous, funny, intelligent, self-deprecating, considerate and any other adjectives you can think of under the subhead "Perfect Man."

I just haven't been able to get this image out of my head. When I walked in I could see him in the kitchen, transferring a saucepan from the front to the back hob to make way for another. His tight-knit black sleeves rolled up to reveal his thick, manly wrists. He turned towards me and smiled that warm and broad smile of his, part-clouded behind a trail of steam and softened further by the gentle curls framing his face. It took every last piece of energy I had not to run and jump into his arms and ask him to tell me, "Everything will be all right."

So every time Desdemona makes one of her subtle digs I cannot help thinking: why is he with her? Can't he *see* what she is like? Actually, it's not so much the words that she says as her subtitles.

Perhaps I should explain. Since our chance encounter on Portobello Road, I have rarely been able to meet her without subtitles playing in my head. Picking up on the *way* she says things in order to tell me what she really means.

So when she tells me that: "Oh Martha, you'll be back on

your little feet in no time, I'm sure," the subtitle in my head informs me that what she really said was: "Oh Martha, you pathetic creature, there is absolutely no hope for you, is there?"

And when she says: "Alex and I are just *so* wonderfully happy together," the subtitle finishes her sentence for her: ". . . which I am *sure* is making you feel sick with jealousy."

And the trouble is, her subtitle is right: it *is* making me feel sick with jealousy. Almost too sick to appreciate the delicate flavors of the hazelnut pesto and definitely too sick to stomach the sumptuous chocolate cake and the oblivion it promises.

Seeing the way she is with Alex, fluttering away like she's on a first date. Bursting into explosive laughter at every single thing he says regardless of whether it happens to be funny.

So by the time we reach the end of the meal, i.e., right now, I am ready to leave. In fact, I was ready to leave an hour ago.

"That food was gorgeous," I tell them, patting my stomach and sighing in the caricature of a person who has just finished eating a filling and satisfying meal. Which, of course, I have, although it still feels like a caricature.

Alex makes a modest face, while Desdemona slaps his knee, leans forward, and says: "A man of many talents." (Subtitle: "He's also a fantastic shag and right after you've gone we are going to enjoy a night of wild and rampant gourmet sex commencing right up against the kitchen wall.")

"So what's this Jacqui person like?" asks Alex, swirling his glass of wine in a sexy way. (Actually, everything Alex has done tonight has been carried out in a sexy way. God, I think he could even blow his nose right now and I'd be wetting my knickers.)

"She's, um, she's a bit of a character."

"A character?"

"Well, she likes to enjoy herself. With men, mainly. She's a club promoter—the Dollar Disco."

"So she's a tart and a drug addict," proffers Desdemona, the red wine bringing out the anger in her voice.

"Well, I wouldn't say that. She just, you know, knows how to have a good time."

"Oh yes. I know, I know," says Desdemona in such an ambiguous way that her subtitle is unclear.

"She sounds like a good laugh," says Alex. A statement which to my guilty delight prompts a reprimanding sideways glare from Desdemona's corner of the table.

"Yes. She is."

Alex and I lock smiles just long enough for my heart to lose its rhythm.

"So, anyway. How's work at the moment, Martha?" Desdemona asks the question in a tone which suggests she already knows the answer.

"Um, work? Er . . . work's . . . work's really good at the moment, actually. It's going really well. Really, really *well*."

Desdemona's chin quivers with unhappy surprise. I must have pulled it off.

"Yes, work couldn't be better. They're even thinking of expanding my column so it can run over four pages."

OK, so I may be lying just a little bit. But what the hey, I'm pissed. There's nothing that gives me greater satisfaction than wiping that oppressive smile off her face. If that makes me a bad person then I'm a bad person. I don't care.

"What about you. How many heads have you hunted recently?" I ask her, claws at the ready.

But, as ever, she shows no sign of weakness. Her headhunting is going great. And she is now starting to speak in her high-powered business-speak, which she knows I am unable to translate. That's the point.

While she is talking Alex gets up from the table to change the music. As he bends over to scan their CD collection I cannot help but notice his arse, accentuated as it is by battered denim. It's the sort of arse you could imagine the Marlboro Man to have after a hard day riding around the ranch or saddling wild bulls at the rodeo. I stick my face in my glass of wine in order to prevent Desdemona from catching sight of my drooling expression. When she has finished her lengthy and incomprehensible monologue my mind is clearly still on Alex and his fine pair of rodeo buttocks.

"Oh right," I tell her. "That's really good to rear . . . Hear. I mean, that's good to hear." Fuck. How much have I drunk?

Desdemona tilts her head to one side causing her blond hair to rapunzel almost to the table. She circumnavigates the top of her wineglass with her index finger and says nothing. Just sits there staring at me with those frosty blue eyes.

I haven't a clue what she is thinking but one thing I do know is this: she is scaring the shit out of me. She lowers her gaze as Alex turns round. Björk's latest album fills the room. And, for some reason, this makes me think about Luke. No, actually, I know why this makes me think about him. Luke *hated* Björk more than any other recording artist on the planet. Not her as such, but her music. He used to call her a "pretentious, wailing hobgoblin" and refused to let me play any of her songs in his presence. I thought he was a bit harsh, and still consider "Venus as a Boy" one of the most beautiful love songs ever written. Despite the fact that it was never one that I could relate to Luke.

But then Alex, like the hero of that song, believes in beautiful things in a way that Luke doesn't. He hasn't told me this but I can tell, just by looking at him now, just by observing that unbreakable smile, as he sits back down opposite me. This might just be the drink talking, but I don't think so. Everything about him spells out inner calm and belief. And then it hits me: Alex isn't just different from Luke, he is the exact opposite. He is the yang to his yin. The Saturday night to his Sunday morning.

He is the anti-Luke.

"I love this track too," I tell him, feeling Desdemona's icy gaze back on me.

"Well, Alex," she says. "Shall we start clearing this all away into the kitchen?"

"Yes, I suppose we should."

I make a move to help them, reaching over to place Alex's plate on top of mine, but Desdemona stops me. "No, Martha. It's all right. You just stay there. Relax. Finish the wine." (Subtitle: "He's mine you bitch, so keep your filthy mitts off.")

So I just sit here, swilling the wine around in my mouth, transferring it from cheek to cheek absent-mindedly. Through my Merlot vision, I turn and watch them both in the kitchen. Stacking all the plates and cutlery in their dishwasher, Desdemona whispering in his ear and stroking his back.

They cannot see me. They cannot see me feeding on this vision of domestic bliss. At least, I think they can't. And although there is a dark little corner of my mind that wants to believe it isn't true, there is no denying the evidence. There is no denying that, right at this moment, they love each other.

"More than anything in the world," I mumble to my drunken self, "they love each other."

# Chapter
# 14

I had never really paid that much attention to Alex at school. Not at first, anyway. As he was a year above me, we didn't have any lessons together. He was just one of those boys you'd always see in the background, playing football on the school field or strutting back from the chip shop with his pack of acne-clad reservoir puppies.

The first time we ever spoke to each other was when I'd just started in the fourth year. On the tennis courts, that was right. I was losing to Desdemona while he was playing doubles on the adjacent court. It was after school, a warm September evening.

Desdemona was acting both as umpire and top seed ("Advantage Desdemona"), taking the game as seriously as if she was up against Martina Navratilova on the center court at Wimbledon. On one of the few times in the whole match when I had managed to get to the ball, I sent it hurtling through the air towards Alex. Unfortunately, he didn't see it coming until too late and it landed, with an audible thwack, on the bridge of his nose. As I rushed over to return the ball and see if he was OK, the pups (and, needless to say, Desdemona) were milking the comedy value for all it was worth.

"Sorry," I offered pathetically.

"It's all right," he said, pinching the bridge and craning his head back in order to prevent a nosebleed. "C-could be worse."

"How?"

He then tilted forward and looked me in the eye. "You could've got my bollocks."

Hardly Romeo and Juliet, was it? But I have to say that from that day on, I developed something of a crush on Alex, and I would wind up thinking about him more and more. I was perfectly happy to keep my thoughts to myself, however, as I knew that he, along with practically every other boy in the school, wouldn't give me a first look, let alone a second.

He wasn't good-looking. Or, at least, not in an obvious way. Not in the way he is now. And he wasn't exactly beating them off with a stick. But he did have something. Something vulnerable that made you want to put your arms around him and tell him, "Everything will be all right."

And I suppose it was that uncommon want which led me, a few months later, to flirt outrageously with him at Paul "Hobb Knob" Hobb's fifteenth birthday party.

It was, if I remember correctly, one of the all-time classic teenage house parties. Hobb Knob, who by now had managed to gain some form of relative control over his spontaneous erections, clearly could not command the same restraint over his houseguests. In fact, at least half of them he could swear he had never seen before in his life.

There were acid heads in "Cool as Fuck" T-shirts chatting up houseplants, hard lads from the Catholic school cruising around like apprentice Goodfellas, baggy shoe-gazers buzzing away to the Charlatans and the Stone Roses, Timberland girls exchanging hairspray tips in the kitchen, and cider-sozzled sixth-formers nearly making it to the toilet in time. Hobb Knob's desperate cries of "My parents are back from holiday tomorrow!" evidently went unheard.

And then there was Alex. Slouched on a beanbag in the corner like a little lost boy. Looking back I realize he must have looked hideous—curtain-coiffed and drowning in his sneakers—but at the time I thought he was perfect. Perhaps it was that vulnerability, that desire to hide behind a hundred masks, that intrigued me. Unlike most of the other boys, who sweated confidence from every pore, Alex was approachable. I knew it wouldn't be too hard to make a move when the time was right. I'd already spoken to him a few times since the tennis court incident, and although it was difficult to tell, he seemed to like me. But the trouble was, in the schoolyard, I was always with Desdemona. Unable to risk rejection and ridicule, I knew I had to bide my time.

As Desdemona was away on a skiing trip with her dad, the party provided me with the perfect opportunity to make my move. And so, when he finally lifted himself off the beanbag, I stalked him all the way upstairs to the toilet in order to "accidentally" bump into him on his way out.

"Yo, Martha, wassup?" he asked me as he zipped up his fly. I should point out at this juncture that this was the period when Alex's role model of choice was Ice T, rap superstar and Original Gangsta. Consequently, while he was living on his parallel planet where the city of Durham bore all the hip-hop hallmarks of South Central Los Angeles, his middle-class English would be punctuated by bursts of Westwood-style street-speak.

"Um, I'm feeling a bit ill," I lied. "I think I'll have to go and lie down."

"Er, do you, um, want me to l-look after you?" he asked, without making eye contact.

"Would you mind?"

What a minx! Anyway, my cunning plan soon worked and we were on the bed together, Hobb Knob's parents, I think, with his arm round me.

And from there, one thing just led to another.

No, that's not quite right.

It wasn't as smooth as that. One thing sort of fell on top of another, that's more like it, and we ended up in full snog.

Kissing in the teenage fashion with mouths open yawn-wide and our heads at right angles to the rest of our bodies. Our lips were probably clamped for about two hours before Alex gently pulled me away to ask, "You're not going to throw up, are you?"

"No, I'm fine. Feeling a lot better now," I reassured him.

And so the tonsil tennis resumed, only this time at a horizontal angle. We fumbled, we groped, we exchanged buckets of saliva. He put his hand on my breast and just left it there, motionless, waiting for something to happen.

"I've f-fancied you for ages," he charmed.

"Me too. You, I mean."

"Have you. Honestly?"

"Yes. Course."

"How much?"

"Er, lots."

"More than Jamie Mulryan?"

"Yeah. Way more."

"More than Daniel?" (Daniel Brown. Alex's then best mate.)

"Definitely."

"What about S-Simon Adcock?"

"Urgh. He's *putrid*."

This was actually a bit of a white lie. Simon Adcock, aka Climb on Bigcock, was drop-dead gorgeous. Short jet-black hair, porcelain skin, and a permanent James Dean squinted expression. Not much between the ears, but then, IQ is not always on top of a teenage girl's shopping list.

"But everyone fancies him."

"Do you?"

"No. Don't be stupid, all you lot do though."

"Well *I* don't. I think he's horrible."

And then, from out of nowhere, he said: "I've g-got a condom."

To which I responded with a coquettish, "That's nice."

We fumbled some more before deciding to lock the door and undress each other.

"This is my first time," I told him, while he wrestled with the strap of my Wonderbra.

"Is it?" he asked neutrally, between the frustrated "fucks" and "shits" as he worked over my shoulder.

Naked, we both slid under the grown-up bedcovers and rubbed our hands over each other, or rather he rubbed his hands over me while I initially held back. Feeling frightened of what I might find, my hands hovered over his body without making contact.

This reiki foreplay didn't last, however. Alex pulled himself closer and I felt his warm skin touch mine, his heart beating a rapid percussion against my chest. Within seconds he was grappling with a condom, trying to work out which way round it should go. And from there, well, you can guess the rest.

Yes, we had sex. Yes, we hardly knew each other. Yes, it was quick enough to set a new world record. But this just wasn't a one-night thing, remember. I'd fancied him for ages. There'd been something between us. And there was something between us then, in the bed. About six inches long. Something I had never seen before, at least not in the flesh, not at close range. Even though it was under the shade of the duvet, I must admit I was slightly frightened by this strange object— with its purple head and curious smile. It just seemed so different to what the concealed bulge in his jeans had promised. Like when you were six and you rushed to open your kinder egg, expecting the jumping frog game but ending up with the plastic parrot.

Not that that put me off. Not really. It was just a momentary flinch, before "getting down to business" as I'd heard other people call it. Mind you, that euphemism seemed strangely absurd in this context. There was no corporate strategy here. No mission statement. This wasn't a boardroom transaction— this was bob-a-job. Dib dib dib. A Youth Training Scheme for the sexually challenged.

Of course, this is hindsight doing the talking. It's strange, isn't it? How memory can turn things into comedy. At the time, though, we weren't laughing. At the time it felt like the beginning of Something Special. I'd laid all my cards down on the table. And he'd laid his. All hearts.

And so, after the five-second roller-coaster ride was over, we kissed some more and agreed to see each other again. The next day, in fact. At the cinema. Now what film was it? One of those nameless Jean-Claude Van Damme bash-them-ups, I think. His choice, needless to say.

Anyway, as we watched oil-smeared muscle men kung fu each other to death for a couple of hours, he tenderly held my hand and threw me the odd puppy-love gaze. And for a whole week at school (which probably counts as the equivalent of seven years in grown-up relationship terms) we were seen holding hands and whispering sweet nothings on the school-yard.

So what happened?

Yep, you guessed it. Desdemona.

After returning from Chamonix she expressed her absolute disbelief that I had swung my bargepole in the direction of Alex Norton. She coerced me. She made up rumors. She told me, in effect, that he was the most vile and repugnant creature ever to have roamed the planet.

"But you don't know him like I do," I had pleaded, echoing the previous night's episode of *Home and Away*.

"Oh pur-lease," she countered. "That's what they all say."

"Do they?"

"Yes. They do."

"Oh."

And that was that. She was the expert, after all. Queen of the home run. Who was I—dark and dreary Seymore, the Addams family cast-out—to contest? And so, weak as I was, I dumped him.

"So that's it, then?"

"That's it. I'm sorry. We're over."

And then, regaining his hip-hop composure: "That's cool, y'know. I'm down with that."

I know, I was pathetic. But then, I didn't have a crystal ball. I couldn't foresee exactly who I was throwing away. Plenty more fish in the sea, so why hang on to this piece of plankton? Indeed, since I had started seeing Alex I seemed to have caught the squinted eye of Simon Adcock. And a week after the split, Simon asked me out (to nowhere in particular) and I answered with a confident, Man-from-Del-Monte, "Yes." Hell, why not. I was late in the game. Had a lot of catching up to do. Alex would get over it. OK, so I had a soft spot for him. But this soft spot was clearly misguided. Desdemona, among many other things, had taught me that.

And, to this day, I still cannot help but feel that the lessons aren't over. That Desdemona's tutelage is, in some as-yet unclear way, only just beginning.

# Chapter

# 15

There is a small wooden box in Jacqui's kitchen, painted pink with a picture on it. Some sort of watered down Pre-Raphaelite job, with sparkly dream fairies and luminous water-lilies. It's the sort of box you would expect to open and find a miniature ballerina pirouetting along to a birthday-card rendition of "Greensleeves."

It does not. The reason I can say this with such certainty is because it is open in front of me, between Jacqui and myself, on the kitchen table.

In fact the box is empty except for a folded-up piece of paper. Jacqui takes this out and moves the box to one side, while I pour myself a second glass of red and top up hers. It takes her approximately ten seconds to unfold the paper, and as she does so her face is deadly serious, as if she is in prayer.

But this is only the start of the ritual. As soon as the powder is visible, brilliant white against the black sheen of the paper, she sprinkles half of it out onto the table.

Bollocks. What the *fuck* am I doing?

Although I am filled with as much self-loathing as the next girl, there are certain aspects of me I feel good about. I am a vegetarian. I always remember birthdays. I have never swallowed during oral sex. Most of all, however, I have never tried cocaine. Never even been tempted.

Along with bungee jumping, Botox, colonic irrigation, and Guy Longhurst, the drug has always been ranked high on my Things Never To Do list. It's not simply because it is one of the most psychologically addictive substances in the world or that it can induce paranoia or heart palpitations or turn you into a complete arsehole in the space of seven seconds. No.

It's a nose thing.

I don't mean to get all moralistic or anything but up till now the idea of leaning forward, like a pig at a trough, and snorting a substance which has in all likelihood been cut with washing powder, seemed about as low as you could go. But at this moment I am feeling slightly different. I mean if, as the song puts it, it really is sunshine in a bag I could really do with some of that sunshine right now.

And this, Jacqui has assured me, isn't simply Getting Off Your Head. It is also, she has decided, Getting Over Luke. And she may have a point. I mean, I've tried other approaches—my own "head under a pillow" method, Fiona's "hairbrush karaoke" technique and Desdemona's "wave my boyfriend under your nose" strategy to name but three—and nothing seems to work.

If love is a drug which promises euphoria and a sense of completeness, then it only makes sense that I should try another chemical with exactly the same promise, doesn't it? To fill the gap.

So I just sit here, watching her, without putting up any sign or resistance. I say nothing, as she chops and spreads the powder into two parallel streaks. Like an equals sign without an answer.

There's just something about her. Just being in her presence you get caught up in her lifestyle. And halfway through doing whatever it is you wouldn't normally be doing you end up saying to yourself, "What am I doing?" but by that point it's too late. You're already doing it.

Like now. As she flashes me her go-ahead grin and hands me the rolled bank note. As I press my finger down on my left nostril and move down towards the table. But then an image of Fiona's Carl on a coke comedown flashes into my mind.

"I'm sorry, Jacqui. I don't think I can do this."

"What?"

"I know you are trying to help me out and everything, it's just that I don't think that this will work."

"Martha. It's a line of coke. It's less addictive than coffee. It's nothing. Just something to pep you up a bit. Hell, I thought you worked on a magazine. You mean you've never?"

"No. Never."

"But everyone does it, even traffic wardens."

Traffic wardens? Where does she get that sort of information?

"I just don't feel like it. I'm sorry."

Jacqui looks at me, disappointed. "OK, OK. Just say no. Be a good girl."

"I'm sorry."

Then suddenly she softens and, although it could just be me, her eyes look close to tears. "Don't be stupid," she tells me. "You shouldn't be sorry. Stick to the wine."

So I do. I bury my head in the glass she has just poured for me and listen as she hoovers up both lines. She then starts to make weird sinusy head noises.

"Are you OK?"

She sits back in her chair, pressing her palm against the side of her face. "On top of the world."

I look at her again. She is now smiling a full if rather shaky smile. And I start thinking, as I watch her rise up, why is she doing this? Why is she so determined to take me under her high-flying wings?

"You and me have a lot in common," she had told me on my first night here. "A lot more than you probably think."

And then we had got talking. Talking about how she believes that the only way to be happy is to live in the present tense.

To forget about the past and ignore the future. Hardly a new philosophy, I admit, but the way she put it across made the argument so much more convincing.

And, looking at her now, in her full kaleidoscopic glory, it is still tempting to be convinced. To believe that she may have all the answers. After all, if the road of excess leads to the palace of wisdom there can be no denying that Jacqui is well on the way to being a very wise woman indeed.

"So where are we going?" I ask her, as she puts the pink box away.

"Oh. All over," she tells me. "I want to show you everywhere."

And she does. During the course of the night we taxi from bar to bar and from club to club, beyond different velvet ropes and past the queens of the clipboards.

Throughout, she acts as my mentor. A loved-up, man-eating, Professor Higgins in a Technicolor dreamcoat. I watch her the whole time, observing how she glides so easily through every protected doorway. How she manages to talk to people she has and has not met in exactly the same way. It feels exhilarating. Walking into these places, feeling your value going up. Being with someone whose name fills every room. The girl with "the hottest guest list in town."

"Are you having a good time?" Jacqui asks me at one point, as we take a momentary pause.

"Yes," comes my voice. "I really am." And the things is, I really am. The music, the people, the shallow glamour of it all. It seems to be having the right effect.

And, by the end of the night, I begin to understand the logic behind that prehistoric cliché, painting the town red. Jacqui has somehow managed to transform the entire gray city into a mass of scarlet. The velvet ropes, the leather-cushioned walls, the spotlights, the bleary eyeballs, the cigarette trails, the MAC-painted glossy lips. Everything shines as red as her hair.

Like one big disco inferno, the whole of London feels on fire.

# Chapter

# 16

Fast-forward three days.

I am with Siraj. At the exhibition. You remember, the Magritte show. Yet another recovery strategy. Standing next to him, my ex before last, watching him do what he does best: stare into rectangles. A canvas or a TV screen, it hardly makes a difference. And when Siraj looks at a painting he always looks straight at it. Unlike me, he never bothers to check the white plaque by the side: *René Magritte*, The Treason of Images, *1928–9, Oil on canvas*.

I recognize this. You know the one. The picture of the pipe and the line underneath telling us *"Ceci n'est pas une pipe."* This is not a pipe.

"So what is it then?" I ask Siraj.

"It's a painting," he tells me, straight-faced. "It's making the point that the image is not the thing it represents. And it was the first time that point was made in the history of modern art. At least in such a deliberate way."

He loves this role, the art connoisseur. And, I must confess, I've always found him at his most attractive when he's like this. When he's trying to make you understand the archetypal imagery in a Rothko or the role of repetition in a Warhol. He's very good at it. Breaks things down. Makes things clear. And he's so passionate. As if there is nothing more important in the world. It's the only time he's like this.

*René Magritte*, The Human Condition, *1934, Oil on canvas.*

Oh yes, I've seen this one before as well. On a postcard, I think. It's the one where a canvas stands on an easel in front of a view through a window. Both the picture and the view depict the same landscape. And the picture exactly overlaps the view itself.

I look down at my exhibition guide. *In this painting the play between image and reality suggests that the real world is only a construction of mind.*

For some reason, standing at this canvas of a canvas provokes me into telling Siraj about my work problems.

"Why can't you just lie?" he asks me.

"It's not as simple as that."

"Why not?"

"Because I'm dealing with real people. Going through real stuff."

He looks bemused, as if that makes no difference.

*René Magritte*, The Rape, *1935, Oil on canvas.*

A woman's body in place of her face. Tits for eyes and a fanny for a mouth. I like this one the best. It makes the most sense. Looking into a face and seeing something else. We all do that, don't we? It's not just men.

And I'm doing it right now. As I'm looking at Siraj. Seeing a thousand different things which probably aren't really there.

"You know," says Siraj, turning away from the painting and towards me. "It'll all work itself out. It always does."

We go for a drink at the gallery bar. Over an Irish coffee and a cigarette I bore him senseless about Luke. About the way he acted at Bar 52. About the mystery woman.

"I know you don't think it now," he tells me. "But you will get over him. You'll just wake up one morning and he'll be gone. Out of your head. You got over me, didn't you?"

"Um, yes. But that was different."

"Thanks," he miffs. "You really know how to make a bloke feel good."

"No. I didn't mean it like that. I *meant* the way we ended. It was mutual. It made sense. We saw it coming."

"I get you," he says, pouring another sachet of sugar into his drink. "But then, as Cilla Black wisely concluded, life is full of surprises."

We drink some more, then get the Tube back to his place, to spend the rest of the night watching TV. I should have gone home. I don't fancy another night on a sofabed. But something stopped me. And now, sitting here next to him, with *Newsnight* blaring from the corner of the living room, I know what it is . . .

"Everything is relative," Siraj tells me, as if he is the first person ever to have arrived at this conclusion.

"Yes. I know. If there was an earthquake right now, I wouldn't give a shit. But that's not going to happen, is it?"

"I wouldn't rule it out. Not altogether. Not with all this climate change stuff going on."

"Are earthquakes affected by climate change?"

"I think they can be."

"Oh. Right."

My attention turns for a second to the TV. "*A Palestinian suicide bomber has killed himself and injured twenty other people outside a café in the small Israeli town of Kiriat . . .*"

Yes. OK. Point taken. I am a self-centered, vacuous individual who magnifies my own problems until everything else seems insignificant.

We continue talking, letting the TV wash over us, blanket us, like it always did. And then the night turns into something else. *Siraj* turns into something else.

"You know what you need? he asks.

"No, I don't," I say.

"Closure."

"I hate that word."

"But it's possible."

But can it be. Can one ex extinguish another?

I recall a piece of advice I gave earlier this year. In the May issue, I think. A heartbroken girl seeking solace in the arms of another former lover. *Don't do it*, I had pleaded. *It would be a very big mistake*. And yet here I am, heading in the same direction.

An hour later, we are talking, sharing a joint, Siraj is saying something about the gaps between things. Between image and reality. Between work and the personal. Between love and sex. He looks so serious as he talks, so pompous, so cute. Like a six-year-old child saying a new long word they have just picked up. *Eggstra-ordinary*.

His voice. That slow-moving, marijuana drawl. It does something to you, doesn't it? And he just carries on, talking and talking, over the TV—some film on Moviemax with Meryl Streep, whitewater rafting—until he has finished his joint. He then sits back, closer to me. My head falls on his shoulder, tired. Stoned.

We say nothing. At least not in words. It feels nice being so close. So warm. So safe.

Before I know what I am doing, I am kissing him. And then, shortly after, he is kissing me. We are kissing. But a few seconds later, in a moment of clarity, I break off.

"We shouldn't be doing this."

"What?" he asks, as if he genuinely doesn't know.

"Kissing."

He looks at me with those sleepy eyes and says, with a cheeky off-center smile: "This is not a kiss."

Fast-forward three minutes.

Siraj is on top of me. Naked. Allowing me to lie back in the passive, patriotic position.

Allowing my mind to wander beyond the Pollock-printed walls of this bedroom.

Allowing me to think of Freud.

More precisely I am thinking of the link he identified between repetition and self-destruction. We repeat ourselves to kill ourselves. Could it be that simple?

"Are you OK?" he asks, between panted breaths, as if checking for a sign of life.

"Mmm, yes. Don't stop," I purr convincingly, placing my arms above my head to form a willowy diamond. I close my eyes and my mind travels back.

*It's certainly true that we go on making the same mistakes, the same ill-starred decisions, but can these be deliberate? Can it really be in our best interests to suffer? Is it possible we feed off our own pain?*

By the time I open my eyes again, he is in full gallop, heading for the final straight, moving in and out, in and out and in and out with ferocious speed. Although human beings are, apart from whales, the only creatures capable of engaging in face-to-face sex, right now I am wondering if this is actually an advantage.

While this gear change has stimulated me out of my Freudian reverie, I can't help noticing what I suppose I must already have worked out. Siraj is, in the most literal of senses, an ugly fucker. In normal life, of course, he is a tousled vision of loveliness, with his soft sleepy eyes and gentle smile.

During sex, however, he has metamorphosed into a different creature altogether. His eyes have cue-balled, his mouth has become hard and small, and his whole face looks under pressure, as if experiencing G-force. It's hard to explain, but as he umphs and pumphs his way towards ejaculation, it's almost like I'm not here.

Sex is often advertised as a way to bring people closer together, but right now all it seems to be doing is creating distance. The artistic flair he used to display in between the sheets has now been supplanted by a philistine desire to get the job done. As his balls slap against me, it's hard to tell whether I'm being viewed as a sexual partner or a masturbation aid.

Not that I'm doing much to dispel the latter possibility. In fact, I am pretty sure that a real sack of King Edwards could exhibit more sexual imagination than me at this present moment in time.

This isn't love.

This isn't affection.

This is biology, that's all.

Seconds away from his solitary crescendo, he bursts into wild speech, scattering the air at random. "Uh, yeah, fuh, oh, c'mon, uh, yeah—" He cranes his head back as the first wave hits, then collapses onto me to ride out the rest of his release.

When we get our breath back, we proceed with a brief postmortem.

"We shouldn't have done that," I say.

"No, I suppose we shouldn't."

As his hand scrambles around on the bedside table, in search of cigarettes, I put my head under the covers.

Perhaps Freud was right after all.

# Chapter
# 17

Closure.

The idea that you can shut something out forever, exorcise your demons once and for all. Pah! In your dreams.

Actually, not even in your dreams. *Especially* not in your dreams. How can you? Oh sure, you can close down the small stuff, like when your dog died (oh Wordsworth, I miss you) or when Desdemona pointed out your wart to the entire swimming pool (the bitch). But the big stuff, the stuff that cuts deep, that's a different story. The more you try to shut it off, the more persistent it gets, like a rejected lover. Or rather, how you imagine a rejected lover to be.

Of course, *my* rejected lover is fine and dandy. In fact, he is so fine and dandy that I am starting to doubt whether I rejected him at all. Don't get me wrong, I am over him. Well nearly. Although shagging Siraj was an undeniable mistake, it has managed to move things on a bit. The selective amnesia which comes with love has almost cleared. I remember him now as he really was. A deceitful, self-obsessed, wandering-eyed wanker. A skinny-framed, shaven-headed arch-miserabilist.

But memory is a funny thing. I mean, you can never really remember things as you experienced them, can you? You can, more or less, remember what happened, but the parts you find significant almost invariably alter through time.

For instance, all the things that used to be significant, all those empty words that used to roll out of his mouth, which I used to hold to my chest like a comfort blanket, have all but vanished. They mean nothing.

Moreover, the things that at the time I barely noticed, all those inconsistencies I glossed over, now come back to me as important road signs I missed along the way. All the small things.

The way he used to correct *everything*.

The way he used to write off any idea that wasn't his own. ("What sort of science is that?" he would ask every time I came up with a new condom theory.)

The way he used to say, "You look *fine*," when I asked him the perennial, Hepburn-inspired question: "How do I look?"

The way he used to write people off on a first viewing and reduce them to simple shades (Siraj—"arty knobsack"; Fiona— "Little Miss Prissypants"; Stuart—"soft lad").

But most of all I remember the way he used to act like a different person around his mates. Even to the extent of adopting a different style of smoking. Inhaling with his head up towards the ceiling, breathing the smoke out of the left side of his mouth, and then patting the cigarette with an aggressive index finger as it hovered over the ashtray (rather than thumb-flicking it from underneath as he did with me).

This is significant. Trust me.

So, my thoughts are of Luke. As they always are. Nothing new there. But now, right now, they are also of someone else. Someone I am at first surprised to see there. In my mind. No. Not Siraj. Alex. Remembering how I felt when I saw him, Alex, with Desdemona, for the first time since school.

When I said he looked completely different, I meant it. Especially the completely part.

Taller.

Broader.

His face had squared out. All his features had expanded widthways. His spots had cleared up too. In their place had arrived a bristly, golden stubble spread evenly across his cheeks.

Even his eyes seemed different. Although they were the same deep brown, they were now steady. The underlying panic I was able to detect a decade ago had been tranquilized. And his dress sense, too, had relaxed. The boat-sized sneakers, baggy jeans, and garish tracksuit tops he used to wear had been ditched in favor of a more sedate look. Battered, tight-fitting jeans and a smart, black, V-neck, tight-knit jumper. He clearly fit into that select group of twenty-something males who have managed to perfect that "I don't really care what I look like" way of looking good.

But perhaps the most obvious difference—at least within those first, all-important ten seconds—was the way he walked. It made it hard to believe it had only been a matter of nine years, rather than a whole evolutionary cycle. The cumbersome, Kappa-clad Cro-Magnon gait had disappeared. He was now, without a shadow of a doubt, a fully fledged human being. (This complete metamorphosis in his appearance made his opening statement—"Wow, Martha, you've hardly changed!"—a little bit worrying. Had we been inhabiting different time continuums since leaving school?)

As the evening progressed I noticed further, nonphysical differences.

He smiled.

He didn't stutter.

He smelled of Hugo Boss rather than Insignia.

He looked into my eyes rather than my breasts when he spoke to me.

He said things like: "It is a sad fact that success nowadays is only meaningful in financial terms."

He didn't say things like: "Yo Martha, wassup, you're looking fly."

And, if it hadn't been for the obvious fact that I was with Luke, I would have had no hesitation in giving him an IFR score of ten out of a possible ten. Oh okay, maybe nine point five. The point five deducted owing to the fact that he'd put on a bit of podge. Only a little bit, mind, around the face. And he was a chef, after all. In fact, the podge sort of suited him. Suited his new self.

Warm. Positive. Comfortable.

So yes, perhaps it would have been a perfect ten after all.

But, as I've said, I wasn't thinking like that. Not really. I had Luke. The skinny-framed arch-miserabilist. The *sexy, gorgeous*, skinny-framed arch-miserabilist. And Alex had Desdemona.

*Has.*

Alex *has* Desdemona. So I wasn't thinking like that. I still can't.

Can I?

So no.

No closure.

# *Chapter*
# 18

An e-mail, from Veronica, subject-lined "Urgent," and cc'd to Guy:

*Martha,*
*Need to speak to you. Today. My office. 3:30.*
*Important.*
*V*

When she signs off with a V, you always know she's pissed off. It's almost as if the act of writing her full name, adding the "eronica," would make her sound too human. Too reasonable. In fact, I'm pretty sure it's intended to represent a two-fingered salute as much as her initial.

Anyway, here I am. A good five minutes early.

I hover at the door, like a man outside a lingerie shop, anxious about what might be waiting for me within.

"Enter," calls Veronica, in her best head-teacher voice.

Inside I am greeted by two faces. One, the head teacher's, is looking at me directly, forcing me to take in the disapproving expression sitting on its sharp angular features. The other, Guy's, is looking slightly more awkward, with its wonky smile and eyes pointing lapwards.

Veronica raises a magisterial arm, a gesture which tells me, "You may be seated," before sitting herself down at the opposite end of the table. I feel as though I've just been beamed up to the Death Star.

I offer a weak smile as a token of peace. It has no visible effect.

"Do you know why you're here?" Veronica asks, in such an abstract way that at first it seems she is pondering the very meaning of human existence. She is not.

"Um, no. I don't."

"Well, to cut to the chase, Martha, I'm a little concerned . . ." She sits back in her chair as her eyes and lips tighten. "I'm a little concerned about your recent contributions to the magazine. To be perfectly honest, your advice has been rather schizophrenic recently, hasn't it?"

So *that* is why I am here.

Guy, who remains mute, crosses his legs and for the first time looks directly at me.

"Well, er, I, I don't know. Has it?"

She crinkles her brow and leans forward to examine me more closely. Feeling the tension, Guy sets about picking invisible pieces of fluff from his shirt.

"In the May issue you told Miss Heartbroken, Cheshire, that when it comes to being unfaithful the only difference between men and women is that men are more likely to get caught out. For the latest issue you declare that, and I quote, 'Women are, by their nature, *faithful*. Faithful to their friends, their jobs, their partners. If there remains a battle between the sexes it is between fidelity and its opposite.' And this is by no means the only inconsistency."

*Defend yourself, Martha. Don't take this lying down. Show them what you're made of.*

"I could cope if inconsistency was the only problem. It's not. It just seems that the suggestions you give are becoming, mmm, how should I put it, *unrealistic*." She stops momentarily in her tracks, to absorb my faltering expression.

I feel anger starting to color my cheeks. What, I suppose, is really biting my burger is the fact that my only crime is to do *exactly* what is in line with the magazine. *Gloss* isn't about truth. It is diametrically opposed to truth. After all, you can't sell truth for £3.50 a month. And you certainly couldn't expect truth to win over the big-name advertisers.

No. *Gloss* doesn't deal with reality, it trades in the young and beautiful fictions we all want to read. It's a "how to" manual for fraudsters, teaching you how to fake it through to the other side. Whether it's faking orgasms or faking hair color the principle remains the same: reality is ugly and tired and in need of a makeover.

In fact, *Gloss* is not just *about* faking it, but it is itself a fake. I mean, the "Your Stars" column isn't even written by a real person. (Couldn't Guy have come up with someone more authentic-sounding than "Astra Horowitz"?)

And then it occurs to me. Maybe I'm not struggling with the truth, maybe I'm just getting worse at telling lies.

"The bottom line, Martha, is that something needs to be done. We've got rival magazine launches taking place every other fucking month eating into our sales. Everything needs to be as tight as—"

*Your arse*, is my unspoken thought.

"—hell. The reason I first took you on was because of your clear and unwavering views on relationship matters. You had an absolute faith in your own judgments; so much so that you didn't really view them as judgments at all, just simple matters of fact. But now you are all over the shop, to be brutally honest."

"So what are you saying?" I ask.

"What I'm *saying* is that, and don't take this the wrong way Martha darling, but to me Martha Seymore isn't a person. Or perhaps I should say Martha Seymore isn't *just* a person. In the context of *Gloss*, which right now is the only context I really care about, Martha Seymore is a *brand*. Do you follow me?"

Erm no, not really. I don't say this of course, but nod a placid affirmative.

"And as with all brands, Brand Martha needs to have coherent, consistent, and easily identifiable brand values."

The phone rings. She answers. "Yup. Yup. Got that. OK. Of course we're not going to ask her about her weight. Yes, ten minutes is fine. Mmm, hmm. OK. *Hasta mañana*." She clunks the receiver back in its cradle. "Fucking celebrities. Now, where was I?"

"Brand Martha," Guy helpfully reminds her.

"Oh yes. That was right. You see the purpose of any brand is to let people know exactly what it stands for. Think Armani and you think of timeless classicism, think Gaultier and you think high-camp irreverence, think Donna Karan and you think contemporary urban chic, think Tommy Hilfiger and you think of the American Dream. OK, so these are all fashion designers, but the same principles apply whatever the brand. There is always one core ideal behind it. Now with Martha Seymore, what do you think of?"

Along with Guy I remain silent, on the presumption that this is a rhetorical question.

"Well, to be perfectly honest our readers don't know what to think," she says. "You just seem to be struggling. One minute you are a bra-burning feminist and the next you are Old Mother Hubbard."

Guy makes a strange high-pitched noise, which I take to be the sound of strangled laughter.

My face reddens, with anger rather than embarrassment.

"Anyway, so here's the deal," Veronica continues. "As I said two weeks ago, we've now got three months to turn the magazine around. And, if by that point there is no visible improvement, I will have no choice but to turn some of the *staff* around. Starting with you."

*Starting with you.* The words arrive in my head as if they have been shouted across a deep and wide empty valley.

"What . . . what do you mean?" My voice has dropped to somewhere between the croaky tones of Macy Gray and Marge Simpson.

"Listen, Martha. I'm sure you know the realities of consumer magazine publishing as well as I do. If our sales figures keep falling at their present rate we'll all be working for *Cross-Stitch World* by the end of the year." Her mouth is puckered so tightly that it makes you wonder how she is managing to speak without causing serious damage to the rest of her face. "So what I am saying to you is that if you are unable to get page sixty-nine back to the way it was, it will have to become something else altogether."

"Like what?" I ask faintly.

"Well, Guy and I have been putting our heads together"—*I bet that's not all you've been putting together*, I muse to myself—"and we've come up with something quite exciting." Her face fractures into an enthusiastic smile. "'The Sex Files.' With 'How to Keep Your Man Up All Night' as a subtitle. Fantastic, isn't it?"

Another rhetorical question, I presume.

And then Guy sits up in his chair, staring straight at me with that oppressively handsome face. "It's a simple concept," he tells me, as if he has ever come up with a concept of any other kind. "Sex advice from real people who have real sex. You know, reader to reader. And we can use it to push the boundaries further. Kick up a bit of a dust. Advice on how to give the perfect hand job, or have the perfect shower sex . . ." He crosses his legs, clearly turned on. "Or the best deep-throat techniques, or how to—"

"Wait a minute. You're going to teach women how to suffocate themselves?"

"No, Martha. The opposite. If we did run a piece like that, it would be teaching the reader how *not* to suffocate herself."

"Oh, I see. And who said feminism was dead?"

Then Veronica chips in. "Martha, come on, these are only hypothetical suggestions."

"I know," I blurt. "It's just that . . . it's just that . . ." But I feel the weight of their combined gaze. "Erm, nothing."

Guy glances back to Veronica, handing over the baton.

"Listen, Martha," she commands, "the bottom line is this. Either you can pull it around or you can't. If you can, great. You stay where you are. Doing what you're doing. We shelve 'The Sex Files' for a later date."

"And if I can't?"

"Well OK. If you can't you'll be faced with a choice. You could either leave *Gloss* behind altogether or we'd have to go back to using you on a freelance basis. For specialized pieces. That's why we're having to warn you three months in advance."

I want to cry. I know that sounds pathetic but I'm feeling really pathetic so I don't care. You see, the thing is, I know I'm going through a bad patch and everything, but I love my job. I really do. It's good money. It gives me a sense that I am helping people out.

It fulfills something as well.

I've always wanted to be trusted. No, that's not quite it. I've always wanted to be acknowledged. Everyone does, I suppose. But with me the wanting is more like a craving. A fundamental need as opposed to a simple desire. To be known for being good at something, to have something valid to offer. Even if it's just advice. It's not that I was unloved or excluded in any way. It's just that I always used to feel like I was defined in relation to other people.

My current role has opened up a wider world. One in which the gravitational pull centers around me for a change. And now that world looks set to be closed off again.

"So, um, how will you know if I've managed to pull it back around?" I ask Veronica (although my eyes are staring into space).

"Well, that will be up to Guy and myself. If we decide that you are providing consistent, realistic, sexy advice—you're in. If not, we'll have to say toodle-pip."

And that is it. No cushion to the blow. No sweetener. As always with Veronica, it's all stick and no carrot.

"Right, um, OK," I mumble, and make to leave.

Then, just as I am halfway out of the door she feels the need to add something. And as she speaks I cannot help but notice her voice soften. "Please don't take any of what I've said personally, Martha. It's just business. That's all. Just business."

# Chapter
# 19

The next day.

"Hi Martha, it's me."

Desdemona always does this, as if she is the only Me in the world. Or, at least, the only one I could possibly be acquainted with. But then again, that genetically modified accent could be recognized anywhere.

"Oh, Des. How now, fair wench?" When we were studying English A level together we would often drop Shakespearean insults and greetings into our conversation. It's quite a wanky-sixth-formy type thing to do, really, isn't it? I should have grown out of it by now.

"In a word, Martha: fanflamingtastic." My heart drops. I'm sorry, it's just that nowhere in my memory can I locate a time when Desdemona's happiness didn't have a negative impact on me.

"How come?"

"Well, I can't really say over the phone. Let's do it over lunch. I just *can't wait* to see your face when I tell you."

"Um, OK. Where?"

"Well, what about the Galgarry? Alex is working today and I'm sure he'd like to see you."

"Right. What time?" My voice is reluctant, the words strangely inevitable.

When the call is over I light a cigarette and inhale deeply. Out of the arch of the church window, all is green and light. There is a bird in the hedge, caught among the tangled twigs. I just stand here, watching it, inhaling deeply. It beats its wings in vain for about thirty seconds, its blinkless eyes in panic, before finally breaking free and soaring off to disappear above the London skyline.

Fast-forward two hours.

When I arrive, the Galgarry is buzzing with the prosperous hum of business lunchers and midday drinkers. Desdemona is already here, sitting at a center table. Although he is not visible, I also feel Alex nearby, behind the far wall.

As I move over toward her, sidestepping waiters as I go, the air starts to thicken and grow heavy. I see my reflection everywhere—in the wall in front of me, in the ones on either side, sliding fast across the kitchen door as it swings open. Altogether there are about fifteen Martha Seymores walking towards Desdemona's table, and for a dizzy second it's hard to tell which one is the real me. I know that this is a mistake, that I should have made up an excuse, a reason why I couldn't come.

If anything she looks better than ever. She's done something with her hair, put it in some sort of ponytail quiff. When I get to the table she puts down the menu and greets me with a smile. Well, I say smile. In actual fact, it's more of a gloat.

She sits very still, her hands on her lap. Full of suppressed energy, like a cheetah waiting to pounce.

We order the soup.

"It's Alex's recipe," she informs me, before telling me about how he might soon be getting promoted. She's clearly building up to something, pacing herself, getting ready to strike the fatal blow.

The waitress comes over with our bowls of soup and, as she leaves, touches Desdemona's shoulder knowingly.

When she has gone, Des swallows and takes a deep breath. For effect. "Me and Alex . . ." She is looking straight at me, feeding off my expression as it switches from forced composure to stifled panic. Her head cocks to the side as she decides to put it more formally. "Alex and I . . ."

Oh God. I know what's coming. I've had this dream, sorry, nightmare, quite a lot recently, but this is all too real.

"Have decided . . ."

Go on, just hit me with it.

"To tie the knot. We are getting married," she confirms, lighting a cigarette.

There it is, the money shot. She sits back in her chair, purring like a cream-filled cat, with toxic pride exuding from every pore. "A commitment to spend the rest of our lives together," she explains, as if I have just been beamed down from the spinster planet Zoog. "Can you believe it?"

"No, I can't. God. That's, um, amazing."

"Look!" she farts, raising her left arm with the speed of a Third Reich salute. "Isn't it fantastic?"

I observe her fingers as they dance a few centimeters above my soup bowl. The ring is truly spectacular, so spectacular in fact that it hardly seems like a ring at all. More of a Las Vegas laser show. A Zsa Zsa rock of rainbow light, causing my eyes to squint away from its expensive glare.

"Yes. It is. Fantastic."

Even though we lost contact for seven years, I think I have always been expecting this moment. This is what it has been about, ever since school. About who would come out on top, who would win the jackpot. Not that Alex had been anything special at school, at least not in Desdemona's eyes. In fact, then he was the booby prize. The wooden spoon. The welly boot.

But of course, that was when *I* had him. As with every other thing I had and she didn't, Alex had been instantly devalued. "Oh Martha, how *could* you?" she had grimaced with theatrical repulsion when I told her about our five-second micro-romp.

In fact, it was down to her that our teenage romance, like our teenage sex, was over almost before it had begun.

No, that's unfair. It was my fault as much as hers. I was weak. Borderline pathetic. I should have been able to say, "Who cares what you think?" and stuck with him anyway. But how was I to know that the awkward sixteen-year-old I lost my virginity to would evolve into a talented chef with mouth-watering good looks and five-star personality?

*Oh God. Speak of the Devil.* Alex strides over from the kitchen and parks his perfect rear at our table. "I've got five minutes," he tells us.

"Aww baby, they do work you hard." Desdemona leans over and plants a soft, showy peck next to his right ear. Suddenly, the whole restaurant disappears. We could be anywhere.

The Sahara Desert. The North Pole. The Moon.

What is happening to me?

Why can't I just be pleased for her?

And what is this feeling, right here in my stomach?

"I take it you've heard?"

"I have, yes. It's amazing. I'm really pleased for you. For both of you. You must be so happy."

Desdemona zooms in towards me, in a final attempt to finish me off. "Oh Martha, you should have seen him. I've never seen anything so romantic in all my life. It was here, right at this table. Down on one knee, string quartet. The works."

"It. Must. Have. Been. Am. A. Zing."

How am I doing? Am I keeping it together? No, I thought not. Whenever I'm stuck for words I seem to hide behind a string of "amazings" and "fantastics," don't I? It's not much of a cover.

"The *best*. He was incredible."

"Steady on," Alex says lightheartedly. "I wouldn't go *that* far." He sends me an embarrassed glance.

"Well, I would," she asserts. "Anyway, Martha, I thought you should be the first to know."

"I'm honored."

"And although we haven't yet set a date, I'd like to ask you to be my maid of honor."

I don't know what to say.

"I don't know what to say."

"Well, 'yes,' of course, you silly little thing."

I successfully resist the primal urge to grab her hair and splosh her head down in the piping hot bowl of apple and white onion soup (that's pretty much the way the dream always ends).

"OK then, yes," I groan. "I'd love to."

# Chapter
# 20

Marriage.
It's one of those words, isn't it. Those big, self-important, deeply unsexy words that hang over us all the time and try to grind us down. Perhaps it's because it is so close to "mortgage," both in sound and connotation, and conjures up all those grown-up values of security and longevity.

Don't get me wrong. I believe in commitment. I believe in being faithful, and staying the whole course. You know I do. Which is why I resent it. It's almost as if it serves to render every other relationship nonvalid, exempt from the rules of fidelity and commitment.

And this is ridiculous, of course. At a time when the divorce rate is yapping ever closer at the heels of newlyweds, when wedding rings are increasingly being used as pickup props, and when "holy matrimony" is starting to sound increasingly like something you could use to drain pasta.

Marriage may be a great invention. But, as Billy Connolly pointed out, so is a bicycle repair kit. Actually, it's not so much marriage that puts me off, as the wedding. The Big Day. Ugh! The whole camcorder naffness of it all: the stupid hats, the fumbled speeches, and all that religious role-play. I, Mr. First Time I've Ever Worn a Suit in My Life, do take thee, Giant

Fluffy Meringue, to be my awful, dreaded strife . . . The horror!

Oh, I know it doesn't have to be like that. As Fiona loves to
remind me, you can get married anywhere and anyhow you
wish—ironically (e.g., in an Elvis jumpsuit at the Chapel of
Love), shamelessly (e.g., on a nude beach in the Bahamas), or
even suicidally (e.g., bungee jumping from the Arc de Tri-
omphe).

But then, as my train of thought chugs along towards its inevitable destination I always end up asking myself: what's the
point? I mean, if the whole purpose is to declare your love and
commitment to the outside world, then why not give the outside world what it really wants—comedy hats and speeches in-
cluded. If I ever do put myself through it, and I'm not ruling it
out altogether, it will be all or nothing. The wedding march,
the peach bridesmaids, the whole, soft-focused shebang.

Yes, I know what you're thinking. You can read me like a book.
And I suppose you can. Of course I'm pissed off. Wouldn't you
be? Your oldest friend marrying your first time. No, it's not
even that. It's more: your oldest friend spoiling your chances
with your first time, coming back years later, parading your
first time in front of you like a trophy, waiting for the worst
possible moment ever in the history of your entire life, and
then asking you to be her maid of fucking honor.

Jeez, I ask you.


An old conversation, between me and Luke:


ME: Would you marry me?

LUKE: Are you asking me to marry you?

ME: No, I said "would," not "will."

LUKE: So what do you mean, "*would*"?

ME: I don't know. Perhaps I mean "could." Could you marry
me? I mean if you picture yourself getting married, am I in the
picture? Could you picture it with me?

LUKE: (pause) I don't picture myself getting married.

ME: Well picture it now.

LUKE: (closing his eyes) Hmm.

ME: Hmm what?

LUKE: Hmm, you're not in the picture.

ME: What? Who are you with?

LUKE: Erm . . . no one.

ME: What do you mean, no one?

LUKE: I mean no one is there, in the picture.

ME: So you're marrying yourself?

LUKE: Yes. I suppose I must be.


A really old conversation, between me and Siraj:


SIRAJ: (Taking a drag on a freshly rolled joint) My dad believes in arranged marriage.

ME: Is that why you don't speak to him?

SIRAJ: I'd say it was a contributing factor.

ME: (pause) But it must be easier though, mustn't it? In some ways at least.

SIRAJ: (marijuana cough) What?

ME: Having it all arranged.

SIRAJ: D'you reckon?

ME: Well, it's more honest, isn't it?

SIRAJ: How do you mean?

ME: Well, a hell of a lot of marriages which don't call themselves arranged, *are* really. You know, they're hardly ever natural. I mean, how many marriages are really sprung from the spring of true love. There's always external factors, aren't there? An unwanted pregnancy or whatever? And how many people are doing it because they feel obliged to marry someone? Because they've got money, or they've been together a long time, or they're the right skin tone?

SIRAJ: (laughing hysterically) That's hilarious. I've never seen it before.

ME: What? What haven't you seen?

SIRAJ: (pointing his joint towards the TV) That advert. The one with the dancing cat. In the nightclub.

ME: Oh.

A really, really old conversation, between me and my mom:

MOM: It was in a pub.

ME: So how did he ask you—did he get down on one knee?

MOM: Oh, it was nothing like that.

ME: So what was it like?

MOM: Well, I suppose it was just like a normal conversation. We both agreed that we loved each other and that it seemed very likely that we would be spending the rest of our lives together.

ME: You knew that after six months.

MOM: I think, to be honest, we probably knew it after six weeks.

ME: That you wanted to marry each other?

MOM: That we wanted to stay together.

ME: So anyway.

MOM: Yes. Anyway. We were just talking in the pub about, you know, the future. About living together and buying a house together.

ME: And he just asked you?

MOM: Well he didn't just come out with it. He just suggested it would be *easier*.

ME: Easier?

MOM: Well it wasn't like now when it hardly makes a difference. In 1972 it was practically impossible for an unmarried couple to be granted a mortgage. Or anything else for that matter.

ME: So you got married to get a mortgage?

MOM: (Pause. Looks out of the window.) Well, yes. I suppose we did.

# Chapter
# 21

In one of the magazines that litter her chaotic coffee table Jacqui is officially recognized as the Hardest-Working Woman in Clubland. What this means in reality is that she makes two telephone calls a day, and turns up on time every Friday night with a handful of drink tickets.

The rest of her diary is filled up with casual sex, casual drugs, and casual conversation. Everything casual. Oh sure, she has to book the odd DJ and do the odd press interview, but most of the hard stuff, the "logistics," is left to the Dollar Disciples, a loved-up coalition of drugged youth, buzzing around Jacqui like she's the Queen Bee. Which, for all intents and purposes, I suppose she is.

But you've got to hand it to her. She pulls it off with style. Flamboyant and spectacular style.

I mean, just look at her.

Getting ready for her Big Night. Moving out of the shower in her chrysalis towel and managing to transform herself into a Ben de Lisi butterfly within ten minutes. How does she do that? I've been getting ready for hours now, literally hours. And, without Fiona's diligent eye to guide me, it's proving really hard.

And so, while the black cab Jacqui has ordered purrs patiently outside, I suffer a sudden crisis of confidence in what I am wearing.

"How do I look?"

Jaqui takes a step back to absorb my star-spangled tunic in its entirety.

"Fantastic," she manures. "You'll blow them all away."

Fortunately, it is impossible to be overdressed at the Dollar Disco. As I soon find out, you could walk in wearing a purple top hat, a foxtrot feather boa, rainbow blazer, and crimson pantaloons and not feel in the slightest bit self-conscious.

Not that everyone is dressed like a Day-glo peacock. There's enough Evisu boys in here to water it down. And man, are they gorgeous. In fact most of them are too gorgeous not to fancy each other, if you know what I mean.

Jacqui leads me through the crowded ground floor, her free arm periscoping above the sea of bobbing heads every time she recognizes someone. It is packed. Every color is distorted or intensified under the ultraviolet.

"Whooooooooh!"

The whole place erupts as the invisible DJ unleashes a new track onto the sound system, the throbbing bassline so heavy it sends vibrations across the floor and up through my body.

Jacqui turns to tell me something but I cannot hear her above the music. I smile and nod my head—it seems like the right response. We linger awhile, Jacqui handing out drinks passes at random, before she takes me upstairs, beyond the velvet rope, to the VIP room.

In contrast to the bouncing bodies downstairs, this womb-like room is relatively sedate. The music is slower and most of the people in here are sitting down within one of the plush crimson alcoves which line the room. Everyone turns as Jacqui enters.

This, according to Jacqui at least, is *the* place to be in London on a Friday night. Where all the movers and shakers of clubland hang out—to do as little moving and shaking as possible by the looks of it.

Jacqui is keen to introduce me to as many people, specifically men, as possible. First on her shopping list is Eddy Thomkins, head of A and R at Large Recordings and proud wearer of a bandanna. Yes, that's right. At the loftiest peak of the new high society, this is what you will find. Pot-bellied middle-aged men in Daft Punk T-shirts with eighties-style bandannas on their head.

We position ourselves among the bevy of blondes who flank him on either side.

"Martha might be able to help you out," she tells him. "She's a relationship expert. A love doctor."

Eddy makes a crucifix gesture with his fingers to ward me away as if I'm an evil spirit. It turns out that he has just broken up with a young DJ agent he had been seeing for two years.

"It's been messy, but now I'm back in full throttle," he says, giving me a Sid James nudge. He then starts to tell us about his record label and all the new acts he's been signing. I almost slip into a coma listening to him prattle on. In fact, I'm sure you could have a more stimulating conversation with the National Rail Inquiries helpline. Jacqui, reading my mind, decides to move us on elsewhere.

"Listen, Jacq, it's great of you to show me around, but you don't have to try and fix me up," I tell her as we reach the bar.

"What, so you're telling me that you wouldn't want to be introduced to him over there?" She nods her head in the direction of an average-looking guy with a crew-cut and a T-shirt blaring the slogan "Only here for the gear."

"Who is he?"

"That, Martha, is Byron Hardkiss, you know, the Boy Wonder, *Mixmag's* DJ of the Year . . ."

"Oh, right. Yeah. Of course. OK then."

We grab a drink each and moochy over. As Jacqui introduces me, he looks me up and down as if I'm a shop window, pricing me up. He's speaking fast, cocaine-fast, so fast that our conversation is over before it has begun. Which is quite a good thing really, considering I didn't understand a word he was saying.

"Anyway, speak later," Jacqui tells him, once he has finished telling her about his move away from hard-Euro-progressive-house towards revivalist NuYorican tribal garage.

"Where are you going?"

"To powder our noses."

And we do. Well, *she* does.

Back amid the throng, I return to my drug of choice, courtesy of José Cuervo.

This will get me in the swing again, I think, as I feel the heat of the tequila reach my chest. And it does. Within seconds, I am feeling alive. Intense. Forget Luke, I tell myself. Forget Desdemona. Forget Alex. They are nothing. Tonight, they don't even exist. Life is too short. Get out there and enjoy yourself. The dance floor awaits, with all its wordless pleasure and untapped potential.

At university there were a number of comedy nights in the different union bars, although I never went to any of them. Instead, I found my comic relief in the Tuesday afternoon Evolutionary Psychology lectures.

For the uninitiated, Evolutionary Psychology is based on the general belief that the psychology of modern men and women has its roots in the behavior of our prehistoric ancestors. So far, so straight-faced. The comedy aspect stems from some of the more eccentric theories put forward by our beardy lecherer, sorry lecturer, Dr. John Flintstone (yes, that was his real name).

For instance, in an attempt to win us over he used to splatter on for an hour and fifteen minutes about how and why men can't find butter in a fridge (because they evolved tunnel vision on their hunting forays) or why women can't understand maps (because they always sat in the caves waiting for their hunter-gatherers to return). Fiona didn't find it as funny as I did. Never the cynic, she tended to take it at face value, rather than see it as a laughable attempt to beat Bernard Manning at his own game. I always kept on expecting him to come out with a mother-in-law gag for his encore.

Anyway, while most of what he used to tweed on about was clearly sexist bullshit, one of Flintstone's theories always seemed to make sense. Namely, the evolutionary psychological theory of dance.

"Dance is not a modern creation," he told us. "I see no reason to believe that dancing is not very ancient indeed, maybe even predating proper spoken languages." It took a while, as always, for him to get round to his point, and Fiona and I passed the time in our usual fashion—scribbling notes on our jotter pads about which meat market we should go to that night.

"There seems to be some mental reward," he suggested, "from moving in a rhythmical and rather pointless way. The fact that humans have an innate ability to enjoy *dancing*"— (when he said the word, he would hold his arms out in front of him as if grabbing a bull by its horns and shake the rest of his blubbery body with a strange violence)—"means that we probably evolved this. Therefore just as our ancestors evolved to like sex in order to pass on their genes, I suggest that there must be some equally good reason why people like to dance. In short, I believe that men and women dance in order to learn about each other. To assess them as a potential mate."

He then started to go off at a bit of a tangent, talking about the close link between a man's dancing and fighting ability (pointing out en route that as well as being the finest martial artist ever, Bruce Lee was also Hong Kong's cha-cha champion).

"I predict that men who are good dancers are more likely to be unfaithful than men who are bad dancers. Already, a number of studies show that people rate the likely future marital fidelity of good dancers lower than for those who dance badly . . ." Although this made sense at the time, now I am not too sure. Luke is one of the worst dancers you are ever likely to meet. On the rare occasions he would step onto a dance floor, he would always draw the wrong kind of attention to himself. His lack of coordination was so apparent he looked like he was having a seizure.

But anyway, that hasn't put me off. The central thesis, about dancing being a way of separating the men from the boys, still appeals to me.

And it is on my mind now. In the middle of the dance floor. As I shimmy along to the samba-infused house music generating from the sky-rise speakers. As I lock eyes with a sleek-headed boy with a high IFR, Travoltaing away like there's no tomorrow.

Jacqui has already headed home, having secured her catch for the night, so I am here alone, but it doesn't seem to matter. Everyone, it appears, is by themselves. I move in closer towards the boy and we dance with more suggestive innuendo than a *Carry On* movie. Although I've never been much of a dancing queen, all the gold tequila I've acquainted myself with tonight is managing to convince me that somehow I'm pulling it off.

Just look at me move.

I turn and, before I realize what I am doing, my lips are on his, the sleek-headed body shaker. Maybe everyone is looking. Maybe they're not. Who can tell? But right now, I couldn't give a broken eggshell. I really couldn't.

Yes, I know what you're thinking.

Slapper. Floozie. Hands off, he's mine.

I don't care. Let me have my moment. Let me, just for once, throw caution to the cyclone. Let me, if you can pardon my French, blow him out of the stratosphere. Let me see if those Elvis hips mean what they say.

We kiss our way outside and into a minicab and then we travel from East to West in the space of a heartbeat. Hey, this is easier than I thought.

The church, my home, is quiet, although Jacqui's coat signifies her presence.

Craving horizontality, we move into the bedroom. When he starts to speak I pinch his lips shut with my thumb and fore-finger. For some reason, he seems to find this sexy.

We kiss. Longer, harder than before. Pheromones on over-load. One of those kisses that travels, taking you from A to B. As our lips wrestle, we make an attempt to undress each other. We fumble on buttons and bra straps, before silently coming to the mutual decision that it might be better if we each take our own clothes off.

It only takes a second to regain the momentum. On the bed I just carry on kissing him, enjoying the feel of his skin against mine and the delicate suggestion of muscle tone underneath. He has a good body. Not one which spends half of its time in a gymnasium, but not one which has spent half its time sitting in McDonald's either. A good, honest body.

We are sitting up now, on the side of the bed. He moves be-hind me and kisses my neck, his legs wide apart as if playing a cello. I watch his vast, gentle hands spider their way up inside my leg, and start to melt as the rough feel of his sandpaper chin on my shoulder contrasts with his soft touch, down there. Inside.

It's amazing. I feel so relaxed.

So safe.

I don't know why. It might be because the condom subject was broached early on, as we entered the house. It might be because I know Jacqui is only a room away if I need her. Or it might be because he is making this feel so normal. No, that's the wrong word. I meant, *natural*. It feels like the most natural thing in the world. With a complete stranger, or as good as. Is that possible?

We lie back on the bed, we bang knees, we laugh. I look at his cock. Wowsa! I'm about to have sex with King Dong. "Careful! You could have someone's eye out with that thing!" We get serious again, bringing the dance floor with us. I look at his face, caught in the half-light. All of his features seem strangely familiar. As if they contain all the memories of former lovers. All the best bits, but deprived of their emotional power. He moves over me and I breath in his scent—a sweet fusion of fresh sweat and Issey Miyake aftershave.

"Are you OK?" he asks tenderly, altering position.

"Yes, lovely . . ."

It soon becomes clear that he is not looking for the quickest route possible. That although he doesn't know me, his enjoyment depends on mine. I like this boy, I tell myself as we start our Kama Sutran odyssey. I don't know him, but I like him. I won't cry when he's gone, but he's certainly proving quite fun to have around.

Until now I've never really understood it. The point of sex without love. It seemed primitive. Dirty. Oh sure, I've had it. I mean, we've all had it, haven't we? God, for some of us it's all we'll ever know.

But, as I said, up until now I've never really gotten it. I've always had, at the back of my mind, even as I have writhed around in fake pleasure, the following query: why are we bothering? Where is this going? All this moany, groany organ-grinding. It just seemed pointless and inauthentic. Kind of like a TV spin-off or a packet of Not Bacon or a postcard Mona Lisa. A watered-down version of the real thing.

And this is what we're meant to think, isn't it. This is what we've been taught as wives or mothers in waiting. Up until recently, of course, when the propaganda has started to swing back in favor of the no-strings quickie. Yes, it is official. The wham-bam-thank-you-ma'am roll in the hay is back in fashion and all of a sudden I am feeling very à la mode.

As he moves carefully inside me, as I observe the arc of his body in the bedroom mirror, I start to understand. I start to see the point of losing yourself to the present. How this, in its own short-lived way, might be just as worthwhile an exercise as shagging for the future. Or the past.

*My God! What does he want to do now? Oh, I see. Yeah, this could work. This could be fun. I hope I don't slip . . .*

Living in the present tense. Yeah, that's right. That makes sense. It's not cheap and dirty at all.

"Yes! Oh yes! That's it! YES! YES! Aaah! YES!"

I'm sorry, you'll have to excuse me for a while.

# Chapter

# 22

"What? You actually spoke to the Boy Wonder?" Stuart is visibly impressed.

"Er. Yes."

We are in Fiona's kitchen—Fiona, Stuart, and myself—putting together a tomatoey pasta meal, while Carl watches TV in the other room, slouched forty-five degrees on the settee. I might as well have told him that I've just had a shower with Cameron Diaz.

His mouth drops. He laughs nervously. And then he does that thing with his hand that he's always doing, shaking it like a football rattle. When he asks, "What was he like?" I'm tempted to tell him, but I don't think he could take that level of disillusionment.

"He was all right."

I'm sorry, but I've never really understood DJ worship. I mean, faced with a crowd of a thousand planet-eyed kids on Ecstasy, how could you really get it wrong? You could spend two hours playing a dusted-down vinyl copy of *The Essential Don Johnson* on rotation and they'd be happy. But anyway, for Stuart at least, this is a truth that dare not speak its name.

Over our food I detect tension, although I am not sure where it is coming from. Stuart is quiet, although he always is when food is in front of him. Carl is also quiet, craning his head back every now and then to see the TV. As I've said before: I don't know what it is about him. That faraway look in his eyes. You can spend two hours in his company and he will say nothing save for a handful of grunted mumbles. When he does talk, it's usually directed toward Fiona, even if it is for the benefit of the rest of the room. Oh yeah, and he's always rubbing his face like at an invisible washbasin. Moving his hands over his deep-set eyes and pale skin as if trying to scrub something away. I'm sorry I can't be more helpful but it's just that it's always hard to tell where he is, you know. But then again, I'm not sure I'd want a postcard.

After the meal, in her bedroom, I realize the tension is in fact coming from Fiona.

"Martha. You *are* all right aren't you?"

"Yes. Course. Why?"

"I don't know. I just reckon you might be spending too much time with Jacqui." She can be blunt when she wants.

"Fee, I *live* with Jacqui."

"I know," she says, gathering her hair back into a smooth ponytail. "But you used to go on about how sad it was to go out all the time, getting off your head just for the sake of it, and how it usually means there's something wrong."

"What are you trying to say?"

Her face crumples and she twists the duvet cover between her fingers. "Oh rubbish. I just don't want you turning into a titwad, that's all."

Now this is rich. Coming from her. Coming from the girl who had chosen to shackle herself down with the cover-star of *The Titwad Digest*. Coming from the girl who used to pop more pills than a hypochondriac chemist. Coming from the girl who manages to parcel out every single unpleasant truth about her own life but who can spot any inkblot on mine.

"You think I'm a titwad."

"I didn't say that."

"You did, you said I'm a titwad."

"No. I said that you might become one."

"Same difference."

"No, it's not."

"Anyway, it's only because you're jealous. Sorry, that should be, you might *become* jealous."

"Jealous?"

"Yes. That I'm going out having a good time. Having *sex*. Not giving a toss, while you're stuck in your anal little world getting ready to be a nice little wifey with two point four ankle-biters tugging at your apron strings . . ."

Of course, even as I'm saying this I'm not thinking about Fiona. I know it's Desdemona I'm angry with. Jealous of. Same difference. I've never wanted to hurt Fee's feelings in my life, but all of a sudden, I don't know. I'm acting like such a, what's the word . . . ah, yes. *Titwad*, that's it. Feeling like complete shit from all the toxic waste in my body. I tell you, if you ever see me going for my tenth tequila you must stop me. You really must.

"Listen, Fee. I'm sorry. I didn't mean that. I'm just, well, a bit on edge at the moment." And then, from out of nowhere, I just start to spill my heart out, the words flowing fast, fluid, without pause: "With Luke and everything, with the time of the month, with the fact that I've got to somehow become the world's greatest expert on relationships overnight when my love life bears every passing resemblance to a steaming piece of dog crap, then there's you who's got everything and you can just be happy and get on with stuff and never let anything get to you and it just reminds me about how pathetic my own life is, but it's not really that it's Desdemona getting married and the trouble is I should be happy I really should I know I should because that's what friends do they are happy when their friends get married and I just can't be and I'm scared because the reason I can't be happy . . ."

By now Fiona is sitting up, back against the wall, cross-legged, and her face has softened and regained its natural warmth. Although she is clearly confused by this stream—no, this babbling brook—of consciousness.

What I almost say is, "The reason I can't be happy is because I love Alex and I love Luke and I can't have either of them." But I stop myself. That can't be right, can it? I can't love both of them at the same time. Can I?

"Because?" Fiona curves her head expectantly.

"Because . . ."

Bang on cue, Stuart cocks his big friendly giraffe face around the door.

"We're going to get a video. Is there anything you want?"

"Erm, we're all right," I tell him.

When he goes we both just sit there, saying nothing. After a while, Fiona shifts herself neatly off the bed and moves over to the portable stereo to put on a CD. I watch her as she runs her finger down the neat stack, her face weighted with thought. She chooses *Moon Safari* by Air and forwards to track three. She knows it's my favorite.

When I get back home I turn my computer on and try to get my mind into gear. Actually, I'm pretty sure my mind *is* in gear (albeit stuck in first). That's not the problem. The problem is this bloody e-mail. It's from a girl asking me about what men, in general, want from a relationship. Her general assumption is that the male of the species is a completely different creature. I am tempted to tell her that men are nowhere near as alien as we are led to believe. I am also tempted to point out only one pair of our twenty-three pairs of chromosomes distinguishes one sex from the other.

But the thing is, we want there to be a difference. In fact, and this I suppose is my problem, *Gloss* magazine is based upon that difference. Men aren't just a different species. They are from outer space. Martians. We have no hope of ever fully understanding their world, that is the general belief. No. Actually, I am giving the wrong impression. *Gloss* is not *always* warning people to "Mind the Gap" between the sexes. In fact, the "Career Confessions" section is founded upon the idea that men and women are capable of doing exactly the same jobs. Radical, huh?

But still, when it comes to love we assume that old stereotypes are still accurate. As far as I can see it, the truth is simple. Men want love. Men want sex. So do women. We know that. But we keep on trying to separate ourselves from each other. Pretending we speak a different language, that we inhabit different time zones. So it's no good. Plato may have been able to recognize that "in their original matter" women are the same as men, but then he didn't have big-name advertisers to keep happy, did he? He didn't have circulation figures to worry about or rival launches to contend with.

So no. I must carry on peddling that old trick-cyclist bullshit of mine. I must carry on telling women that their men *are* in fact from a different planet, because that is the security blanket we have chosen to wrap ourselves with. After all, it's usually much easier than facing up to the real reasons why loveboats often end up on the rocks.

Yes, of course, I hear you.

Luke was unfaithful. Behind my back. With another woman. Now that's rather a stereotypically male thing to do, isn't it? Yes, I agree. It is. And of course, I couldn't see it coming. So what does all this mean? Is Luke a fluke? Is he the only one from another planet?

I don't know. I haven't worked that one out yet.

# Chapter
# 23

"What's this?" I ask the next afternoon, although it is perfectly clear that what Jacqui has just handed me bears all the hallmarks of a plane ticket. Heathrow–Ibiza. This Friday.

"*That*, Charlie, is your golden ticket," she says, in a voice which I suppose is intended to resemble Willy Wonka.

"But what, but—"

She cups her hands around her mouth to form a megaphone and launches into a bellowed voiceover: "This Friday, Dr. Martha Seymore, Ph.D., of Boringville, Boringshire, is being flown away on an all-expenses-paid trip to the party capital of the world to soak up the sun and get completely out of her tree for what is going to be the biggest weekend of the year."

Oh no. Fiona was right after all. Jacqui *is* dangerous. Certifiable, in fact. I know that right now I should be smiling. I should be looking happy. Thankful. But I'm not. I don't want to go to Ibiza. I want to stay here, completely in my tree, and have a very small—no, a *microscopic* weekend. This is what I am thinking as the words "I can't" feeble their way out of my mouth.

Jacqui raises her arm and does the speak-to-the-hand gesture beloved by guests on American talk shows.

"Listen. It will be fantastic. Three nights, flying back on Monday. We're staying at the new Hacienda hotel, it will be full-on. It's the Powder Records party at Pacha on Saturday night which is *always* a right mash-up." Or at least I think that's what she says. The only words I take in properly are "full-on," "powder," and "mash-up," which—as with the rest of her Essex rave-speak—sound weird spoken in her syrupy Surrey accent. And although they might have done something positive for me once, they now strike my twenty-five-year-old heart with dread.

"Listen, Jacqui, I can't accept this. It's lovely of you, it really is, but it's not possible." Jacqui says that's fine. If I can give her ten reasons for not going, she'll leave it. I get stuck on number three.

"That settles it," she says, before umpalumpaing around the room in triumph.

I phone my mom and tell her:

"Mom, just thought I'd let you know, I'm going away at the weekend."

"Away?" she gasps with deliberate melodrama. "Away where?"

"Um, Ibiza," I say, with a defensive flinch.

"*Ibiza?*"

I can remember telling her before the last time I went. With Fiona. She'd nearly passed out. She'd wanted me to go somewhere with more middle-class connotations. Somewhere Second or Third World. India. Thailand. Cambodia. Macedonia. Or to go Inter-railing, like Jenny from next door.

"Yes. I'm going to Ibiza."

"Really, Martha. I thought you'd got all that silly stuff out of your system."

"Mom, I'm going for free."

"Free?"

"It's all on Jacqui."

"Hmm. This Jacqui girl sounds like trouble if you ask me."

"I'm not."

She releases an exasperated sigh.

"I don't know what's got into you lately."

"Nothing's got into me. It's just that I'm twenty-five. I'm old enough to make my own decisions, aren't I?"

"Evidently not."

"Mom, please. Don't be unreasonable."

"Dad won't be happy."

She always does this. *Dad won't be happy*. Projecting her own annoyance onto my father. The fact is, though, my dad will be completely indifferent. As he always is.

I say nothing, waiting for her.

"Are you still doing your yoga classes?" she asks obscurely.

"Um, yes," I lie.

"Well, I suppose that's something."


Round two. Fiona.

"You're going to Ibiza?" Fiona asks, echoing my last sentence.

"Uh-huh."

"But . . . but . . . *Ibiza*? *With her?*"

God, she's as bad as my mom.

"*We've* been to Ibiza before, remember?"

"Yeah, I know. Years ago. I wouldn't want to go now though." She sits back on her bed and crosses her legs in the yogic huff position.

"Why not?"

"Well, I don't know, it's just something you do when you're younger, isn't it?"

It's almost as if Fiona owns some sort of chronological chart which tells her exactly how much fun you are allowed to have at every age.

"Fee, it's only a weekend. And I promise, I'll be a good girl."

I throw a smile at her and, although she is resistant, she volleys one back seconds later.

"I'm sorry," she says. "I only worry."

# Chapter
## 24

Salinas Beach is, according to Jacqui, "the place in Ibiza to hang out during the daytime." By "daytime" she means that time from around five P.M. when people have managed to finally shake off the night before and drag themselves away from their pillow. By "hang out" she means, well, just that. Let them dangle in the breeze.

Not all of the beach is nudist. The bit next to the car park is filled with respectable Spanish families. But we have traipsed down half a mile in the scorching heat to watch the in crowd parade their bits in front of each other. Even here, however, nudity is optional, not compulsory, and so I decide to go semi, leaving my forestation within my Missoni briefs (well most of it, at least).

Jacqui, as ever, goes for the whole-hog option, causing every nude male on the beach to avert his gaze (after all, the "it's a gun in my pocket" line wouldn't exactly hold up in this context). When I told you about Jacqui's contagious beauty I was, as I'm sure you realized, talking about her fully clothed. The naked version is a completely different kettle of fish, if you can pardon the phrase. I feel like a Citroën 2CV parked next to a gleaming Ferrari. A gleaming Ferrari, I should add, with absolutely no spare tires. Look at that bodywork. Those golden globes and the extravagant pubic topiary.

As I lie back on the beach mat, squinting away from the sun, my mind rewinds to my first visit to Ibiza. A few years ago. With Fiona. I can't remember it all. Just snapshots. The odd conversation, nightclub or beach.

It had been a package. Not one of those fuzzy-duck wet T-shirt packages but a package all the same. It just seemed like the easiest way to do it.

I remember Fiona's disappointment the first time she came across the Café del Mar ("it's just a load of rocks"), and how that disappointment faded as we sat and watched the most spectacular sunset of our lives. All those violent reds and oranges as the sun sank behind the still, shimmering sea. We knew this had become a cliché, used to help sell thousands of island dreams and mix CDs, but we didn't care.

I can remember that night. We had an E each. We danced for about seven hours at Amnesia—completely, and wilfully, lost in the music. Back at our hotel we were still gushing:

ME: That was the most amazing night of my life.
FEE: Me too.
ME: Me three.
FEE: Me five million.
(Hysterical laughter for approximately two hours)
ME: It's incredible, isn't it?
FEE: What is?
ME: How you can feel like this. This happy. This complete.
FEE: Without sex.
ME: It's like we've found the secret key to the universe.
FEE: Without men and their big bollocky bollocks.
ME: It's great.
FEE: I think, just as long as we can remember this night, we'll never be able to be unhappy again.
ME: I love you.

FEE: I love you.

ME: Don't you think, really, we are the same person?

FEE: We *are* the same person.

ME: That's what I said.

FEE: There's no difference.

ME: No difference at all.

FEE: I love you.

ME: I love you.

FEE: Do you want some water?

Unfortunately, the next day we woke up only to find the secret key to the universe had been stolen from under our pillow.

But still, it was a great holiday. Yes, we got off our heads. Yes, we felt like crap for two weeks afterwards. But there was something sweet about it. Everything was new. Untouched.

Now, lying on this beach with *her*, the Porn Princess, and surrounded by this gallery of well-oiled cocks and hairsprayed pubes, I can see the earlier holiday as a pocket of innocence.

After two hours on the beach we head back to the villa. Freshen up. Listen to Basement Jaxx. And, don't judge me too harshly, I end up having a line of coke (don't ask me where she got it from). Yes, I remember what I said. I know I'll regret it later. But come *on*, I'm in Ibiza. They don't call it the white island just for its beaches, you know. And anyway, everyone does it. Even traffic wardens. And out again. A few bars. A few nameless faces. Then on to Ibiza town and Pacha. A Moroccan-style, cavernous netherworld set to house music. Drink. More cocaine. And then, just for a second, we settle.

My eye pans across the dance floor. There must be two thousand bodies out there, close-packed and pulsating in time to the music—one endless track of beats and wooshy electronic chords.

It is hot in here. I mean literally. Even though I am standing motionless on the side platform—the orbital loop around the dance floor—my whole body is soaked with sweat. Jacqui too, is glistening. She shouts something incomprehensible in my ear.

"WHAT?"

She shouts louder: "LET'S GO OUTSIDE."

I follow her crooked path through the mass of people, who are now all simultaneously clapping their hands above their heads as the DJ hardens the pace. Jacqui flashes her VIP smile at a serious-looking Spanish man with a walkie-talkie to get us through to jet-set central. We climb some narrow, white-washed steps before emerging onto the roof terrace. Here, people are either sitting in one of the many mosaic-tiled al-coves or leaning against the egg-shaped bar. A beautiful Spanish girl, standing behind a stall selling Pacha merchan-dise, plays with her corkscrew hair, looking bored. It is after four and light is just breaking through, making everything look like an old, faded color photograph.

"Isn't it great up here?" Although her question is aimed at me, her eyes are on a caramel-tanned man by the bar, chatting up a couple of random blondes.

Wait a minute.

No, it can't be.

It must be all those chemicals rushing around my brain, swapping faces like mischievous children.

I close my eyes and try to shake off my gear goggles. It's no use. He still looks the same.

And then an old recording of Veronica's voice starts to play in my head: "*We're going to be sending Guy off to cover the big Ibiza weekend for our club section and maybe get some juicy material for a holiday sex article . . .*"

But just at the moment I realize that yes, Mr. Caramel Love God is in fact Guy Longhurst, it is too late. Jacqui is at the bar, less than two meters away from him, sending out more signals than an air traffic controller.

I cower behind Jacqui, hoping that her glittery presence will render me invisible.

"Oh. My. God. Martha—is that you?"

I turn and he is standing there, his mouth agape in exaggerated shock. He looks as nauseatingly gorgeous as ever, dressed in Versace black and with his hair slicked back with gigolo confidence.

I try and speak but all the words come out scrambled: "Arba—nah—yah . . ."

"It *is* you."

Jacqui has now turned away from the bar as well and she is looking at me as if I am completely gone out. Which, incidentally, I am.

Somehow I manage to gather the mental effort needed to form an intelligible sentence (well, almost): "Wow, Guy. Amazing. Um, coincidence. What are you doing here?"

"I'm, um, talent-spotting," he tells me, casting an eye down Jacqui's curvilinear physique.

"Aren't you going to introduce me?" she asks.

"Um. Yeah. Sure. Jacqui, this is Guy, Guy, Jacqui . . ."

"How *you* doin'?" he asks her, in his best Matt Le Blanc.

Jacqui then leans forward and shells a hand to his ear in order to whisper something. As she does so, Guy's face momentarily freeze-frames with pleasured shock.

"So you're doing fine," he says, almost embarrassed. I say "almost" because embarrassment, as far as I am aware, is not something Guy has ever been able to feel. What with all those voices in his head telling him how fabulous he is all the time.

The conversation then starts to head back in my direction. Guy asks me why I'm here. I tell him I don't know. And then Jacqui, helpfully, tells him it's to get me back in the saddle. When his eyebrows start to dance with puzzlement, Jacqui strikes the fatal blow.

"You know, after she split from her boyfriend."

Look, I know it's not her fault. I mean, how was she to know that Martha "Get It All Off Your Chest" Seymore would keep something as BIG as that all to herself. That I would have been spending the last month acting as if nothing had happened and inventing believably bland Friday-night boyfriend stories.

"You're kidding me, right?"

And then, just to make sure every nail in my coffin is hammered in as tightly as possible, she adds: "What? You honestly think she should have stayed around after he went and did that, do you?"

"Did what?" he asks.

As I have learnt from Fiona that the enemy of crisis management is denial, I decide to tell him myself, in order to save any further assault on my relationship-guru reputation.

"He slept with someone."

For a split split second it seems as though Guy's face is about to explode into hysterical laughter. He stifles the urge, and instead creases his forehead as part of a look which I suppose is intended to be sympathetic.

"That's unbelievable," he tells me, raising his hand to my shoulder in the Robert De Niro style. "When did it happen?" I tell him the truth, while Jacqui stands on the sidelines wincing with guilt.

"But you're—"

"I know."

"And you said—"

"I know."

Jacqui now turns back to the bar to order us some drinks.

"All that stuff—"

"I know. Bullshit. All of it. My love life is a disaster zone, OK. All that stuff I wrote—you know, all those ways to spot if your relationship is on the rocks. Guess what! I didn't spot one of them. Not a single one." By this point I couldn't give a fuck, I just carry on blabbing in the same kamikaze spirit. "Hilarious, isn't it? The getting cheated on and then trying to cover it up, acting as if everything is all hearts and flowers."

"Well, I wouldn't say it's hilarious," he says. "But it is kind of ironic, babe, isn't it?"

Jacqui hands me a vodka and coke and then starts glugging her own.

"Yes. It is. Very ironic. But you'll, um, keep it to yourself, will you? I mean, I will tell Veronica, you know, about breaking up with Luke. But I think I might leave out the him being unfaithful stuff. You won't tell her, will you?"

"What's it worth?" he asks with an off-center smile.

"My job. My self-respect. My whole life."

"Well, in that case," he smugs, "I'll think about it."

"I'm sorry," Jacqui mouths, as Guy turns to say good-bye to two men I have never seen before in my life.

"It's OK," I tell her. "You weren't to know."

Jacqui is then pounced on from behind, by a couple of girls. One is dressed up as a pipe-plaited schoolgirl, while the other is spacehopping around in a cowgirl costume. They are chewing so fast that they are probably creating enough kinetic energy to power the entire island.

"Awright Jax you nutbag! Fand you at last!" gurns the schoolgirl.

"Facking mental!" squawks her spacehopping friend.

Jacqui introduces me to them.

"Marts, these are two of my star Dollar Disciples: Lisa and Shola."

"Pleased to meet you."

"Awright!"

"Facking mental!"

"'Ere Jax," says the schoolgirl, 'Jear Coxy earlier? Played a blinder! Bosh, bosh, bosh! Mazin! Wiped the floor. Blew the roof off! Bladdy wicked wannit?"

"Facking mental!"

"Yeah. Bladdy wicked! Bass in your face! Bangin'!"

Unable to speak fluent spacehopper, I decide to leave

Jacqui to it and turn back to the bar, where Guy is ordering himself a drink.

"You know, Martha," he says as he waves a fifty euro note in the direction of the barman, "you've got every reason to hate me."

"I know, I do."

"But I'd just like you to know one thing, babe. If it was up to me, your job would be the safest of the lot. I love having your face to look at every Monday morning."

"So, um, why did you propose that feature on keeping men up all night or whatever?"

"Ah, yes, good point, babe, very good point. You see, at the time I had no idea Veronica would use it for page sixty-nine."

"Oh, come on."

"No, I can assure you. Scout's honor." He gives me a three-fingered salute.

I smile. I'm sorry, I can't help it.

OK, I know. This man is Guy Longhurst. The man who has never done me a single favor in his entire life. The man who has, in fact, been trying to make my working life as difficult as possible from day one. The man who has been plotting, like a fake-tanned Iago, to replace my advice column with a glossy piece of prick worship. The man who thinks the whole world is one big amusement park made in his honor.

But right now I can't help thinking he is also someone else. Or at least, some*thing* else. Oh sure, it's hard to tell whether he isn't really looking in my eyes to check his reflection, but I'm willing to give him the benefit of the doubt. And anyway, who cares. He's beautiful. Although I've always known that, I've never really *appreciated* it, having never seen him on this side of a hangover. But through my vodka-vision, I can fully understand now. How that dangerous man-beauty can suck you under. It's probably because I've never been this close to him before. I mean, physically.

"Anyway, Martha, babe, let's not talk about work. Not tonight. Let's talk about, *me*. Yes. Let's talk about me."

You see, while Guy is clearly a wanker he is, at least, a self-aware one.

"Yes. What else? Let's talk about you! Tell me about yourself, Mr. Guy. Tell me, tell me, please."

"All right, Martha. Cut the sarcasm. It doesn't suit you," he says, flashing me an expensive smile. "I just think you might have got the wrong impression of me."

"And what impression would that be?" I say, leaning coquettishly back against the bar.

"Well you probably think I'm a self-obsessed egomaniac who doesn't give a shit about anybody."

My eyebrows maneuver into the "got it in one" position.

"But I'm actually a self-obsessed egomaniac with a creative side. Bet you didn't know that?"

"No. But thanks for the newsflash."

"And . . . I bet you didn't know I'm in the process of writing a book. My life story." He stands back as if waiting for applause and a bouquet of flowers. "It's going to be an *Angela's Ashes* for the chemical generation. I'm just trying to think of the title at the moment."

*The Unbearable Lightness of Being a Body Fascist* is my unspoken suggestion.

"So, erm, where are you at then, with this book?"

"Chapter One: A Croydon Childhood. It's actually quite traumatic, writing a lot of it."

Trauma? Guy? The only trauma you could imagine him having would be the kind you suffer after falling asleep on the sunbed. That said, I'm finding it fun playing along.

"You had a difficult childhood?" I ask him.

"It was terrible," he tells me, pinching the bridge of his nose for dramatic effect. "You see, I haven't always been as gorgeous as I am now. I used to have ears like Mickey Mouse. The kids at school used to say that you could pick up incoming aircraft with them . . ." By this point he is close to crocodile tears.

"So, um, what happened?"

"Well, by the time I reached eleven things were really hard and so my mother checked me into hospital. I came out two days later with these streamlined beauties and I've never looked back."

I look with mock-admiration at his right ear while he talks me through the later stages of his personal history, but to be honest with you I'm not listening. After all, with Guy, the less you concentrate on what is spilling from his mouth the better. He is not about conversation. He is about a beautiful body and a beautiful face. And right now, that's all I'm after. Who cares if they're both fake?

No, I mustn't. I mustn't let him have his wicked way. It would make those Monday-morning editorial meetings even more unbearable. Mind you, I wouldn't be the only one. By now half the office has been there, done that, and bought the "I did Guy" T-shirt (designed by Gucci of course).

"Martha, babe, what are you doing after this? Are you carrying on?"

"Er, I don't know, it's up to—"

Shit. Where is she? She was there five minutes ago. I scan the crowd, looking out for her flame-red hair among the Eurotrashed bodies.

No sign.

"I, uh, don't know," I repeat.

Guy gives me one of those power stares. A Jedi mind trick, I'm sure of it. Those dark, chocolate eyes are shining like a shop window.

"Because I was just wondering if you fancied having a look at my . . ." he looks down toward his crotch ". . . er, villa?"

And then my Obi-Wan Kenobi voice kicks in: *Resist, Martha, resist. Do not succumb to the Dark Side. You'll only regret it in the morning. You'll only regret it every morning for the rest of your life.*

"Yeah. That sounds great," are the unlikely words I find coming out of my mouth.

"Fantastic," he says, as if clinching a deal. "We'll have the place to ourselves if we go back now."

"OK."

And so we walk back downstairs and through the crowded dance floor, past the podium goddesses, around the champagne-swilling Mafiosos, over the drugged floor-crawlers, and underneath the stilted transvestites. Then back outside, sidestepping the door whores and clipboard pimps, across the road to the car park, and before getting in Guy's hired Jeep, I breathe in the clean air, in the hope that the fusion of salt water and distant pine will revive my senses.

The villa is just on the outskirts of Ibiza town and so we are there in no time. Unlike every other villa we have passed this one is pink.

"Did Mortimer cover this?" I query, as we walk past the kidney-shaped swimming pool.

He flexes an incredulous smile and says, "Come off it, babe. What do you think? No, I've got rich friends."

There is still time. I could still get out of here alive.

"Fancy a dip?" he asks, as if reading my mind. Then I realize he's referring to the swimming pool.

"OK. You first." God! What is with me! Within a nanosecond Guy is there in front of me naked. A work of art. A Rodin. Smooth and pumped. I tell you—what with all the vodka, cocaine, and confessions I'm feeling just a little frisky.

I watch him as he prepares to dive in. His buttocks a marvel of physical engineering. Solid, square, pointing skyward. With the muscular hollow at each side looking as though it has been shaped using an ice-cream scoop. My gaze moves upwards, to take in the architectonic form of his back. Delicately curved and triangular. Broad enough to project a cine-reel onto.

He disappears under the water with a Hockney splash.

"You coming in?" he asks, on surfacing. I turn my back towards him and start to strip.

Strangely, I don't feel in the slightest bit self-conscious. You see, I don't care what he thinks of me. What he thinks of the Malteser mole on my back or the Australia-shaped birthmark on my front. After all, I hate his guts.

I approach the pool and edge my way in. Fuck! It's freezing!

"Wairgh!" I splurge, as I launch into a breaststroke with my face a good ten feet above the water. For the next five minutes, I am standing in the shallow end with my arms folded against my ice-cold breasts watching Guy try and butterfly his way into my affections.

"I'm getting out," I say, through chattering teeth.

We are sitting inside the villa on a sofa. A now boxer-shorted Guy has wrapped me in a white cotton towel and is rubbing my back under the pretense of trying to get me dry. In reality, I think he is hoping for the opposite.

"Sorry about that, babe, should have told you the water isn't heated."

"It's OK," I say, taking a swig from the glass of Vina Sol he has just produced. There's something about this place, this villa, that instantly weakens you. I don't know what it is. Perhaps it's all the phallic cacti standing at every window, or that screaming red artwork on the wall. Anyway, there's no doubt about it. I'm being sapped of resistance. To such an extent that when Guy leans over and plants a kiss on my lips I kiss him back. Not with passion, but as a reflexive gesture. I don't believe what I am doing. Cocaine and Guy Longhurst in one night. I might as well book the Botox, bungee jumping, and colonic irrigation for tomorrow.

"So," he says between kisses. "Am I forgiven?"

"No," I assure him. "I still hate your guts."

And I still do hate his guts. But hate can be as sexy as love, can't it? The tension or inertia caused by finding someone physically beautiful and psychologically repulsive can probably inspire as much lust as anything else. There's a thin line, after all.

He's actually quite a strange kisser. Not how I expected. His bottom jaw moves from side to side, rather than up and down, and he keeps on nipping me every now and then. Little lip-bites. And his tongue tastes weird. A blend of white wine, chlorine, and something else. Something I can't quite put my finger on.

He carries me into the bedroom, caveman-style, kissing me as he walks. Then he drops me down on his bed and climbs on top of me. And all the time I am hearing this voice: *You are going to have sex with Guy Longhurst. You will hate yourself but it is going to happen so enjoy it while you can . . .*

He pulls off his boxer shorts and starts a running commentary, describing every action as he does it. His hand slides under the top of my towel, he gets a firm grip, and then pulls upward, causing me to roll, three hundred and sixty degrees, into nakedness.

I grab the back of his head and pull him closer and make every effort to forget about Monday-morning editorial meetings. But then, just as we have passed the point of no return, I start to realize something is up.

Or rather, isn't.

Guy, positioned on all fours, starts to realize it too. We both look down to see, between his body-built thighs, a tiny, flaccid cock, frowning at us with disapproval.

For a few seconds we say nothing. Guy squints and then takes another look, as if he can't believe what he has just seen. He then springs to life (Guy, not his penis), sitting bolt upright on the bed. In a desperate resuscitation attempt, he starts yanking it and shaking it and stroking it. "Don't worry, babe, the old boy will be fine in a minute," he tells me, as he pummels away. For an anxious moment I even think he's going to suggest mouth-to-mouth. But Guy soon realizes that nothing will wake his little princeling. In fact, if anything, it seems to be getting smaller. Tortoising back into its shell.

And then, feeling the intense pressure of the moment, we start to exchange a barrage of floppy clichés:

"Sorry, this has never happened to me before."

"Don't worry about it. It happens to every man from time to time."

"I must have drunk too much."

And so on.

But somehow, they don't seem to help him. His face crumples into that of a little boy and for a second I think he's about to start crying. And, hard though it is not to laugh my head off, I try my best to look sympathetic. For someone whose entire *raison d'être* involves being able to muster an erection at any given opportunity, this must be Armageddon.

I move off the bed and walk, stark naked, back outside to the pool to collect my clothes. By the time I am fully dressed, Guy has gained a form of relative composure.

"I'm sorry, Martha, you must think I'm pathetic." His voice is different. The smugness has evaporated. He almost sounds likeable.

"Listen Guy, seriously, it doesn't matter. In fact, it was probably for the best. I mean, think about it. What *were* we doing?"

He shrugs. Deflated.

About half an hour later he drives me back to Jacqui's. All of a sudden he seems very keen to talk about work. Trying to decipher whether or not I will keep his little secret safe. Impressed as I am with his new babeless vocabulary, I'm not too, ahem, hard on him. That said, I do leave him guessing.

When I get back to the villa, Jacqui is in bed. Splayed out like a starfish. Asleep. On her own. Before going to bed I take a shower. A cold one. Putting my face right up to the nozzle so that water streams over my nose.

When I slide into bed I pull the white sheets over my head and try to sleep. It's no good. My mind is in hyper mode, flashing images of mad spacehoppers, frowning penises, and crowded dance floors.

There's no way I'm getting to sleep. It's already a quarter into tomorrow. I writhe about some more in that lethargic breakdance I always do when insomnia sets in. And even if I do manage to slow my mind down, I won't be able to block that noise out. It's either tinnitus or crickets, I'm not sure which. So I decide to give up, and start to eat my pillow.

# Chapter
## 25

A few hours later Jacqui shakes me out of bed. I can't tell if I've been asleep or not. We walk into town, buy a liter of water, and melt under the wobbly heat.

By dark I have managed to bury my hangover under five glasses of Tequila Mockingbird, a crimson drink with the potency of a horse tranquilizer. Don't ask me where I am, I haven't a clue. There are some boats, some palm trees, and some weird floaty objects moving around in space. That's about as much as I can tell you.

And all I've got all the time in my ear is Jacqui. Yammering on about everything and nothing. Telling me all her theories. And boy, has she got a lot of them.

First, there's her Getting to Know People theory. "You know my theory," she begins.

"No, I don't," I slur.

"The more you're with someone the less you get to know someone."

I pause, waiting for the words to gain meaning.

"That's quite a contro . . . contro . . . controvershial theory."

"Well, I'm quite a controversial person."

"So exshplain it to me."

"Right. Well. It is my general belief that every single piece of information you get about someone—be it their name, their job, their criminal record, their taste in music, whatever—all that stuff, it actually gets you further away from the core person. The person you first set eyes on, or shagged in the toilet or whatever. It's like you, with that Luke. I mean, there you were, living out of each other's pockets for two years or something, knowing absolutely everything there was to know. Star sign. Shoe size. First memory. You could probably even predict when he was going to take a dump."

A vision of Luke on the toilet, in Rodinesque pose, passes affectionately through my head.

"But you didn't know that all-important thing, did you. You didn't have that one crucial piece of information. The piece of information that cut through to the heart of who he is."

Then, over a cigarette and our sixth Mockingbird, she spells out her Lost the Plot Theory: "People sometimes tell me that I've lost the plot, but you know what I tell them?"

"Uh, no."

"I tell them that there was never any plot to begin with. But that's the trouble isn't it?"

"Is it?"

"People want their lives to read like a book. They want plot, they want structure. A beginning, a middle, and an end. They want things to be ordered. But life isn't like that. There is no structure, not really. I know people try to build one, to follow a pattern, to fall in love, to get married, to have children, in that order, but how often does it really happen naturally? And even when it does, there is still no pattern. No plot."

Then, finally, there's her Falling Off a Bar Stool theory. Oh no, that's my theory. Actually, it's not so much a theory as a practical example.

"Are you all right?" she asks, helping me to my feet.

The whole bar is looking in my direction.

"Don't worry. Slippy cushion, that's all," I say, as I feel a sharp pain shoot up my spine.

\* \* \*

Fast-forward two hours.

"What time's the plane?"

We're in a car. A very *fast* car. I haven't a clue who's driving it, but Jacqui seems to know him. A mad-looking bloke with bulging eyes, salami neck, hair pulled back in a loose ponytail, wearing a loud Hawaiian shirt with ultraviolet palm trees. He is sweating like a maniac and clearly off his head.

"We should have been at the airport twenty minutes ago," she answers him.

The car takes a violent swerve to the right, following the road sign. A picture of a plane with the number seven next to it. My head bumps against the window. There is less traffic on this road. The odd green light of a free taxi. That's all.

"Fuck!" Salami Neck swears as we pass a Guardia Civil jeep moving in the other direction. If we don't end up dead by the roadside in a mangled piece of metal we will be arrested. And who knows how many illegal chemicals are in this car. The Guardia keep moving.

"Bigger fish to fry."

"We miss it, we miss it," muses Jacqui in a *que sera* voice.

No. We cannot miss the plane. We've got to get this plane. I don't want to stay on this island a minute longer than I have to. I want my bed. Hell, I want any bed. So long as it's empty. I want London. I want Fiona. I want Richard and Judy. The car takes another swerve. Oh shit. I feel ill.

In-flight.

"I can't believe you did that."

"What?" I ask her, half-conscious.

"Threw up all over the back seat."

"I'm . . . sorr—"

Sleep.

# Chapter
# 26

The day after I get back my mom phones. Midway through the conversation her reason for calling is clear.

"We're ever so worried about you."

"Mom. There's nothing to worry about, I can assure you. I'm fine."

"Your dad can't sleep with worry."

This I find hard to believe. My dad, on more than one occasion, has been known to fall asleep standing up. He can drop off anywhere. In the car. On the settee. In his office. At the supermarket.

"But Mom. Honestly, everything's fine. Can I speak to him?"

"Sorry?"

"With Dad. Can I have a word?"

"Dad, Martha wants a word with you." She anxiously hands the phone over.

"Hi Marty," he breezes.

"Hi Dad."

There is a strange muffled sound at the end of the line, which is followed by him telling me (in a more somber voice than before): "We're ever so worried about you."

I sigh. "I know. Mom said."

And then, in the background, I hear my mom's prompt: "*Ask her about work.*"

"Er, we've been wondering how you're getting on at work?"

"It's, um, going really well. The magazine's going from strength to strength."

Again, I pick up my mom's voice: "*Ask her about Luke.*"

"I haven't seen him," I say, before my dad has time to ask.

Later today, I am in Boots. Waiting to get served by a girl with no eyebrows or customer service technique. I'm buying, if you must know, a new antiaging cream which is really meant to do the job. Results proven under dermatological control and all that. It's got AHAs. Sun Protection Factor. Retinol. And all these clever unpronounceable chemicals like cholorplorodoxymene which are meant to be able to combat all those free radicals. Prevent them from getting together and staging a revolution on my face.

I am also in a world of my own. Planet Martha. Thinking about what to write in the next batch of responses. Thinking about how to tell people to be happy in love. How to have as smooth a ride as possible. But the advice fountain, after months of functional operation, has now run completely dry. There's nothing there. Just an empty, black hole.

"*Hello stranger.*"

My heart stops dead and I jump, visibly, out of my skin. The voice is Luke's, whispered into the back of my neck.

I turn and face him, taking in his too-familiar features, faring well under the brutal light.

"God. You gave me the shock of my life," I tell him.

"It's your turn," he says mysteriously.

"What?"

"To pay. At the checkout."

"Oh. Right. Yes." I turn back and pay for my antiwrinkle miracle cream.

"Jav an Advantij Card?" asks the eyebrowless girl.

"Um, no," I say, signing the credit slip.

The girl checks the signatures for what seems like ages. Trying to find a point of similarity between the smooth loopy signature on the back of my Switch card and the spiderly scrawl I've just produced. She decides to give me the benefit, and so I make way for Luke to pay for whatever it is he's come in for.

Not condoms, that's good. That's very, *very* comforting. A packet of razors. Disposable. Wilkinson turquoise. For sensitive skin and extra *glide*. This, I know, is not an opportunist purchase. Luke takes his shaving routine extremely seriously. He's tried the three-blade options. Mach 3 and the like. He's even tried electric. But he knows that the Wilkinson twin-blade sensitive disposable, used in conjunction with shaving gel, is the closest he can get to a perfect shave. Close, but without skin irritation.

As he roots around in his wallet for the correct change (he'd always prefer to spend three hours digging out two pounds and sixty-two pence than round it up to three pound coins and wait for the thirty-eight pence in return), a vivid image enters my head. Luke in front of the mirror, head arched back, eyes forward, making the razor glide under his chin with feminine precision. Naked, except for a damp towel miniskirted around his waist.

We bustle outside.

"How've you been keeping?" I ask him, fearful of the response. Fearful of too much information.

"Good," he abbreviates. "You?"

"Good."

"Good."

It's amazing, isn't it. Two months ago we could talk about anything. The Middle East peace process. Product placement in TV sitcoms. The way instinctive behavior, such as yawning, is contagious. Anything at all. No topic was off-limits. But now we can't even put a sentence together. Eventually, though, Luke manages to break the verbal constipation.

"You know how I acted that day at the Bar 52?" (Luke always does this: puts an unnecessary "the" before words which don't need one.)

"Uh-huh."

"Well, it was exactly that. An act. You know, like you always said the first sign of feeling insecure is acting like you couldn't give a flying fuck. So I could."

"Could what?"

"Give a flying fuck. I was just, you know, testing the water. Seeing where I stood. I didn't mean a word of it. All the time I was sitting there saying how glad I was that you'd made me see sense, I was really just dying to tell you how fucking shitty I felt. I mean really. Like shit."

I knew it. Hah! He hadn't fooled me for a minute. Not really. Of course he's been fucked off. He would have been in pieces. Well and truly Humpty-Dumptied, as Fiona always likes to say.

"So, um, why didn't you just tell me? Or phone me? Or something?" I sidestep to the left in order to avoid a hypomanic mother wielding a Trojan pushchair at about twenty miles an hour. Luke does likewise.

"Well, I don't know. Didn't want to fuck you up any more than I already had, I suppose."

"I wasn't fucked up," I lie. "You know. Was just a bit of a shock. That's all. Took a bit of getting used to."

"Listen," he tells me, catching his reflection in the shop window. "You know, if you ever want to talk it through. Just call me and come round. You always know where to catch me."

I smile. Could version 1.0 have returned? Probably too early to tell.

"I'll keep it in mind."

A six-foot glamazon catwalks past, provoking a flurry of excited head-turns and car honks. Luke's eyes stay fixed on mine.

"Yes. I'll definitely keep it in mind."

# Chapter
# 27

It's the second of August.

The date Jacqui shouted into the air weeks ago.

"What about it?" I asked reasonably.

"What are you doing?"

"Um. Nothing."

"Well in that case you can come with me to the Boy Wonder's big summer garden party."

"I hardly know him."

"So? He told me to invite as many as possible. Bring thingummy as well."

"Fiona?"

"That's the one. As many as you like."

"So what is it?"

"Well, he does it every year. Simple idea. Outside. In the garden. One of the biggest gardens in the whole of Surrey, actually. Overindulging as much booze and what-have-you as is humanly possible. Everyone's there. All the DJs. All the top bods. It's great. Loads of babies and stuff."

"But I won't know anyone."

"Hey, it may be celeb central. But it's an easygoing bunch of people."

* * *

I'm at Fiona's.

"I'll be about five minutes," she says, before disappearing back into her bedroom. I wait in the living room. Stu should be here in any minute. I've asked Fee if Carl's coming and she goes a bit weak and fluffy before telling me that he's got "work commitments."

Stu arrives, sporting baggy combats, baggy T-shirt, and an even baggier smile.

"Oi, Seymore, there going to be some fit women at this party or what?" he asks me, before crashing onto the sofa.

"Stu, with your natural sophistication and gentlemanly charm, I should imagine you will be able to take your pick."

"C'mon!" he enthuses, before doing that football-rattle thing with his hand. He then dives into his Large Recordings record bag and pulls out the latest copy of *FHM*. A few pages in, he folds open the tester flap from the Calvin Klein Obsession advert and rubs it under his chin. ("Got to smell the part.") He speed-flicks through the rest of the magazine, pausing halfway in order to show me a semi-naked portrait of Carmen Electra.

"Hey Smarts, look at the bazookas on *that*."

I give him a mock-appreciative smile. "Lovely, Stuart."

As Fiona's car carefully tortoises up the driveway we are met by a vision of a whitewashed Georgian mansion.

We park and make our way round to the garden, which is essentially a national park equipped with a swimming pool. Some decks have been set up outside and the music is blaring. There must be about two hundred people here, and I would say about one hundred and ninety of them look over in our direction as we walk round. At first, I don't recognize anyone. It's just a mass of garish shirts and Gucci shades. Then a few faces come into focus. Some from magazines, others from the Dollar Disco. Eddy Thomkins is laughing raucously with a couple of other Day-glo grayheads. A group of B-list couples stand near the barbecue, clutching onto their C-list babies and champagne glasses for dear life.

"This is the bollocks," observes Stu, before immediately heading over to grab some free food.

I spy Jacqui, threading a path towards me and Fiona.

"Hey, you're here!" she sozzles, hooking her arms around our necks. "Isn't it fantastic!"

"Yes, it is," Fiona and I chirp in unison.

Stu returns with a plateful of charcoaled meat, and crimsons into silence when Jacqui greets him with a loud and lary "Oi oi, big boy!" In fact, Stuart remains uncharacteristically quiet for the rest of the afternoon, especially when introduced to the Boy Wonder himself, "Fan . . . Fan . . . Fantastic party," being all he can squeeze out of his quivering lips.

Which, incidentally, is a much better effort than what he ends up blurting out to Lara Broxfield, *Blasted* magazine's July Babe of the Month. "Um . . . I . . . ah . . . hi . . . oh . . . God . . . TITS! . . . um . . . sorry!" She was only *that* far away from slapping him around the head. I think she would have done it if I hadn't rushed to the rescue by explaining that he is suffering from an acute strand of Tourette's syndrome.

"Keep working that charm, Stu," I assure him. "And she'll be eating out of your hand."

And, from here on in, the afternoon trollies even further downhill. Fiona, who as a professional networker could normally mingle for England, is clearly not in top form. In fact, now I come to think of it, she hasn't been in top form all week. I tell her she should have a drink, and she reminds me she's driving.

"Are you OK?" I ask her eventually, when we are sitting in one of the garden chairs by the pool.

"Uh-huh."

"Are you sure?"

A trace of anger ripples across her face.

"I'm sorry if I'm letting you down, Martha," she huffs. "I'm sorry I'm not as wild and crazy as your newfound celebrity friends."

The word "friends" is barely audible owing to the fact that the Boy Wonder has just provoked a huge cheer by somersault-diving into the pool fully clothed.

"Don't be stupid."

"I'm not. I'm just saying."

A minute later, Fee turns to look at me and smiles. "I'm sorry. I'm just feeling a bit bollocky at the minute. I think I'm PMS-ing on, that's all."

"Sure it's not me?"

"Sure."

But as I smooth my back against the silver chair I feel like a complete titwad. I shouldn't have pestered Fee to come, not if she didn't feel up to it. Then again, I can't help thinking she's being just a tad unreasonable. After all, she's always dragging me to things I don't want to go to, with people I don't want to be with. In fact, if it hadn't been for her, I'd never have met Jacqui in the first place.

It's always like this. I always get caught in the middle between friends. I suppose that's why I usually try and keep them separate. They invariably seem so disappointed in me when they see my other selves.

I watch as Stu navigates his path from the barbecue to where we are sitting, balancing a whisky and Coke and his third mountain of meat. His tongue is protruding in concentration. He must have drunk loads, even by his standards.

As he approaches us, he clearly becomes distracted by a collection of sun-worshipping celebrity bazookas lined up on the other side of the pool. He smiles nervously in the direction of their owners and gets blanked in return.

*Careful!* Shit, we're about to lose one of those C-list babies under his size twelve Birkenstocks. "Stu!" I call. "Watch out!"

He looks down as the tot crawls towards him, and takes two giraffe steps to the left. The baby is plucked away from the pool's edge with a parental glare up towards Stu.

"Sorry, sorry!" he mumbles pathetically. "Sorrrrraggghhh!" He loses his footing along with his glass of whisky and plate of meat, as his arms windmill, and he falls backwards into the pool.

*Splash!*

*Fuck!*

Now all two hundred guests are looking in either his or our direction. The cheers which accompanied the Boy Wonder's fully clothed dive are quickly replaced by scornful giggles and heads shaking with disapproval. There are obviously clearly defined rules as to who is allowed to act like a twat and who isn't, and Z-list plebs like us must fall into the latter category.

Fiona turns and looks at me as if it's all my fault, before walking over to the pool. After four unsuccessful attempts Stu manages to haul himself out of the water, leaving the floating pieces of meat behind him.

"I'll get my coat," he says, once he is out, although there are clearly no *Fast Show* fans present.

I scan the crowd of hostile faces to look for Jacqui, but she is nowhere to be seen.

"Let's go," I say to Fiona, and we head back to the car.

# Chapter
# 28

Jacqui's TV is of the backless variety. You know the type: a large flat screen apparently floating in midair. It's also got a surround-sound capability which really lives up to its name. When you are watching a film or televised drama the actors' voices come from all over the room. Anywhere, in fact, other than from the TV itself.

She is still in bed. My watch tells me it's eleven fifty-two, although it is increasingly unreliable. God knows what time she left the party last night.

I am watching an old episode of *Friends*, the one where they have all gone to Las Vegas and where Ross and Rachel get married because they are drunk. When the phone rings in Chandler's hotel room I wonder why he isn't answering it. And then I realize: it's Jacqui's phone.

"Hello?"

"Martha?" It takes a second for me to place the voice.

"Yes?"

"It's Alex."

"Alex, hi." For some reason I find myself whispering.

"I need to talk to you face to face."

"What about?"

"Please. Can I tell you when I see you?"

"Curiouser and curiouser."

"Are you free tomorrow afternoon?"

"Um, I can be."

"Good. Good."

Twenty-five is the age now. The point of no return. When everything starts to go wrong. It used to be thirty, but they must have moved it forward.

And I'm starting to think that they may have a point. I mean the signs are already there in my face. All that skin damage. I've read (in *Gloss*, needless to say) that if you wore Factor 50 every day from the day you were born, if you coated yourself with it, you wouldn't show any visible signs of aging until you were sixty. Could that be true?

Just look at that forehead. Those creases. No laughter lines yet though. That must tell you something. And it's not just my face either. It's the whole package. It's getting baggy. I can feel it. It's as if I've got a size twelve birthday suit for a size ten body. Under my arms and at my elbows. A loose fit. I don't think they've got an exchange policy worked out yet though. Not that it should be too long before they do have one. What with all that DNA testing and stuff.

"Am I starting to look old?" I ask Fiona on a regular basis.

"No. Am I?" comes her invariable reply.

But it's different for men, isn't it? They've got the fact that ninety-nine percent of Hollywood screenwriters and directors are male on their side. This means that saggy relics such as Michael Douglas, Sean Connery, and Richard Gere have become the archetypes of male virility. Men can wear their bus passes as a badge of pride. They could probably zimmer on down to your average meat market aged seventy-five and stand a fair to middling chance of copping off.

I sometimes fantasize that it's the other way round. That the sequel to *Driving Miss Daisy* featured Ewan McGregor as the love interest. That old women could be shown on celluloid shafting their young male employees up against the filing cabinet. OK, so there was *The Graduate*. But that was centuries ago. And Anne Bancroft was hardly Thora Hird, was she?

So yes, I'm scared of getting old. Or rather, scared of *looking* old. Becoming one of those invisible old ladies munching on sandwiches in the park. Who has given up everything in order to live on memories and ham and pickle.

And all of a sudden everything seems to be moving so fast. I reckon the last 365 days would be able to fit quite comfortably within one of those old schoolday afternoons. So while you may think it's strange that one week nine years ago could still mean anything, to me it is perfectly understandable. In fact, it means more now than it did then.

It's a hot day: that kind of rare London August heat that sticks to the back of your throat and turns all the buildings to rubber. Green Park. That is where he wanted to meet me. Over the road from the Galgarry, after all. Actually, today it should probably be renamed Green and Yellow Park in tribute to the thirsty patches of mown grass emerging away from the shade.

Through my squinted gaze I watch him as he moves toward me, his image overlapping with the dancing knots in my eyes. He looks beautiful, the strap of his satchel cutting diagonally across his blue cotton chest, accentuating its natural form. As he gets closer I can take in his face—a furrowed brow contradicting a warm, greeting smile—framed by those cherub locks.

And, for a reason I can't yet identify, I feel terrible.

Guilty.

Unclean.

I am doing nothing wrong, I know that. Not really. I am just meeting a friend for a talk. A talk and a walk. Nothing bad about that, is there? Not in and of itself. True, I have had sex with him. But that was lifetimes ago. Centuries. OK, OK. I do have *feelings* for him, even if I am unsure over their exact nature. And this man, this visual feast, is Desdemona's future husband, and she would very probably be wearing a tailor-made Seymore-skin overcoat within a week of finding out about this meeting. But hey, what she doesn't know and all that.

"It's good to see you." Alex greets me with an awkward peck on the cheek.

"You too."

The park is busy with a mix of first-time visitors and seasonal Mayfairers, looking around with interest or indifference accordingly. A young French couple walk by, laughing at nothing in particular. Probably just married. On honeymoon. A Couple in Love. As they pass us they hook each other closer and move in for a kiss. They are doing it out of spite. I know it.

We just walk for a while, saying just enough to get by. And then, as I brake to light a cigarette, he turns and says: "You broke my heart, you know."

He doesn't say it dramatically. His tone is matter-of-fact. Flippant, even. He might as well be making a comment about the weather.

"No, I didn't know that." I inhale deeply and put my lighter and Marlboros back in my bag.

"It doesn't matter," he says. "I'm over it now. Just." As he says that last word, he screws his eyes up and levers a clenched fist toward his heart. Is he taking the piss?

"Are you taking the piss?"

"No. I'm not. I am over it. But at the time I was besotted with you. You know. You were more than just a mate. I don't know if it was love or what, but I was totally fucked. And when you started dating Simon Adcock, that was it. I just kept on asking myself what does he have that I don't. I couldn't do my homework or anything. And senior year as well. It wasn't the best timing." He pauses, as if running the next sentence through his head before playing it aloud. "It was *my* first time as well, you know."

"Now that," I giggle, "has taken me by surprise."

Unlike Guy, he is not too proud. He laughs with me, although first he seems reluctant to do so.

"I don't think my second time was much better," he concedes.

"Now. Who was that with?"

"Er . . . Alison Shipley."

A scary vision of a girl in a baggy Kappa top with an impossibly high-fringe flashbulbs into my mind, sending a school-yard shudder down my spine.

"You didn't."

"I'm afraid I did."

"But she was a psychopath."

"What can I say." He shrugs playfully. "I was on the rebound . . . She was easy prey." And then he lifts his head up with feigned nostalgia. "A right dirty one if I remember rightly."

"All right, all right," I say. "Get the picture."

We carry on like this for a while, prodding each other with half-forgotten teenage memories. Soon, and almost accidentally we move out of the park and onto a quiet, shady side street. And our conversation shifts with our environment, as if provoked by the orange-bricked architecture and the quiet smell of money it exudes.

We talk about Luke. About my feelings. I am honest. I tell him I love him and hate him. And feel completely indifferent. He seems to understand that these are not contradictions.

"Are you thirsty?" he asks.

"Yes, I am."

We go into a pub. It is dark and, except for two lone drinkers, empty. The barman seems almost too tired to serve us, as if he's doing us a favor.

"A pint of . . ." Alex leans back to survey the ranges of lighted beer pumps. "Carlsberg Export, please . . . No, actually, make that a whisky and Coke." He turns to me.

"Vodka cranberry."

We take our drinks and journey over towards a mauve alcove in the far corner. He sits down opposite me and takes a sip of his drink.

"I think Desdemona is being unfaithful."

The words just hang there in the air for a while, floating between us. As if waiting to be collected, along with the used glasses on our table.

"What?"

He repeats the sentence again, only with full stops between every word.

"You're not serious?" I suggest.

"I am," he tells me, stone-faced. "Dead serious."

For the first time since I met up with him an hour ago his smile has gone. His wide, honest features now wear a darkened expression.

"But, but . . ." My mouth is in guppy mode again. "You're getting married."

He shrugs. A shrug that seems to say, *I know, unbelievable, isn't it?*

"But what makes you think so?"

"She keeps disappearing. I keep coming home and she's not there, even when she's not at work. She gives me pathetic excuses. That she's been window-shopping, trying to get sorted for the wedding. But it doesn't ring true. We haven't even set a date."

"This is hardly conclusive evidence."

"No, I know, I know it's not. But it's not the fact that she keeps making up lame excuses, or at least not *just* that. There's all this other stuff, like the way she looks at me sometimes and some of the things she says."

"Such as?"

"Oh, I don't know. Lots of things. 'Would you still marry me whatever happened?' Stuff like that."

This is a textbook case of relationship insecurity, and I can hear that shrill psychologist voice ring clear in my brain. Alex is on the cusp of making the most significant step of his life, and he is starting to have doubts. Unwilling to face up to his own ambivalent feelings, he is starting to project them onto Desdemona. It's easier for him to deal with it this way. All those fears of what may or may not lie ahead. All those unwritten chapters of his life. Yes, that's it. It's probably just a classic example of that most common of all male afflictions, commitment phobia, kicking in just that little bit too late.

I've covered this topic quite a few times, and I know how I should respond. Take a deep look inside and ask yourself if this is the real problem. If you are still convinced it is, bring it out in the open. Confront her with these fears as carefully as possible. See how she handles them. Listen to what she has to say. Talk it through. Get to understand each other better. Set up a commune. Yada yada yada.

I can't say any of this of course. I'm involved. He's making sure of that.

I get up to order our second drinks, which gives me a bit of time to consider how to play this. At the bar I look back at him and catch his eye; we hold our gaze just that bit too long.

"Thanks," he says as I sit back down.

"Listen," I tell him authoritatively. "You asked Desdemona to marry you. You couldn't have had any doubts then." My inflection goes up at the end of this sentence, turning it into a half-question.

He ducks his head to the side, in order to let my words go straight over him. "Can I have a cigarette?" he asks.

"You don't smoke."

"Well, I don't. Not really. But I've never ruled it out."

"It spoils your taste buds," I remind him.

"Taste buds are overrated when it comes to cooking," he tells me. "Other stuff is just as important. Smell. Texture. The way the food looks on the plate."

Under the table I feel his leg, or rather his jeans, fall against mine. This could be an accident, but he is making no attempt to move away. I hand him a cigarette and light it for him.

He splutters as the first take of nicotine hits his lungs.

"What would you do if you did find out she was unfaithful?"

"It would be over. No question. Just like you and Luke. You didn't forgive him, did you?"

"Er, no. But don't you think there are a lot of gray areas? I mean, what if Desdemona could see us now? Having a drink together. Talking like this. What would she think? She wouldn't be happy, that's for sure."

"But we're just talking."

"What. So you're going to tell her?"

"Well, no. But that's not—"

"Exactly."

I look straight at his face. He is a good person. You can see that. Essentially positive. But just look at those eyes. Those deep brown-black mischievous eyes. Right now they are suggesting a different side to him. One which wasn't detectable nine years ago. One which has been developed through experience.

"So you're saying that just by the fact that we're here, talking like this, I'm being unfaithful?"

"In a way. In principle."

And then, with no apparent warning, he leans across the table and kisses me. A closed-lip kiss. Sexless. Friendly. That's all it is. But all of a sudden I want it to contain more.

To go further.

"I'd, um, better go," I fluster, as my head moves away.

"I'm sorry. I didn't mean—"

"I know. I know. I just need to be getting back."

And then, caught in those eyes, I move forward again. Within a second I feel his lips press on mine. Nothing is holding us together. There is a table between us. But for some reason I can't pull away. The fresh nicotine on his tongue tastes beautiful, corrupt.

But now, in my head, Desdemona appears. I watch her face crumple and fall apart. This will hurt her. She does not deserve this, I tell myself, as I lift my arm up to Alex's shoulder and push him gently away.

Standing up, I try and blanket the situation with words: "This didn't happen; and Desdemona loves you. She hasn't been unfaithful. You are getting married."

Alex says nothing, and makes no attempt to follow me as I walk out of the pub.

Once outside, I am walking fast, but in no clear direction. I get to Green Park Tube and walk straight past—for some reason I want to stay aboveground. Eventually, I find myself on Oxford Street. I get a bus, number 25, and travel east to Fiona's.

# Chapter

## 29

What I need right now.

I'll tell you what I need right now. I need to hear Fiona's soothing voice at the other end of this intercom. I need to see her face, as warm and perfect as ever. I need to tell her everything and then for her to tell me everything back, with sugar on top.

But what I need is not what I get. I should know that by now.

For a start, the voice coming through the intercom is Stuart's, not Fiona's. And even over the crackle I can tell something is wrong. I know it at once.

"Stu, it's me."

"I'll buzz you in."

When I get to Fee's landing, my heart sinks and anchors in my stomach.

Something has happened.

Psychologists generally have no time for the sixth sense; they say five are enough, and have the experiments to prove it. But I am not so sure. Not at this moment, not as I feel myself moving into another, darker orbit. A physical feeling, terrible and goosebumpy.

The door opens and Stuart, or rather someone or something possessing Stuart's body, is standing there.

"What is it? What's happened? Where is she?" My questions are fired fast and shoot into the air at random.

I move in as Stuart makes way. The living room has been hit by a tornado. Everything is either on the floor or broken. Or both. As in a *Crimewatch* reconstruction.

The rich black earth from the two yucca plants has been sprayed diagonally across the shiny wooden floorboards the length of the room, like a scar. The plants themselves are lying horizontal, in fractured pots, where they have crash-landed next to the standing lamp (which, along with the TV, is the only object in the whole room which appears intact and in its normal position). The sky-rise CD stand has been knocked over, along with the self-assembled, totemic bookcase. A copy of *How to Have What You Want (and Want What You Have)* lies at my feet, face down with the author's Californian smile beaming up from the back cover. Other self-help and psychology manuals litter the floor, covered with soil and broken glass.

"What the—"

I am scared. My thoughts read like the *Daily Mail*: *I am witnessing the aftermath of a violent burglary*, I tell myself, *undertaken by a gang of youths out of their brains on heroin, looking for a means to finance their next fix. This is Tower Hamlets, after all.* But a second thought tells me this is not the case. Nothing is missing. Everything is out of place, sure, but it is all contained within this room.

Then I hear a sound. A quiet but painful whimper, coming from the bedroom. The feeling in my stomach turns to nausea. It seems like a lifetime since I entered the flat, this parallel universe, but it must only be a few seconds. Ten at most.

As I stagger into the bedroom, trailing a wordless Stuart, things are beginning to fall into place. The sound, the whimpering, is coming from Fiona. She is there before me, sprawled facedown on the bed sobbing into the duvet. Her hair, which normally sits so tidily, is a wild mess. She has a dressing gown on.

Sensing my presence, or at least someone's presence, in the room, she tries to gain some form of relative composure. I can see and hear her try to stifle her tears by burying her face deeper into the duvet, but it is obvious that snot and salt water are still breaking through.

"Fee, it's me. Martha." There is no immediate response. I look at Stuart, his eyes soft and lachrymose. "What *happened*?" The question is now delivered more carefully, and on target.

The answer, although inevitable, still makes me shudder. "Carl." Stuart nearly chokes on the name. "It was Carl."

Although this is an attempt at an answer, it still makes no sense. And then Fiona slowly pulls herself up, twisting around to sit towards us, on the bed. The sight makes me flinch, and I produce a faint noise at the back of my throat.

Her face is transformed.

The light beige monotone and symmetry of her skin are gone. There are new colors there now, around the left side. A purple bruise and an angry pink scar. A white hospital patch is stuck to her forehead and one eyelid is swelling shut.

The real shock, though, is the way she is looking at me. It is a look I don't recognize, or at least not one I have ever seen her display. Her eyes, or rather her one good eye, is glazed in surrender, as if it has seen too much to try and pretend otherwise. She is lost, distant. Looking at her mouth, which is frozen downward, it is hard to imagine her smiling again.

I move forward and climb, awkwardly, onto the bed; my arms envelop her and she nestles delicately into my shoulder. I am gentle, as if handling a fragile parcel.

"I'm sorry," she says obscurely. "I'm so sorry."

I look at the hairbrush on the bedside table; the one which has doubled, on so many occasions, as an imaginary microphone. An image of her on this same bed, equipped with Elvis strut and lip-curl acting out her Las Vegas '68 video, flashes into my mind. Feeling the immense sense of pathos and nostalgia which can be brought on by an everyday inanimate object, I bite back the tears.

There is a funereal pause and then Stuart starts to tell the story. "He did this. Beat the fucking crap out of her, smashed the whole fucking place up. Fucking cokehead." He is visibly shaking with rage and fear as he speaks these words.

Fiona lifts her head up to smudge away her tears.

"When did you get here?" I ask Stuart, in a deliberately steady tone.

"Half an hour after it happened. As soon as Fee called me."

Over the next ten minutes he tells me the whole story, with Fiona occasionally correcting the odd detail or groaning at the memory.

The core facts are as follows (I will try and be as objective as possible with no glossing over). Earlier this week Fiona found that Carl had been taking money out of her bank account to spend on cocaine. She previously knew he had a "bit of a problem," but had no idea of its magnitude. Following a weekend bender, she decided to confront him. A big mistake, as it turned out. Carl erupted into a fit of rage. He attacked the apartment and then turned on Fiona, grabbing her hair and throwing her to the floor. Dizzily she got to her feet, her heart hammering. But it was not over. She was dragged, again by the hair, through the carnage of the living room to the kitchen. He hit her. He laughed. She pleaded. He hit her again. She fell back against the unit. On the floor, the room spinning, she watched as he stood over her. As he unbuttoned his fly and pulled out his penis. He was going to rape her. He thought twice.

When Stuart got her phone call he was in the pub, enjoying an after-work drink. He was round in twenty minutes. He pleaded with her to go to the hospital and tell the police. After a shower, she went to the hospital, although she hasn't told the police. Stuart says she won't. That it will make things worse. After dressing and bandaging the cut on her forehead, the nurse at the hospital told her no further treatment would be required; most of the damage was, sorry *is*, "superficial."

They got back here an hour ago.

Stuart is on the bed now as well. He is smoothing his sister's shin affectionately, his face a blend of hurt, incomprehension and anger.

There are things to sort out. The flat. The issue of where Fiona is staying tonight. Carl.

"It's going to be all right," I tell her, although the words sound strangely pathetic. It's almost as if the silent air is providing its own response, to contradict me.

*It will never be all right. Never.*

# Chapter
## 30

I never knew what Fiona saw in Carl. That doesn't mean there was nothing to see, just that I never saw it. But then, perhaps she too only saw one side.

The Halo Effect. That's the psychological term. Taking one personality trait of someone and then interpreting *all* their behavior as essentially good or bad depending on whether the trait is positive or negative. Of course, this is most common in situations where love is involved. So much so that some have even argued that falling in love with someone is the least effective way of getting to know them.

And what he has done—specifically, what he did exactly one week ago—has made love and its halo effect harder for her. More distant. This may prove to be his biggest crime, and one for which he could never be tried.

Not that the police have been involved at all. They never will be. We have argued. We have pleaded. But she has decided: it would make things worse. I don't really see how, but she is entitled, more than anyone, to that decision.

She has moved out, to Stuart's. She didn't have to. It was her place as much as his.

"Too many memories," she said. "Too many memories."

So now she is holed up in a glorified shed in Whitechapel,

surrounded by a thousand glossy images of Kelly Brook and Angelina Jolie smiling down at her.

And we are here now, the three of us, in Stuart's bedroom. The fusty smell I remember is still there, although disguised underneath the chemical musk of Lynx spray-on deodorant.

"I'm sure you'd be able to stay at Jacqui's. She'd understand, if I just explained, you know, the situation—"

"No." Fiona's voice is urgent. "No, I don't want anyone to know. I'm fine here."

"Martha, there's no one here for the next three weeks," explains Stuart, lying on his bed. "Jim and Webby—his housemates—are still in Australia."

"But, and don't take this the wrong way, Stu, is this really the best place for you right now, Fee?" I look around at this preserved testament to teenage testosterone. The *FHM* posters, the bazooka babes, the *Top Gun* memorabilia.

"Well, yes," she says, looking at her brother. "This is the *only* place I can be right now."

Her face is still damaged. The bruising has almost disappeared and she is no longer wearing her hospital patch, but she has that same, surrendered look in her eyes. Defeated.

I can sort of see why Stuart had wanted to wait for Carl to return. To exact vengeance. To cause him pain. To "kick his fucking teeth out." But I think I did right to avert that situation. To help Fiona disappear and to use the threat of getting the police involved if Carl ever came near her again.

And, as much as I can, I've been here for her this week. Trying to talk about anything which can take her mind off it. This strategy hasn't really worked. Oh sure, to the untrained eye she seems quite normal. She isn't bursting into tears every five minutes or pining out of the window or listening to The Smiths or quoting Sylvia Plath.

But she isn't playing hairbrush karaoke, either. And she's gone a whole five days without saying "fuck-a-duck" and "bollocky bollocks." And she's not smiling. Not her usual shiny happy PR girl smile, anyway. She has occasionally widened her mouth in the style of a sad old widow having a good day, but that is all.

She is not, in other words, her old self.

But then, neither is Stuart. As I look at him now I realize that he too has changed over the last week. Grown older and wiser. Taking care of his sister seems to be civilizing him. For instance, he now calls me by my proper name rather than by some laddish nickname (Marts, Seymore, the Seymore, etc.).

Oh yeah, and he's started pouring his lager out into a glass before he drinks it.

These may seem like little changes, but I can't help thinking they could hold a wider significance.

And then there's me.

Although I wouldn't say this whole situation has changed me in any fundamental way, I have started to see things a bit differently. I have had to acknowledge that there are more things in the world than having sex with people you shouldn't have sex with. I have realized also that cocaine is best left to traffic wardens. And discovered that in my head the image of Luke with another woman is not as painful as the image of Fiona suffering at the hands of Carl.

Nowhere near.

When something like this happens there are no silver linings. There is no bright side. But there is perspective.

And now, today, I can see things a whole lot clearer. I see, for instance, that there were never one hundred thousand Lukes. There was just one. The one I loved.

The one I would argue with during our weekly shop.

The one who would say, "It's a load of bollocks," to everything, but then a doubtful "Isn't it?" as if he needed confirmation.

The one who would protect me during sleep.

And yes, the one who was unfaithful.

But, come on, I've been a bit unreasonable, haven't I? I

mean, perhaps Jacqui is right. Perhaps people are only as faithful as their options. Only not quite in the way she intended.

Look at Alex. Nice guy. No, great guy. The *best* guy. But I can't pretend that just because I am the subject, not the object, of his infidelity it makes it any different. And, if I am being completely straight with myself, when I first saw Alex again I too was unfaithful. In my head, at least. And although head sex is a lot less risky than bed sex, it is no less dirty. So, Martha Seymore, it's time to graduate. It's time to forgive (Luke) and forget (Alex). It's time, at long last it's time, to really talk things over.

The real world awaits. And it's only a Tube journey away.

# Chapter
## 31

The last time I was here I knew I was never coming back. You remember. That was it. I'd got my stuff, so had no need to return. But that was then.

I've decided, nearly two months too late, to heed my own advice. Talk it through. You see, although I used to say it all the time I suppose I must have never believed it. That things are not black and white. That life, more often than not, is shot in Technicolor.

He's fixed the window.

I try to see in from the other side of the street but the blinds are down. He might be out. Four-thirty. Yes. Could well be. Perhaps I should have called, like he said.

Oh fuck it. I'm here now.

I cross over and press the metallic silver button marked Flat 2. No answer. Mind you, it always did play up. It's probably a sign. That's what Fee would say. Telling me I should give up. Go home. Forget about it.

The keys. *My* keys. The spare set. The set I'd neglected to leave with my good-bye note. He's never asked for them back. Probably doesn't even realize.

I take them from my pocket and open the main door. It shuts behind me with a loud metal clunk. So here I am. Inside the communal hallway. With that smell: cheap disinfectant mixed with expensive perfume. The black mailboxes are on the wall to my left. Out of Luke's box there is a bundle of brown envelopes half-sticking out. Folded over like paper fajitas. As the lift is silent and there are no footsteps, I go over and have a look.

Bills. Junk. Something from *Internet Planet*. A check probably. An angry-looking envelope from the student loans company. And that's it. I don't know what I was expecting. A love letter from Miss X, Sealed with a Loving Kiss? I mean, come on. Get a grip.

I push the envelopes back through the slot and start to walk up the stairs. A vision of Luke, stark bollock naked and calling my name from this very spot, comes back to me. I smile. A few seconds later I am on the landing, inches away from his door: the door I have opened and closed behind me one thousand times before.

I pause awhile. Standing still on the beige fitted carpet. I look down at what I am wearing. I've worked hard at looking like I haven't made an effort. An überchic Paul and Joe T-shirt offset with low-key denim. After a quick hair realignment, I knock on the door.

The moment I do so my heart starts to canter. He is in. I know he is. I can smell him. Any minute now I am going to hear his heavy step move towards the door, the lock will turn, and he will be there. Mouth open. Pleased to see me. I must control myself. My first words must not be: "I love you Luke, I forgive you, please take me back, or I will die a lonely, bitter old lady."

That might look needy. Anyway, I am here to talk, that's all. Two completely imperfect human beings having a chat. Nothing else. But then, suddenly, I want it to be more.

I have been stupid. I made a rash decision and stuck to it. As a result I have nearly lost my job, nearly destroyed my oldest friend's marriage before it has begun, and, as if that weren't enough, turned myself into a complete shagaholic. Luke's the one I should be with. I mean, God, at least he told me. That must mean something, mustn't it?

There is no answer.

My forced smile fades and falls.

I am about to go when I hear the faint sound of music coming from somewhere within the apartment. I knock again. There is still no answer.

Oh fuck it. I'm here now.

With the same twisted logic that makes those horror-flick heroines lost in the woods think it would be a really great idea to investigate where that strange screaming sound is coming from, I push the key into the lock and twist it open.

Inside, the music hits me. Prince, "When Doves Cry." A remixed version. I didn't even know he had it. Shit. Has he moved out? He never used to play music this loud. Not in the flat.

My insides are in freefall. "Luke. Luke. It's me." No answer. Probably can't hear me above the noise. I move forward, past the bathroom on the right. Not in there. I tilt my head around the bedroom door. Nope. No sign.

And then I hear it, breaking through above the eighties' guitars and synthesizers. That unmistakable miaow of pained pleasure.

I step back two paces to look through the thumb-wide opening in the living-room door. There are two candles on the windowsill, bathing the room in a soft, golden light. My heart is now a drum-roll. I swallow my breath and silently change my angle, to take in the whole room. The hall is dark so I should be invisible. I see the bookcase, the kitchen movie posters, the Art Deco ashtrays.

And there it is. The mind's-eye picture come to life. Luke on the floor naked with another woman. The Other Woman. She, head down, her angular body saddled on top of him, in full gallop. As her head arches back, allowing me to glimpse her face, I cannot help but release an audible gasp. Audible to me at least. When I catch sight of those ice-blue eyes, I feel my whole body freeze over. She lets her head fall again, Desdemoaning with delight.

My head at first fails to make sense of it. I am just standing here, trying to see what this image means, as if I am looking through the dots of a Magic Eye poster.

I see Luke.

I see Desdemona.

I see Luke underneath Desdemona.

I see Desdemona on top of Luke.

I see Luke's arm descend towards a bowl: the black and white one I used to eat my Crunchy Nut Cornflakes out of. I see his fingers emerge, dripping oil, and I pick up the smell. What is that? Lavender? Lavender and ginger? I see a bottle on the floor, closer to me. Ylang-ylang. Luke doesn't even believe in aromatherapy.

This is incredible.

Luke's familiar hand is now on Desdemona's right breast. Smoothing more oil around her glossy nipple, then moving down past her ribs and around to her bouncing buttocks.

What am I doing to myself? Why am I still here, watching this live horror pornography? This unplugged aromasex? But I can't help it. I am fixed to the spot, caught exactly halfway between the impulse to leave and the impulse to barge right in and rip every single strand of her sunny blond hair out of her sunny blond head.

Despite the mangled cacophony of sex groans and crying doves, a voice enters my head. An old recording. "Wow, Martha, haven't you done well." And then at a slightly higher pitch: "Oh Martha, lighten up. It was only a bit of fun. And anyway, I can't help it if I have such an effect on boys, can I?"

But as I hear this voice, looping continuously around my brain, I am looking at Luke, his face clenched in aggressive pleasure. A face so much more animated than I remember during *our* naked adventures. The neatly shaved cheeks and stubbly chin may be familiar, but nothing else. And the room, too, seems transformed.

Oh sure, the kitsch movie posters and modernist furniture remain in place. But the negative energy I detected before is now overpowering, making everything seem ugly in the flickering light. The invisible war is now plain to see.

"... *haven't you done well* ..."

My eyes pan back up to Desdemona and zoom in. In contrast to Luke, she remains beautiful. Feeding off his gaze as her fingers comb through her hair. Their bodies are confident with each other. Too confident for a first time. Or even a second.

I am still struggling to believe it.

This is the room where we have lain on the floor, like two little kids, playing PlayStation, where we have had tickle fights and boxed with cushions. This is the room where we sat and ate together, night after night, for nearly two years. Where we curled up together on the settee, that settee there, and watched videos or crappy daytime TV or Channel 4 news.

With no candles. No essential oils. And no sex.

I look again at the floor. No clothes anywhere to be seen. This is not a spontaneous thing. This is preplanned. The bowl. The music. The whole setup. I wouldn't be surprised if there are some strawberries and ice cubes somewhere around. And this is a prolonged entertainment. Whatever she has said to Alex, she has made a full day's worth of excuses. After they finish, they will wait, recharge, and begin again. No doubt about it.

And then, still firmly in the saddle, her head turns slightly towards the door. Towards me. Her eyes are half-closed and I am standing in the dark. She is lost in pleasure. But even so, I am sure, just for a second I am sure, that she is looking at me. That she can see me.

She doesn't flinch. She maintains that look of ecstatic triumph. Her fifteen-year-old voice returns again: "Love ... advantage. Game, set, and match, Desdemona." And here she is, still killing me for her sport.

A second later I realize my mind may be playing tricks. She

wouldn't be able to see me, would she? Not here. In the dark. And there's no way they'd be able to hear me above the music.

I cannot stay though. I realize that if I do I have lost completely. And Luke will not be able to hold out for much longer. No matter how hard he may be trying to keep up appearances, it won't be long before his own ylang-ylang will shoot its load.

I take a silent step backwards, still keeping sight of their bodies, their naked skin flickering gold, then turn and walk towards the door. As I reach to turn the lock the Prince CD finishes. I leave to the wailed chorus of their combined climax.

Once the door has shut behind me, I am back into light. I move quickly down the stairway and back outside.

# Chapter
## 32

If this was happening in a film it would be raining right now. Not soft London rain, either. No. It would be pissing it down with all the force of a tropical storm. Umbrella-less pedestrians would be splashing past me with newspapers over their heads while I let myself soak in wet misery.

But this is not a film. Or at least if it is it is someone else's.

My state of mind has absolutely no identifiable impact on the climate. The sun is out and there is a warm, gentle breeze. Small, cotton-wool clouds pattern the narrow blue sky, so still they seem like they have always been there.

A funky dread in a suit swerves past me on the pavement, smiling. And he is not alone. In fact, the whole of Notting Hill is wearing one big goldtoothed grin today. Making the most of what is probably going to be one of the last sunny Saturdays of the year.

Desdefuckingmona.

I know my proof is inconclusive. I know there is a possibility that Luke had told me the truth. That the person he had sex with behind my back was a complete stranger, to him as well as me. I know also that they would never admit it, not unless it could be tortured out of them using some kind of medieval contraption designed for causing as much physical pain as possible. But that is unrealistic. Where would I get one from?

And besides, I don't need hard evidence. I *know* that Luke was unfaithful to me in the same way that Desdemona is being unfaithful to Alex. That is to say, he was unfaithful with intent. He knew what he was doing, and who he was doing it with. How long he was doing it for, now that's a different question entirely. Your guess is as good as mine. Well, maybe not *quite* as good as mine actually, now I come to think of it.

You see, I have a little more knowledge. I know, for instance, that Luke went to see her two months before his confession. This was, I assumed, perfectly innocent. He told me he wanted to interview her for an article he was putting together on the state of the high-tech job market. Even though the article never appeared, I wasn't suspicious. Why should I have been? He often had articles pulled at the last minute. But now I am seeing things differently. Now I am starting to wonder about the type of jobs they were discussing. Could it have started then?

Probably. Possibly. I don't know.

But that's Luke for you. Now you see him, now you don't. I now well and truly believe that the Lying Cheating Bastard is capable of anything. *Anything.*

And so am I. I realize that now.

Where am I going?

Why am I still walking?

The nearest station is in the other direction. But here I am heading towards that turquoise door. Is this a good idea?

Of course it's not, I tell myself as I ring the buzzer. But then, the world is full of bad ideas, so why should I be left out. I'm in shock. I'm traumatized. I can't think straight. These are my excuses and I'm sticking to them.

There is only one man in the world I want to see right now. And he is behind that door, I know he is. I can feel him. He has always been there, hasn't he? The first one to say "I love you." Before all the others. Luke, Siraj. And all those meaningless one night stand-offs. My original ex. Not that I know him. I've never known him.

But then, I never knew Luke either, did I? And, as Jacqui says, the virtue of knowing people is highly overrated. I know his face. That's the main thing. Those features which have broadened with age. The eyebrows which have grown thicker. The jawline which has gained strength. And this is the face I have in mind now. Mature. Confident. Inviting.

But when he opens the door he is sixteen again. The nervous lips and vulnerable eyes I remember so well have returned, sending me back through time.

"Thanks for coming over," he says. Actually, he doesn't even manage to say that because by the time he's reached "over" my lips are on his, pushing him back into the flat.

"Martha," he gasps, coming up for air. "Wait!"

But I am not listening. I've got him against the wall, his head awkwardly positioned against the glass frame of the Miro print in the hallway.

"We can't—"

"We already are."

And then more passionate lip-wrestling ensues. God, he's a good kisser. It's as if he's spent the last nine years taking a Ph.D. in the subject. Such subtlety. Such depth. The fish-in-a-washing-machine technique he once practiced is barely detectable now. These are adult kisses. Not well-thought-out, carefully considered grown-up kisses, but hot, urgent, intense adult ones. My eyes are shut. But then they open, just for a second. Enough time to snapshot his expression, to take in that look of pain and torment and pleasure.

My lips direct us into the living room, Alex's feet shuffling backwards. By the time we have reached the settee we are half undressed. All traces of resistance have now evaporated.

And I can feel Desdemona everywhere. In every object in

the room. The TV, the pine chest by the window, the Stonehenge speakers, the glass coffee table, the Oriental rug, even the settee itself—all are witnesses. Each one, I feel, will be able to tell her what happened. The whole room is on her side.

But I don't care. Not right now. Even Alex doesn't seem to. And this is a bigger thing for him. A bigger crime. Oh sure, he's expressed his doubts. But he doesn't *know*. He hasn't seen what I've seen.

I could tell him, of course. I could let him know that, right now, Desdemona and Luke are enjoying a postcoital cigarette together.

It has to be like this, though. I have to know he's doing it for the right (that is, wrong) reasons. That he is willing to be unfaithful for me. That he is not just fucking me on the rebound.

So, is that what I'm doing?

This is the question passing through the back of my head as Alex moves his hand from my breast to my legs, then navigates his way upwards. As I am panting kisses into his ear—a tactic, by the way, he seems to be enjoying.

But no. It's not like that. Not entirely. I am not going to pretend that this is not about Desdemona. Of course it is. In part, at least. If it wasn't then why would the theme tune from *Rocky* be blaring in my head? Da-da daah. Da-da daah . . . Seconds out. Round fifteen.

If it wasn't, then why would I be so determined to make sure this is better than what they were having? More real. Intense.

So yes, it's about Desdemona. It's about Luke. And, dare I say that word, *closure*. But this is also about unfinished business and the chance to start again. Not to mention living for the moment, and letting nature, just for once, take its course. Most of all, however, it's about those eyes, inviting me in, letting me delve further.

Even though we are not completely undressed, we are ready for sex. His hand is through my legs, his fingers on the base of my spine, and he can tell. I move back, he releases his arm, and I lower myself onto him.

As I feel him inside me, I think for the first time: she could walk in at any moment. She could walk in, and we wouldn't even hear her. The Other Woman face to face with the Other Woman. I could just open my eyes and find her standing there, ready to kill. Like I was.

But then a voice enters my head, with Jacqui's accent: *What better way to go? Death in the saddle.* Now that would be a climax.

I look down and see Alex lost in the present. Concentrating on nothing but pleasure, his and my own. And I soon realize it's not just his kissing that has advanced. This boy can really cook up a storm. All the ingredients are there. The drive-thru experience of nine years ago has been replaced by a Michelin-starred banquet, so I just sit back and lap up the service.

*If only this feeling could last,* I think to myself, *if only this feeling right now could be sustained, preserved indefinitely. If only it could be bottled to be available on tap for the rest of my life. If only . . .*

When it is over, however, I see regret in his eyes. Still inside me, his face crumples and he starts to sob. "What have I done?" he asks, as if he genuinely doesn't know.

"You've just had sex," I inform him. "With me," I add, as clarification.

"I hate myself," he tells me, on his withdrawal.

"Boy," I say, trying to lighten the tone. "You really know how to make a girl feel good."

"No. It's not you, Martha. You know it's not. You're great," he blubs.

"I'm"—sob—"getting"—sob—"married." He stands up, peels the condom from his half-mast cock and dresses himself.

"I know you are," I tell him po-faced. "To Desdemona."

A cloud of panic crosses his face: "She could be back at any minute."

"She won't be."

"How do you know?" he asks, wrapping the used condom in a man-sized Kleenex.

"Well. Where is she?"

"She's, um, she's shopping."

"Window-shopping?" I raise a doubtful eyebrow.

"Er, yes. She is, as it happens." He disappears into the bathroom with the Kleenexed bundle in his hand. I put my jeans and top back on. The toilet flushes. He emerges seconds later.

"You said she's been doing a lot of that lately."

"What?"

"Window-shopping. For the wedding."

"That's right, that's right . . ." He wipes his eyes and attempts to regain composure. "And I believe her now, I really do."

There's a big question hanging in the air, so I decide to bring it to life: "Do you love her?"

He pauses. The big question must lead to an even bigger answer. After all, love is a complex thing. So complex, the Greeks had nine different names for it. That must have just about done it. Trying to contain it in a single, four-letter word was always going to lead to problems.

"I'm *marrying* her."

"Do you *love* her?"

He pauses again. Confused. Perhaps failing to realize that love and marriage are not synonymous. "If I didn't love her would I be marrying her?" The tone of his voice indicates that he may genuinely not know the answer.

"That depends."

"It does?"

"It does," I tell him with authority.

"Well, in that case, I don't know." This is what I have wanted to hear. Doubt, uncertainty. Not because I want Desdemona to get what, and who, she deserves, but because I don't want Alex to get hurt. I really don't. I want to protect him, but at the same time I want him to know the truth. Actually, now I come to think about it, that amounts to the same thing.

I light a cigarette, my last one, and inhale deeply.

"Let's go," I tell him.

"Why? Where?"

Two car horns screech aggressively at each other outside the window.

"Window-shopping."

# Chapter

## 33

I wasn't going to tell him. For some strange reason, I wanted him to find out like I did. In full color. I wanted him to find out by walking in and seeing and smelling what I saw and smelt only just over an hour ago.

But, as I lead him out of the flat, I am already having second thoughts. He might go completely mad. In my head I may enjoy the sight of Luke getting his nose broken, but in reality? I don't think so.

So when Alex asks, for the second time, "Where are we going?" I tell him.

When he asks, "Why?" I stop him and say: "You were right." A response which leaves him bemused, as if I am speaking in Latin. "About Desdemona. You were right."

"What do you mean? Right about what?" He looks at me with frightened, little-boy eyes which seem to be telling me he might not want the information I am about to give him.

"Desdemona *is* seeing someone else," I say, trying to take all the subjectivity out of my voice. He gulps, in an attempt to swallow my words.

"What do you mean?" Although he is clearly taken aback, he is also aware that there are other people on this street and so retains a calm face.

"Well, you said that you thought Desdemona is being unfaithful and I can tell you that you were right. She is."

"But you can't *know*."

"I've seen her."

"With another man?"

"With another man."

"But that doesn't mean—"

"Alex, listen to me. I've seen Desdemona, *your* Desdemona, doing what we were doing back there on the sofa with another man."

"W-what other man?"

Perhaps this wasn't such a good idea, after all. Perhaps I should have just left him to feel guilty. But no. Contrary to popular thinking, ignorance *isn't* bliss. Ignorance is a disaster waiting to happen. A time bomb.

"*My* other man."

I watch as the news travels across his face. It reaches his eyebrows first, moving them closer and corrugating the skin in between. Then it hits his eyes, widening the lids and dilating his pupils. The mouth is the last to go, falling open to the sound of a dropped penny.

"You. Don't. Mean?"

"I'm afraid I do."

"*Luke?*"

I give him a slight, single nod.

"No no no no no." His voice is a whisper.

"Yes. I've just seen them."

"Where?"

"Luke's."

He pauses, lost in thought. "But . . . we're . . . getting . . . married." He is not really speaking to me, but just voicing his thoughts aloud, into the air.

"Alex. Listen to me. If you were really wanting to marry her why did you say all that stuff to me the other day? Why did we do what we just did? You've known for ages it was never going to work out. And you've had your doubts about Desdemona from day one . . . I mean, *haven't you?*"

Oh please say you have. Please say I haven't completely fucked this up.

But I am not going to get an answer. I don't think he has even heard me. He's totally glazed over. I speak again, more forcefully. Almost with anger.

"Alex. You were getting married. Yes. And that would have been the Biggest Mistake of All Time. Wouldn't it? I mean, come on, Alex, for one second, just think about it. If you loved Desdemona as much as you sometimes pretend to love her, then why the fuck were you having sex with me when you hardly know me? I mean, not really. I've only seen you what, once, when you haven't been with Desdemona. I mean, think about it. I could have been anyone. It didn't matter."

This time the words have an effect. Although he remains conscious of the fact that he is out on a populated street in daylight, he is visibly close to tears.

"It *did* matter. And, for the record, I *did* love Desdemona."

I cannot help but notice the tense. "And now?"

He stares at me, as if through a fog. "I don't know."

We resume walking.

"I'm sorry I had to tell you."

"Don't be." He slows down and then asks me the one question I really don't want to answer. "If you hadn't seen them together would what happened today have happened?"

I quickly run through possible answers:

*Yes. Of course it would. It was always going to happen.* No, too much of a lie.

*No. Of course it wouldn't. There was no way I would have done that.* No, too much of a truth.

*Maybe. Who can tell? If you'd wanted it too.* Too weak. Wishy-washy.

Eventually, I plump for: "I honestly don't know. But I would have wanted it to."

This seems to do the trick. At any rate, the trick of not making things any worse than they already are.

"But Alex, are you sure we should be going around now?" I ask him, even though this had been my idea in the first place.

"Of course we should."


And what do we see when we get there? Just put it like this. Never has the phrase "It's not what it looks like" seemed less likely to be taken seriously.

At first, Alex does nothing. Nothing at all. Just stands there taking it in, completely separated from what he is watching. As if looking through a one-way mirror. And then, bizarrely, he starts to nod his head. *Mmm, I see*, he appears to be thinking, *so it's like this.*

"Martha!" (Luke)

"Alex!" (Desdemona)

"But how? How did you get in?" Luke is breathless, and I don't think it's just from the shock.

I pull my hand out of my pocket and jangle the answer in front of him. "You can have them back," I say, and throw the keys to him.

Alex, still silent, turns and starts to walk out of the apartment.

"Alex, wait!" Desdemona's face is a picture. "The Scream," to be precise. A swirling pool of open-mouthed panic. The sunny color completely washed from her cheeks. She is halfway dressed and Luke is not far behind.

I follow Alex out of the door, down the communal stairway, and outside. When he gets there he three-sixties and looks straight at me.

"What are you thinking?" I ask him, trying to read his expression. His whole face now seems in a state of conflict, torn between anger and something else.

"I . . . don't know." And then in an attempt at clarification he adds, "Lots of things."

And, just at this moment, I feel terrible.

What was I hoping to achieve, bringing him here? I mean, who was I really doing it for? Alex? Come off it, Martha. So OK, he might have been in a bit of a state back there on the sofa, but that hardly justifies it, does it?

Before he has time to give me a proper answer, Luke and Desdemona fall out onto the pavement, still dressing themselves. A man with a baby strapped to his belly is walking on the other side of the street, trying his best to pretend he is not looking in our direction. Which of course he is.

Alex turns to Desdemona. For one second I think he is going to Othello out of control, and strangle her on the spot.

He does not.

Neither does he go over and break Luke's nose. Instead, he masterfully manages to retain a steady simmer and starts to speak in song titles: "How long has this been going on? Can you fill me in?"

Desdemona and Luke answer simultaneously:

"A week." (Desdemona)

"Three months." (Luke)

*Three months*. Now where would that take us back to?

"My birthday," I think aloud. Fabric. Losing them both on the dance floor.

"Look, let's not make a scene," says Desdemona. A statement which seems strange coming as it does from a woman wearing only one shoe, and who has a purple bra sticking out of her armpit. "Alex, please darling. I love you. I *love* you. I love *you*. Please understand, Alex, please."

Alex looks at her with disbelief. "It really looks like it, doesn't it, Des?" he says, now starting to bubble over. "I mean that's what I thought when I walked in on you. I thought, God, is there no end to that girl's sense of love and commitment? She must really love me, I thought. I'm so lucky to be marrying this person who has currently got some wanker's cock in her mouth."

"Hey. *Hey*," says Some Wanker, rather pathetically.

"But Alex, I couldn't give a flying fuck about Luke. I love *you*."

Luke's eyes widen in disbelief. "You what?"

"Oh come off it, Luke, you're the most miserable bastard on the face of the earth."

"But you said—"

This is getting better.

"What? And you believed me? You really thought I was going to leave Alex for you—get real." As Desdemona's words hit him, Luke's face contorts with pain. "You honestly thought I'd choose *you* over *him*." I notice her voice. The accent has changed. Or rather, been recovered. I haven't heard her sound like this since we were in school.

"No. I think you wanted us both." A relative calm has been restored to Alex's voice. Desdemona hobbles forward, narrowly missing a dog turd. Her blond hair flies vertical on a warm gust of wind.

"Don't you see, don't you *see*, this isn't about Luke. This isn't about you. This is about . . . this is about . . ." Unable to tell us exactly what this is about, she turns and looks at me; her ice-blue eyes freeze on mine.

"Oh, I bet you're fucking loving this, aren't you? Eh? Aren't you? Seeing me. Like this. For once in your sad little fucked-up little sad fucking *sad* life you've got one on me." Strange as it may seem, I have never heard Desdemona say the F-word. Not even at school. To hear her say it three times in the space of five seconds therefore comes as quite a shock. "Well, well *fucking* done."

She pants, exhausted. There is a pause. Luke has his back to us, to chastise himself. ("O fool, fool, fool!" he warbles, like the lead player in an amateur dramatic production.)

And then, prompted by the look of hatred clouding her face, I proceed to give Desdemona the facts:

Fact one, she started seeing my boyfriend behind my back on my *birthday*. (Nice touch, by the way.)

This led smoothly to fact two, the breakdown of the relationship between myself and Some Wanker.

Fact three. She decides to marry Alex while carrying on fucking away behind his back.

Fact four. She has taken every single opportunity to rub my nose into the stinking fact that her life is so fucking fantastic and even asked me to be her maid of honor.

And then, fact five, she still keeps having a go even though she has completely fucked up three people's lives.

"And fact six, fact *six* . . ." I'm sure there is one but right now it is not coming to me. It doesn't matter, though. Five seem to have done the job. She is silent. For a second, it looks as though the ice in her eyes is about to melt away. I hate her. Of course I hate her. I suppose I always have. Just like she must always have hated me. Underneath all that shiny pretense of friendship. It has all turned out to be as false as her Sloanified accent and too-blue eyes.

As I look at her now—hair all over her face, Donna Karan T-shirt on back to front, purple bra now at her shoeless foot—I can see her almost as she really is. At the animal level. And, although I am still feeling hate, it is mixed with something softer. Not pity exactly, but something in the vicinity.

"It's over, Des." Alex's voice slices through the air and cuts her to pieces. "Not because of you and Luke, but because of me and Martha."

*What?*

"What?" ask Luke and Des at the same time.

Alex continues with a plausible stutter. "Me and Martha . . . Martha and I . . . well, we, um, we love each other." He then takes two paces across the pavement so as to be at a snoggable distance. He looks straight at me, winks with the eye invisible to our dumbstruck audience, and plants a huge red sunset kiss on my lips.

I kiss him back, in an equally over-the-top style, and move my arms around him in a body clutch. We are a deliberate cliché of passion.

"You *bitch*," wails Desdemona. "You villainous whore." (An insult left over from our Shakespeare-quoting days.)

*Aaargh!* I feel my head yank back away from Alex's mouth. The woman who didn't want to make a scene has now got me by the hair and is shaking me about like a demonic puppeteer. *Fuck!* It really fucking hurts.

Alex somehow manages to release me from her schoolyard grip. When I am free, I notice that a small crowd has gathered on the other side of the street, clearly under the impression that a traveling production of the *Jerry Springer Show* is in town.

"Are you all right?" Alex asks, with heart-throb concern.

"I'm fine," I tell him. Shaken, not stirred.

It's enough to make you sick isn't it? And from the disgusted expressions on their faces, it looks as though Luke and Desdemona are about to empty their guts right onto the pavement.

"Come on Martha, *let's go*," says Alex, grabbing my hand. Then as we start to walk off he turns his head and tells them both. "We'll be seeing you."

As we turn right at the corner of Montano Street I too look back, and Luke catches my gaze. He is just standing there, looking straight through a bedraggled Desdemona, asking a question with his eyes that I am unable to answer.

Once we have turned the corner Alex and I are still holding hands. I turn and look at Alex: his eyes are fixed on an imaginary horizon.

# Chapter

# 34

Spin the bottle.

When I was thirteen years old, this sequence of three words provoked only one emotion: fear. Pure and undiluted fear.

You see, it wasn't that I was scared of boys. I was, by this stage, completely fascinated by them. I would watch them, normally from a substantial distance, to see how they interacted with each other. I would look on with anthropological interest as they gave each other dead arms, played heads and volleys, and lassoed their lunch boxes into the air.

It was the kissing that scared me. Or rather, the snogging. I sort of knew about the kissing, but snogging—now that was something else. I'd witnessed it, of course. But no matter how many times I would see Desdemona lock jaws with her boyfriends I still felt unsure as to whether or not I would be able to pull it off. I had no idea what went on in that dark, mutual space beyond view. Between lips. So I was petrified I would get it wrong. Be laughed at. Ridiculed. Branded unkissable.

But then I had an equal fear. That I would die, aged ninety-nine, having never snogged anyone. Already, even at thirteen, I was in a minority. One of the last remaining Unsnogged, a

species slowly but surely becoming extinct in direct propor-
tion to the growing popularity of Spin the Bottle parties. In
truth, I would have been more likely to go to a *Deer
Hunter*–themed Russian roulette evening than put myself
through the humiliation of Getting It Wrong. But as I've said,
the thought of my ninety-nine-year-old lips resting in peace
after a whole lifetime of doing the same also cast a shadow in
my mind.

So much so that by the time I had got my fifth invitation to
an STB party, I decided to accept.

"What, so you're actually going?" asked Desdemona,
splayed out on her bed among her cutesy teddy bears and
Pound Puppies.

"Mm–hmm."

"First time for everything."

"Mm–hmm."

My stomach was in knots. Only two days and my fate would
be decided. I just sat and stared at the Athena posters on her
walls, trying to find comfort amid the black and white images
of biceps and babies.

"Are you OK, Martha?"

"Mm-hmm."

"You seem a bit nervous about something."

"It's . . . nothing."

She gave me her "I don't believe you" look and then
smiled, as she always did whenever I was in a state of visible
torment. "You're nervous about Saturday, aren't you?"

"No," I replied, far too quickly to be believed.

"Thought so," she clucked, with a teddy clutched tight to
her stomach.

"No. Honestly. Des. 'Snot that."

She nodded her head in the style of a doctor who has just
managed to identify a patient's condition. "You are scared of
playing Spin the Bottle," she diagnosed (correctly, of course).

"No . . . no . . . I'm not."

Then, and I can remember this vividly, she put the teddy

bear up to her face and spoke from behind it, as if the teddy, rather than herself, was doing the talking. She even disguised her voice, adopting the pseudo-aristocratic tone she now deploys on a full-time basis.

"*Martha Seymore, it has come to our notice that you have never snogged a boy before. Is this correct?*" She peeped over from behind the teddy to watch me nod a sad affirmative. "*It has also come to our notice that you will be forced to snog lots of boys on Saturday night. Is this correct?*"

"Mm-hmm."

"*And so, you are worried as to whether or not you will be able to Get It Right. Is this correct?*"

"Mm-hmm."

Yup, that's right: I had been cajoled by an upper-class teddy bear into revealing the truth about my snogophobia.

Desdemona threw the teddy aside. "Ha! I knew it!"

"Des. Please. Don't be horrible."

And then, just as I thought she was going to run into the streets of Durham with a loud hailer and broadcast this shameful truth, she did something completely out of character. She said something nice.

"It's all right, Martha. Your secret's safe. But why are you so scared? There's nothing to worry about, you know."

I watched her on the bed, combing her mid-length blond hair through with her fingers. Staring right at me, not saying a word. After about thirty seconds, just when I was starting to feel the awkward pressure of her clear blue gaze, she said, "I could show you."

"Huh?"

"I said: I could show you. How to kiss."

At first, I thought this was a buildup to another one of her cruel games. But then I realized she was one-hundred-percent serious.

"How?" I asked tentatively.

"Bernie."

"What?"

She picked up the aforementioned teddy bear. "We could use Bernie."

I looked again at the teddy. At Bernie, with his furry ears, his one eye and his stripy dungarees, seeing no more than a passing resemblance to Jamie Mulryan and the other boys who were going to be there on Saturday night.

"You think I should practice on a cuddly toy?"

"It might help you. Why not just try it? I'll take you through the steps."

I smiled. "But I might not be his type."

"Bernie's not fussy," she told me, only half joking. "And anyway, I'll go first."

"OK then."

Desdemona stood the lanky teddy upright in front of her and puckered up.

"Right, first you must make eye contact. Like this." She fluttered her eyelashes playfully.

"Is that important?"

"Yes."

"Why?"

"It just is."

"Oh. OK."

"Then, once you've done that, you wait for him to make a move and, when he does, you close your eyes and open your mouth. Very slightly. Like this." She brought Bernie towards her and kissed him with feigned passion, supporting the back of his stuffed, furry head with one hand.

"So, um, what are you actually doing? With your mouth?" I asked, with sincere interest.

She broke off from Bernie. "I'm following him."

"But he's not doing anything."

She then stuck her tongue under her bottom lip and pushed it out to make a duh-brain face. "I'm Pre. Ten. Ding."

"Sorry. Do you use your tongue?"

"That depends." Her voice was now back to the tone of authoritative tutor.

"On?"

"On whether he does."

"Oh. Right."

"But one thing you always must do is this." She slid her bottom jaw from side to side in slow motion. "And make sure it is you that always finishes first."

"OK."

"So. Now your turn."

She walked Bernie over across the bed and positioned him in front of me. "*Well hello*," she said, in her aristocratic teddy voice.

I laughed. What was with her? She was never like this. I relaxed my face and then went through the snogging method she had just taught me. Eye contact. Wait for his move. Close eyes. Open mouth a fraction. Follow his lips. Wait for his tongue. Move bottom jaw from side to side. Bring snog to close. Snog over.

But as my lips wrestled with Bernie's damp, matted face I realized that this would be nothing like The Real Thing. As I pulled my mouth away I couldn't help but notice that Bernie's one plastic eye now seemed in panic. If I had this effect on an inanimate, cotton-brained teddy bear, with an appalling dress sense, what would happen to the poor unfortunate boys for whom fate (disguised as a spinning bottle) would decide that I was to be their snogging partner? They would probably die on the spot.

"Well?" asked Desdemona.

"I don't know. What do you think?"

"Hmm. Not sure. Hard to tell." Her index finger rested on her chin to signify that she was deep in thought. Then her face switched into an expression of sudden enlightenment, like that of a cartoon character with a lightbulb in a thought bubble above his head.

"I know!" she said.

"What?"

"Why don't you try on me?"

"*What?*"

"Why don't you pretend I'm a boy?"

"Eh?"

"Well, you're never going to be able to do it right if you only practice on Bernie, are you?"

I distorted my face in repulsion. "I can't kiss *you*."

"Why not?"

"Because . . . because . . . you're a *girl*!"

"OK. Suit yourself. I was only trying to help. If you want to make a complete div of yourself I'm not going to stop you."

"But if we did that we'd be lezzies."

"Don't be stupid! We'd only be lezzies if we *enjoyed* it. Don't you know anything?"

"No. Sorry."

"Just pretend I'm a boy. It won't be that hard with your eyes shut."

"Um . . . um . . ."

"All right, fine. Do what—"

"No. OK. Perhaps I, perhaps we should."

She smiled and put her hands on my shoulders, in the style of a football coach pep-talking a new recruit. "Now listen. I'll be the boy so you've got to wait for me and make eye contact." I quickly looked around her room, at all the sentimental, monochrome images. The soft-focus muscle men cradling babies. Looking out, towards the viewer. Towards me. Watching us. And then I casted my eyes down, onto the bed, at the audience of Pound Puppies.

"I don't know if I can."

"Course you can. Just close your eyes."

"I—"

But before I had time to say another word I felt her lips on mine. And that is where the memory stops. I cannot remember anything about the kiss itself. The snog. I can *imagine* it felt weird and dangerous, but that is all. I sometimes think it might not even have happened. It did, though. I'm sure of that now.

Even though I can't remember how it felt, or how long it lasted, I can recall how it ended.

A parent's voice. Her mother's. From downstairs.

"Girls. Your tea's ready."

And that was it. The snog tutorial was over. We went downstairs, ate our pizza, oven chips and salad, and never said another word about it. Ever.

# Chapter
## 35

"I'm sorry. That's hilarious."

Jacqui is in a fit of laughter. And when I say fit, I mean it. Her whole body is convulsing with spasmodic giggles. She is having to hold onto the kitchen chair in order not to fall over.

I just stand there waiting for the laughter to subside, before asking, "Why?"

I am genuinely interested in where the comic value in finding out your ex-boyfriend had cheated on you with your oldest friend could be.

"I just keep seeing your face as you walked in on them." She opens her mouth and eyes wide in mock-shock, laughs some more, and slaps her thigh.

"Well, you know, at the time there was nothing funny about it, I can assure you."

"Oh no," she chortles. "I'm sure there wasn't."

It suddenly occurs to me that Jacqui is in her dressing gown. I look at my watch. Four thirty P.M. Now, I know she likes her weekend lie-ins but this is ridiculous.

"Jax." The voice is male. Possibly foreign. Someone I don't recognize. "Ready when you are."

Jacqui looks coy. Or at least, as close to coy as she ever gets. And when I turn round I can see why. A blond, blue-eyed demigod in bulging boxers has just stepped out of her bed-room, his pumped body looking unreal in the light from the stained-glass window.

"Martha, I'd like to introduce you to . . ."

"Stefan." Mr. Lunch-box flexes me a smile.

"Hi, um, pleased to meet you."

"Sorry Martha, duty calls." Jacqui makes her way back to her boudoir (as she always refers to her bedroom in the presence of male company).

And then, just as she is about to get there, I hear another voice, this one definitely foreign. "Vee wait on you, sexy!"

Oh. My. God.

The second voice belongs to Stefan's exact replica. Only this one isn't wearing any boxers. In fact, except for one silver nipple ring, he isn't wearing anything at all.

"Oops, I was not knowing you was having company." Although he is surprised to see me, he makes no attempt to conceal his manhood.

"Double trouble," Jacqui says with a predictable wink, all trace of coyness now vanished, as she claps her manicured hands against their identical buttocks. "You can join us if you like. I'm sure the boys wouldn't mind. Would you, boys?"

"No! Baby, come join us."

"The more . . . the more happy!"

"You know what," I tell them. "Thanks for the offer but I think I'll pass."

"Suit yourself," says Jacqui, disappearing into her bedroom with the Scandinavian lunch-box twins. Actually, maybe they're not even twins. Maybe she's just discovered the same DNA they use to make boy bands and she's conducting her own Frankenstein-style experiment. Developing a whole army of anonymous blond love gods from a chemistry set underneath her bed.

And perhaps that would be the answer. The perfect way to separate sex and love. Grow your own sex slaves.

Mind you, for Jacqui I don't think it's ever been hard to separate the two. Sex and love, that is. In fact I don't think love's ever been an issue for her. Not *love* love. Not the painful stuff that makes you wake up in the middle of the night in a cold sweat. She's stayed well away.

Two men at the same time. That should do it. That should keep it at a safe distance. None of the emotional hazards which can be found with the more conventional ménage-à-deux experience. There'd be too much going on, wouldn't there?

Bloody hell.

I can hear them already. I can *smell* them already.

I grab my denim jacket and head outside into the polluted West London air to clear my thoughts. I don't have a clue where I'm going. I'm just walking in as much of a straight line as possible. Past all the cozy Sunday evening houses, past all the early pub-goers and aimless, arm-swinging couples.

It's funny. I don't really know how to explain it. It just seems that London has reverted to its full scale again. Being with Jacqui the whole city had contracted to become a microcosm of itself. On all those nights out she made it feel like everyone knows everyone. Hopping from club to club, seeing the same familiar faces all over town, was sort of like joining the dots. It brought everything together and gave it a coherent shape.

But now, although I am less than a quarter of a mile from where I live, London is back to how it always was before. Completely disconnected.

In fact, if anything, it feels bigger than it ever did. Big enough to make you feel dizzy. And everyone has become unfamiliar. Not just those unknown faces walking by but also the people in my head. Jacqui. Desdemona. Luke. Alex. Everyone I know. Or rather, don't.

Suddenly I get the strange, but very real feeling that there are one hundred thousand other Martha Seymores in this city. They are my alternate selves, the lives I have denied myself or ruled out as a realistic possibility. I see them, in my mind, those who are swinging kids in the park, soaking in foamy luxury, sweating it out on the pavement. I have the even stranger premonition that these parallel lives are no less or more real than my own. I am living them all simultaneously, or at least they are all still options open to me.

Finding myself at Notting Hill Gate I decide to take the Tube across town to see the only person in this city I can honestly say is not a stranger.

When I get there and tell her about it all she knows exactly what I want to hear, namely: "What a *bitch*. And Luke—God, he's even worse."

"Thanks, Fee."

"But what about Alex?" she asks while filling Stuart's kettle.

"Oh," I groan. "I don't know. He, um, took it better than could be expected. But then again, he'd have been a bit of a pot-calling hypocrite if he hadn't."

"True," she says, with a sigh.

"Mind you. I suppose I haven't been much better behaved, have I?"

"No, young lady, you haven't." She smiles. Not quite her old, broad, childlike grin, but a smile all the same. If nothing else, my farcical love life has at least managed to divert attention away from her own heavy problems.

"So there's no chance of you and Alex walking off into the sunset together?"

I laugh. A defensive laugh. "No," I say. "There's no walking off into the sunset. That was just for Luke and Des. It wasn't real." I have a strange feeling of regret as I say this, but I'm not sure why.

"Oh," says Fiona, nodding her head.

"Where's Stuart?" I ask, suddenly realizing he's not here.

Fee mimes her "drinking a pint in the pub" gesture.

"Good to see some things never change."

Seated on the sofa, clutching a hot mug of coffee, I also find myself complaining about Jacqui.

"I'm starting to think you've been right all along about her. And the trouble is it's not just like I live *with* her, it's like I *live* with her. D'you get me?"

"Er, no. Not really."

"Well, it's like I've just got caught up in her whole life. You know. All the sex, drugs, and, well, more sex basically. I don't know how to explain it, I just sort of feel swallowed up."

"So you're thinking of moving out?"

"Well, no. I haven't been. Not really. I mean, I just can't be bothered dealing with all that hassle again."

By "all that hassle" I am, of course, referring to my half-hearted attempt to find that mystical Place of My Own.

"Yes, I know you can't. At least, not by yourself." Fiona, sitting in her mumsy jog pants and pink T-shirt, looks down into her coffee as if staring into a crystal ball.

"What are you saying?"

"Well, I can't stay here forever, can I?"

I look around the room, taking in the peeling posters, the pyramids of Stella, and the whirlpool wallpaper.

"But I thought—"

"No. And anyway, his mates will be back before I know it. So I was thinking perhaps we should get a place together, you know, like the old days."

Ah, the old days. It might as well have been a lifetime ago. Our first year in London. We spent the entire time singing and dancing if I remember correctly. Which I'm sure I don't. It couldn't all have been *Mary Poppins*, could it?

Before I have time to respond to her suggestion, a key turns, the door opens, then bangs shut. Stu clodhops his way into the room, scratching his face like a gibbon, throwing his keys onto the coffee table and cock-flicking his way to the sofa.

When I get back home to the church, I am hit by a wall of sound. And on top of the house music blaring at full volume, I can hear boisterous male voices. It is clear that a good time has been had by all. And here she is, the Good Time: Jacqui, sitting between the two tank-torsoed Vikings (now fully clothed) slamming tequilas like there's no tomorrow. Because, the way Jacqui sees it, there *is* no tomorrow.

"Oh sssssshhhhh! Ssshhhh!" she says, using her hand to wipe the smile off her face. "Serious faces! Serious faces!"

"You would like tequila?" asks the twin with the definite accent.

"No. I'm fine actually. I'm probably just going to crash. Could you—" I look at Jacqui and mime the turning-down of the stereo.

She gets to her feet (an action which takes approximately five minutes) and turns the sound down by half a decibel. When she returns to the table she has another shot waiting for her.

"TEQUILA!" she roars, before swigging back.

"Good night," I say, aware that my tone of voice has just aged by ten years.

"Good night," Jacqui says back. Or at least, I think that's what she says. It's hard to tell when she's sucking on a lime.

"This isn't working," I tell her the next day.

"Huh?"

"This whole sharing a place together thing. It's not working."

"Huh?"

"I mean, it's been very kind of you and everything. And I'll pay all the rent I owe you. It's just I think I'm going to have to move out."

"Move. Out?"

"Yes. Move out."

"Well, that's just great," she says melodramatically. "Just *great*. I take you in, I show you how to have a good time, I pay for you to go to Ibiza . . ."

"I know, I know. You've been very kind. You really have."

"I let you embarrass me at the most important party of the year. With your stupid friends."

What? Embarrassment. Jacqui. Not the most obvious word-association.

"Well I'm *sorry*," I say, before giving her a piece of my mind. The piece which contains all that negative information, the stuff which disproves her stupid theories. I tell her about how living for the moment is a self-defeating strategy. I tell her to move into the middle lane once in a while because she might be able to appreciate the view. I tell her a million and one other things too, because this is a very *large* piece of my mind.

"Have you quite finished?" she asks eventually.

"Yes. I have."

And then, as I walk out of the room, she bursts into manic laughter, as if I'd just told her a punchline to a very long joke.

# Chapter
## 36

One year ago. Mortimer Publications. Veronica. Raked upright in front of me. The first time I had seen her in the flesh. Or more accurately, in the bone. I was trying to get to grips with the position she was offering.

"So it's um, like an agony aunt?"

This, it transpired, was hilarious.

"Please. That makes you sound like Dear Deidre or one of those dried-up old grandmas on daytime television. This is the twenty-first century, darling, not the nineteen-bloody-eighties. *Gloss* is a magazine for the contemporary woman. You know: sexy, strong-minded, postfeminist. Women like us."

Women like us? My God. What a scary thought.

"So what am I then, if not an agony aunt?"

"Well, Martha, I prefer the term relationship consultant."

"So, um, what's the difference?"

"There is an infinite difference, Martha. An *infinite* difference. It is the difference between our generation and that of our mothers. Our grandmothers, rather. Well, both really. Our readers are confident, Martha. They know what they want, and by and large they know how to get it. Just as we do. They just need a little . . . *consultancy* from time to time. Advice from a peer, not some washed-out old widow."

"Right."

"I suppose ultimately it comes down to a question of morality."

I raised my eyebrows inquisitively.

"The generation gap is really a morality gap," she informed me. "The contemporary woman is no longer burdened by the morals agony aunts have always been employed to enforce. The morals which succeeded in keeping women miserable for centuries by confining them to the kitchen and denying their right to reach orgasm. No. Women like us know that all that is bullshit. We want our cake and we want to bloody well eat it too. Morality means fidelity and thinking of England at all costs . . ."

She was now talking as if I wasn't in the room, as if she was acting out some internal monologue to herself. I realized that, for Veronica, this magazine served a purpose beyond high circulation figures and advertising revenues. Well, that's what I thought, anyway.

Now, of course, I realize things are completely different.

OK, so here's the deal.

Veronica wants rid of me. That's obvious. You worked that out ages ago. And Guy? Well, that speaks for itself, doesn't it?

So I reckon that whatever I produce this month, that is it. Game over. End of story. In the immortal words of Samuel Taylor Coleridge: I've fucked it, big-style.

What this means, I can now deduce, is that I have nothing to lose. Next month I will be back to writing freelance for the likes of *All Woman*, *Take Five!*, and *Readers' Lives*. Cobbling together stories on miracle babies and evil stepfathers and neighbors from hell. Never again will I be called upon to nurse the broken hearts of the undersexed and overattached.

I don't care. For once, just for once, I'm going to submit the truth. Not *the* truth but *my* truth, which I now feel inside, burning like indigestion.

I wait as my laptop beeps and burps into life before checking the e-mails.

The first one I come to is from a Miss Confused, Newcastle, Aged 24. It reads:

*I have been seeing my boyfriend for six months and I love him very much. My friends like him, my mom and dad like him, and he's very good-looking. Our sex life is perfectly fine too. The only problem is I feel something is missing, but I can't seem to put my finger on exactly what it is. Sometimes my boyfriend just seems distant and sometimes we will just start arguing for no reason. I don't want to lose him and go back to being single but I don't want to carry on feeling like this. What should I do?*

Hmm. A tricky one. Bit vague, isn't it? I should probably click straight through to the next one. But then, there's something about Miss Confused that's drawing me in. This, I reckon, is a girl in need of some good advice.

I start typing.

*This is a common dilemma. You obviously love your boyfriend but retain certain doubts about your future together. The first thing you need to do is sit your boyfriend down and express these doubts to him. If . . .*

I look at what I have started to write. Advice as neat and tidy as the Helvetica font it is written in. Oh come on, Martha. Give the girl a break. I hit "delete" and start again.

*Perhaps the first thing you should realize is that you are not alone. Many women, and people in general, feel like this at various stages in a relationship. You need to weigh up in your own mind the pros and cons of your perfect situation . . .*

Ugh.
Even worse.
Highlight. Delete.
OK. Here goes. Two tears in a bucket, and all that.

\* \* \*

*You are not in love with him. You are in love with the idea of being in love with him. You are in your mid-twenties so you are feeling a load of pressure. From parents, from friends, from books, from magazines, from us, from me. You have been led to believe that completeness is only possible within the confines of a loving relationship, and yet each time you think you have struck gold, he turns out to be the tin man—full of oily charm and rusty promises. But that's not his fault. It's yours. For wanting him to be more in the first place. The only way you will be able to find happiness is to be honest with yourself. Stop comparing your situation to other people's and start looking deep inside. After all, if there's one thing scarier than the idea of being alone, it's the idea of being stuck in a relationship which is pretending to be something it never was in the first place.*

*Get out while you can.*

There. They'll never go with it, but who cares? That felt good. I could get into this. I save and click onto the next e-mail.

Oh dear. Oh deary dear.

I can't even bear to read it out.

This girl. This poor girl. I can't believe it. She reckons her boyfriend will finish with her unless she learns how to give him a proper blow job. She says sticking his manhood in her mouth makes her feel sick, and that her boyfriend never lives up to his side of the bargain. What should she do? I think a brief one-liner will cover it:

*Tell him to suck his own.*

A bit girl-power, but I'll stick with it.

Right. Next one.

*My boyfriend is addicted to cybersex. What should I do?*

Erm, let's see.

*Dump him. Via e-mail.*

And I keep going through my in-box like this, providing immediate answers to every single query.

*Am I too fat to find true love? Should I tell my parents that I am gay? Will I ever have an orgasm?*

Et cetera. Et cetera.

A near-endless cyberstream of neurotic voices.

And then, as soon as I am done, I cut and paste them together and do a word count: 9,432. Hmm. Might need editing down just a little bit.

So I go back through. Looking for signs of weakness. For any pambified, feel-good whitewashing. And find quite a bit to chop. Highlight. Delete. Highlight. Delete. Highlight. Delete.

There.

I scroll down the remainder. Not proofreading as such, but picking out key words and phrases. *We are all faithful . . . looks-obsessed age . . . you are not in love with him . . . blow job . . . your parents need to decide . . . friends fall into two categories . . . whatever turns you on . . .*

And when I reach the bottom of the document I smile at the final answer. The answer that contains more truth than anything I have ever written. A three-word response to a question I can hardly remember.

*I don't know.*

I. Don't. Know. Perfect. Isn't it?

# Chapter
# 37

Well, it had seemed perfect.

Now as I face the day of reckoning I am not so sure.

As I walk down Denmark Street my head is in something of a rotten state. Why the *fuck* did I send them in? I could still have stood a chance. The fat lady was only warming up her vocal chords backstage. The crowd wasn't even on the pitch. I may have thought it was all over.

But it is now.

Glendower House. Fifty meters in front of me. Looking different, exuding a strange, ramshackle beauty as it reflects the late-summer, early-morning sunshine. And I wonder: what is waiting for me inside? Stupid question. An ax-wielding Veronica, ready to make the necessary chop. The death of Brand Martha. The First Day of the Rest of My Life. And all that crap.

Here we are. Those overfamiliar revolving doors, showing absolutely no mercy.

"Morning," mumbles the miserable old codge who has had to spend his entire lifetime (and possibly many others) behind that desk. Monitoring the in-flow and the out-flow. Watching his black and white screen. Keeping track.

"Morning."

I wait for the lift and observe its progress as it meanders between floors. The doors open with a halfhearted ping and I step inside, press five, and journey up. When the doors open again I have to check that I am on the right floor. The normal Monday-morning drone has been replaced by a chatty buzz. What's going on? Has news of my departure reached them before it's reached me? I see Zara and Kat already in Veronica's office, notepads at the ready, and make my way over. Surely Veronica won't break the bad news in front of an audience. Will she? She'll dismiss them and call me back. "Martha, a word." That is what she'll say, just before bringing the ax down.

But she is not here.

Aside from Zara and Kat, there is only Guy. Mr. Floppy. (I'm sorry—that wasn't very mature, was it, for a relationship consultant. For an *ex*-relationship consultant.) Wearing black trousers and a black shirt open almost to the waist revealing a twenty-four-carat chest. He flashes me an awkward glance and then clears his throat.

"As you probably already know, Veronica is not here and, judging by the nature of her accident, she is unlikely to be here for some time."

*Accident?* Did he just say *accident*?

Guy picks up my expression and realizes I haven't heard. And then he tells me the following piece of information: Veronica fell off her horse over the weekend and broke her leg.

My mouth falls open. I picture her flying through the air, her face in panic. Hurtling towards the ground.

"So what this means," Guy continues, "is that I'm placed in charge of seeing the October issue through to publication. The buck stops with me."

As he says this, his eyes narrow and his teeth flash. For a brief moment his trademark vulpine grin has been restored to his face. He continues talking, his mouth keeps moving, but I am not listening.

*The buck stops with me.*

If Veronica is out of the picture, there is still hope. Perhaps only a glimmer, but hope all the same. I can still turn this around. I may have only one card to play, but it's an ace.

I watch Guy as he briefs Kat, one of the last remaining *Gloss* überbabes he has as yet been unable to get his predatory paws on. But he'd like to. You can tell from that gleam in his eye, from the way he runs his hand through his glossy mane every time she looks in his direction. He's just biding his time. Waiting for an opportune moment. Like he did with me. Like he did with Zara (when her father died, it was Guy's body-built shoulder that she chose to cry on).

All it would take would be one word to ruin his chances. Not only with her but with every remaining female in this building. One word.

I remain mute. Just keep staring at him. Ratcheting up the tension until the air's thick enough to slice. And then, just as he looks like he has finished with Kat, I pop the question: "Er, Guy. If you don't mind me asking, have you had a chance to look at my contributions this month?"

His whole face becomes flaccid.

"Ah, yes. Martha. I do, er, need to, um, talk that over with you. But I think it would be better if we had a private chat after the meeting."

*I bet you would.*

"Oh, I see. I just thought that this was an editorial decision which affected the whole of the issue and so I thought it would be better if we discussed it in front of everyone. But if you would rather keep it between us, then that's fine."

He looks flummoxed, unsure of what his next move should be. "No, no. It's all right. If that's what you feel is best then I don't have a problem."

My bottom lip swells with triumph. "Fantastic. So what did you think?" I tilt my head to the left and my eyes don't waver from his.

"Well, you know, Martha, ba—" Oops. He nearly said it.

The B-word. And in an editorial meeting too. Yup. No doubt about it. I've got him by the short and curlies. "The thing is, I think you probably know that we'd be unable to publish your responses this month, don't you?"

"Erm, no. I don't."

He shifts in his seat, smiles nervously at Kat and adopts a reasonable tone. "Martha, the responses you gave are just completely unsuitable and, as Veronica told you, you had three months."

"Mm-hmm."

He then tries out a few different sentence openers:

"Now, if it was up to me—"

"I didn't personally have a problem—"

"If *I* could keep you on—"

"But it *is* up to you," I remind him.

"Arhm, ahm, yes, but . . ."

I've got nothing left to lose. "The *buck* stops with you."

"Martha, look, come on, you can't expect me to publish this month's submissions and recommend the renewal of your contract. I mean, can you?"

I shrug my shoulders and puff my cheeks.

"Look. If I published your responses the October issue would . . ." He pauses.

"*Flop?*" I suggest, to his evident discomfort.

"Well, no. Not necessarily, but it may be detrimental to our profile and ultimately lead the circulation figures to . . ."

"*Shrivel?*"

His skin color shifts from mandarin to blood-orange. So this is the question. Whether it is nobler in his mind to let me off the hook or to risk the slings and arrows of an impotence slur.

"All I'm saying is that we can't risk *anything*. If the circulation slips below two hundred thousand it might be tricky to—"

"Get it back up?" I bring my hand to my face and let my little finger drop. A trace of anger flickers in his eyes, clearly provoked by my juvenile tactics. Kat and Zara look completely bemused.

"All right, all *right*. We'll do it. We'll let them through this issue."

"And the recommendation?"

"I'll, er, have a word with Sally."

"Thank you, Guy," I say, with a mischievous smile. "That would be really great."

# Chapter

# 38

Later today I am at Stuart's. Which, from the inside, is almost unrecognizable. There are no empty beer cans or computer manuals littering the carpet. There are no pizza boxes anywhere to be seen, the ashtray is gleaming silver, and even the airbrushed bazooka babes are in shorter supply.

And then, there's the smell. Or to put it more accurately, there *isn't* the smell.

Now this means either one of three things:

1. I am in the wrong house.
2. Stuart drinking out of a glass was only the first step on his route to becoming Mary Poppins.
3. Fiona is back to her old self.

Number one is ruled out by the view from the (now transparent) window. Number two is rendered highly unlikely by the fact that Stuart's spoonful of sugar (for his freshly made cup of tea) misses its target and lands on the kitchen unit. So, it must be the third.

"I'd thought I'd sort it out a bit," she explains.

"You've done a good job," I assure her.

She smiles in gratitude.

"There you go, girls." Stu hands us both a cup of tea. And I say tea in the loosest sense of the word (I think somewhere along the way it involved a tea bag and some hot water). He accidentally spills a bit from Fee's cup on her immaculately washed and ironed jeans.

"Oh, bollocky bollocks!" she exclaims, to my delight. She *is* her old self.

"Soz, sis," offers Stu pathetically.

"That's all right. Just be careful."

Stu slumps himself down on the settee next to his sister.

"I've told him," says Fee.

"Told him what?"

"That I'm moving out."

"I've had enough of her anyway," jokes Stu. "She messes the place up."

"Me too," I say. "I've told Jacqui."

"How did she take it?"

"As you would expect."

Fee nods and places her cup on the small coffee table. "So, um, are we definitely going to do it?"

"Do it?"

"Get a place together."

I pause for a second, to make sure I really mean it. "Game if you are."

Her eyes light up and her mouth blooms into a full, un-reserved smile. "So when shall we start looking?"

"Tomorrow?"

"Tomorrow."

"Tomorrow's good."

I look at her, as she sits upright next to her slouched brother, feeling an urge to protect her. And, at the same time, I realize this urge has come too late. But I will make up for it. I will try. That is all that matters. Because right now I understand that this is not an ending, or a return, but the beginning of something else.

Something beautiful.

Something real.

And as I get up to leave, to go back, to start packing; as we laugh at Stuart readjusting his boxer shorts, our words are left to decorate the air.

Tomorrow.

*Tomorrow's good.*

# Chapter
# 39

The rest of the day is equally successful. So successful, in fact, I even decide to give my mom and dad a ring before going to bed. Now though, as I dial her number, my *joie de vivre* is starting to wear off. The thing is, I've been a bit off with my mom recently. You've probably noticed. We had a small tiff last week actually, now I come to think of it. About my boyfriend situation. Or lack thereof.

So anyway. Better give her a call. Ten o'clock. They should still be up.

My mom answers the phone, breathless.

"Have I, um, disturbed you?" I ask anxiously.

"No"—huff—"it's"—puff—"fine"—huff. "We are just"—puff—"having a bit"—huff—"of an early night."

"Oh. Right. Sorry."

"No, no, it's OK," she pants. "I meant to phone you anyway."

"Oh?"

"Yes. You'll never guess who I bumped into today. In town."

I run through a silent list of suggestions:

The Dalai Lama?

Kofi Annan?

Marilyn Manson?

Brad and Jennifer?

"I dunno. Who?"

But the name she gives makes me jolt far more than any of the above would.

"Desdemona."

I can feel my face move into close-up as the room shrinks around me. Like Janet Leigh in the *Psycho* shower scene.

She lives!

"Arba-bada-ahm . . ."

My God. The last time my mom bumped into Desdemona was when we were at school together. About ten years ago. She doesn't half pick her moments.

"What did she say?"

Shit. She could have said anything.

She could have said I destroyed every chance she had of happiness by running off with her intended husband. Which I suppose in a way must be how she sees it.

"She said the wedding's off. But I suppose you already knew about that, didn't you?"

"Um, yes. Yes. I did. She told me about it the last time I saw her. Um, two weeks ago now. But I, but I—"

I'm finding it really hard to breathe. I must need a cigarette.

"Anyway," my mum interrupts. "She seems completely fine about it."

"She does?"

"Oh, yes."

"Did she, um, say anything else?"

"Well no. Not really. But I did get to meet her new boyfriend. You know, the one you used to go out with."

Oh my God. A horrifying image of my mother bumping into Desdemona and Luke in Durham city center. It takes every piece of energy I have left in me not to pass out.

"Are you still there?"

"Um. Yes. Still here."

"Simon. That was his name," she tells me.

"Simon Adcock?" I gasp, with relief.

"Yes, that sounds right. Ever so handsome. They said they'd only just met up again. While they were both back in Durham."

The feeling of relief suddenly turns into something else. Déjà vu. Simon Adcock. My number two. I picture him, as he was then, with that fixed, squinted expression.

"And Martha, you didn't tell me how beautiful Desdemona's become. She looks amazing!"

"Oh, didn't I? I must have forgotten."

When I wake up the next morning I lock myself into my room and try to get on with some work. I sit at the end of my bed hunched over my laptop, and run through the subject lines. When I come to one ambiguously marked "Glimmer of Hope" I decide to click through.

*Dear Martha,*
*I recently confessed to my long-term boyfriend that I have been un-*
*faithful. He did the natural thing and walked out on me. Recently*
*though, it seemed like he was starting to forgive me. The only thing*
*is, the small detail I neglected to tell him was this—the person I*
*have been unfaithful with is one of his closest friends. Now he has*
*discovered this fact for himself, with his own eyes, it seems unlikely*
*he will ever forgive me.*
*I love him very much and realize that I have betrayed his trust.*
*While there is still a glimmer of hope for our future together, I want*
*to try and win his forgiveness.*
*How would you suggest I go about doing this?*
*Yours,*
*Miss Perplexed*

So here it is. The Big One. The e-mail I have been waiting for, to test the strength of the new and improved Brand Martha. And I am ready, I tell myself as I click on "Reply," I am ready.

*Infidelity is a fact of life. We are all unfaithful all of the time, only some of us manage to keep our infidelities locked up in our heads. Some even manage to bury them in the unconscious, but they are still there. You see, we live in an age of comparison shopping—we always want to make sure that we have got the best deal. Our consumer society tells us every day that we should not be happy with what we already have—be it our mobile phones, our wardrobes, our bodies, or our partners. Indeed, magazines like this have traditionally served only one purpose: to make us yearn. We yearn for more, for the best that we can get, and sometimes we foolishly pretend that we can find it in the arms of another.*

*You made a mistake. You acknowledge that. You had sex with someone else. A someone else your boyfriend knows. Now that you realize that it was a mistake, the love for your boyfriend is likely to be stronger than it ever was before. You realize that you already had the best deal. The greenest grass is right underneath your feet. But you are now worried that it may be too late. However, you can also see a glimmer of hope. If your boyfriend really loves you he should at least, in the long term, be able to understand this. If he does not, he may be projecting his own insecurities about the relationship onto this, albeit significant, lapse of judgment.*

But then, just as I am starting to get on a roll, just as I am starting to *believe* in what I am writing and the implications it has for my own life, I stop.

I spot the subtext, which in this particular case is conveniently located in the "to" box. It reads:

*Miss Perplexed <luke@internetplanet.co.uk>*

Miss Perplexed? Miss Computer Bloody Illiterate Internet Journalist more like. Nice try, Luke. Nice try. I delete my previous response and start afresh:

*Sometimes there are no soft facts, just hard ones. And here is one to get used to: there is no glimmer.*

# Chapter
# 40

This is the first editorial meeting since the October issue came out and I realize it is probably going to be my last.

I don't know for sure if they will fire me. After all, people generally don't get fired from Mortimer. They get sent sideways, demoted, reassigned, or forced to quit, but rarely outright fired.

If Guy's still at the helm I will probably survive (for obvious reasons), if it's the V then it's going to be a different story.

Well, in approximately five seconds I will find out.

Five, four, three, two . . .

I open the door and there she is, standing behind her desk. Or at least, I think it's her. She looks so different. And it's not just the potted leg bulging out of her Incredible Hulk trouser suit, either. Her whole face has changed, her cat's-arse pout having been replaced by something not altogether unlike a smile.

She looks, what's the word? *Human.* Yes, that's it. She looks like a human being. Perhaps she's on medication. Do they prescribe Prozac for broken legs?

And there is Guy, next to her, looking his usual Guccified self, his trademark smug grin having returned to his face. Zara, Kat, and all the other *Gloss* girls are here too, each looking so

relaxed I half expect them to close their eyes and start chant-
ing "Om" at any moment.

They don't.

Instead, they wait for Veronica to start proceedings. Which,
for all I know, could involve the ritual sacrificing of Martha
Seymore, *Gloss* magazine's relationship consultant turned rav-
ing mad pen-wielding psycho.

"OK, people," she begins. "As you can see, although I may
not be in one piece, I have at least made it."

*My God. She's trying to be funny. I'd better laugh.* "Hahaha-
hahahahhaha!"

Oops. I think I've overdone it. The whole room is now
looking at me.

"Right, well," she continues. "This is it . . ."

*This is it: the sacrifice. Prepare to die, Martha Seymore.*

"This is it, we're at the three-month mark, and so we have
come to that make-or-break time."

*Break, it's definitely break.*

"And, although we're not out of the woods yet, I'm pleased
to be able to tell you all that we have made significant
progress."

I stick an index finger in my left ear and wiggle it about to
clear the tubes. I must be hearing things.

*Significant progress?* That can't be right. Veronica carts her
potted leg over to the printer and reaches for the printout.
"Now, here we go," she says, giving nothing away. "The
figures for last month show relatively little difference . . ."

I knew it. I'm doomed.

"But the projections for this month are up considerably.
Although it's too early to know for definite, we could be getting back to three hundred thousand."

Well fuck-a-duck, as Fiona would say.

"And the reason we are back on track is down to our secret
weapon." She then raises her hand towards . . . towards . . .
Bloody hell! Towards *me*! "Yes. You, Martha." She is looking at

me and nodding her head like a proud parent. I think I am about to black out.

"Me? Really? Me? Buh . . . I . . ."

"Martha, you've started a virtual marketing phenomenon."

"A what?"

"Apparently we are selling thousands of copies owing to word of mouth. Word of mouth about your column!"

"I, um, thought I was going to be fired."

"Fired? *Fired*? You deserve a bloody medal! I've had advertisers on the phone saying they want to pay extra just so they can be next to your page! Thanks to you, and Guy's courageous editorial decision to run with your responses, it looks like not only are we going to be in the clear, but we're going to be able to charge premium rates!"

Courageous. Now that *is* funny.

I'm waiting for the "only joking" but thankfully it doesn't arrive. Zara and Kat glare at me with disdain.

I gulp back and swallow my hat. "Wow, um, thanks!"

"And in fact," Veronica says, surveying the rest of the room. "This is the way forward. I think we should all take a leaf out of Martha's book and go for reality. Go for a bit of truth. The advertisers love it. There's no point carrying on trying to compete on everyone else's terms. Let's move the bloody goalposts. Readers don't want to aspire any more, they're fed up with it. It's not good for their health. It's not good for their sex. It's not good for their looks. And let's face it. It's not good for ours, either."

I haven't seen her like this since she first offered me my job. Full of missionary zeal. And that expression. Her Concorde nose up towards the ceiling, eyes fixed on those high-fire-risk tiles.

"Anyway. We are back in the game. So let's not blow it. We've got to inject the whole magazine with the sort of hard-hitting, straight-talking attitude Martha has perfected in her column. A glossy, girly magazine which completely undermines the whole founding ethos of glossy, girly magazines. It's fantastic, isn't it?"

She then briefs us all on the way forward and lays out her commandments. When she is finished she calls me back to run me through the details of my new package. More money, more space, more time.

And then she hands me a big question: "Where did it all come from?"

"Sorry?"

"The idea to tell the readers the truth?" She asks this in a neutral tone, with no trace of irony.

"I, um, don't know. It's just that I've found out a few truths myself recently and, you know, I just wished I'd known them all along. It's better to tell people how it is than how they want it to be."

She smiles and shakes her head as if I've just unraveled the secret mysteries of the universe. That is *so* profound, she appears to be thinking.

But even as my head is visibly swelling with pride I also feel strangely empty. In the peripheries of my mind I realize that there is no way on earth a relationship consultant, or anyone else for that matter, can even approach the truth as it relates to other people. And then I realize: I am about to face the biggest lie of all. And what is more I am going to greet it with a full smile and a firm handshake.

But hey, I'm getting paid.

# Chapter

# 41

Alex is, officially, Over It.

He told me so on the phone. He has also told me that Desdemona has moved out. He hasn't a clue where. Even if he owned one he "couldn't give a flying monkey." And, bizarrely, his tone of voice seems to suggest he genuinely couldn't.

"That's good to hear," I told him, because it was. I've been worried about him, I really have. He was getting married, for God's sake, and if it hadn't been for my interference, he probably still would be. Probably, I don't know.

"So. You still want to meet up?" he asked tenderly.

"Love to," I said. "Love to."

So now, we are doing exactly that. We are meeting up. At that new tapas place near Marble Arch. He is early, I am late.

"Sorry," I say. "Got stuck on the Tube."

"No worries," he tells me. "I've ordered a selection. All veggie."

I survey the table full of stuffed olives, *patatas bravas*, and Spanish tortilla.

"Great. Looks lovely."

Sitting opposite him, I immediately relax. It's his face—that familiar warm smile and gentle look in his eyes—that puts me at ease.

"I'm moving out," I tell him, as an opener.

"Moving out? From Jacqui's?"

I nod.

"How come?" he asks, harpooning an olive.

"It just hasn't really worked out. I think I've realized that we are two very different people."

"Right. So, what are you going to do now? Where will you go?"

"Well. I think I've worked that one out. I'm going to move in with Fiona. We're planning to get somewhere new!"

He stares at me and shifts his smile. He seems to want to tell me, or ask me, something. And, although he does ask something, I cannot help thinking there is another question on his mind.

"Do you ever think you'll get back with Luke?"

I shake my head while I swallow a mouthful of omelette. "No. At least, not in this lifetime."

He laughs and looks down at the table. We talk some more. We talk, openly, about how we felt when we saw Desdemona and Luke together. He tells me that he was surprised he hadn't gone "completely ape," and I tell him he had probably been numb with shock and anyway what he did, what *we* did, was the best possible response anyway.

"It was, wasn't it?"

"The looks on their faces!"

But although his mouth is smiling, and his voice is confident, his eyes tell a different story. One which has less of a happy ending.

And then he says, straight out of the blue: "I love you."

His sad eyes are still directed down towards the table and for a moment it is difficult to tell what is going on. Who is he talking to—is it me or the *patatas bravas*? After about five seconds it finally strikes me: it is me. He is talking to me.

"No," I say to my own surprise. "No, you don't. You don't love me." There is nothing in my voice. No sadness, no regret, no doubt, no melodrama.

Alex looks at me, bemused.

He wants to believe he loves me. I want to believe he loves me. Hell, even the *patatas bravas* want to believe he loves me. After all, it would make things a whole lot easier, wouldn't it? It would round things off nicely. If we could just eat up, pay the bill, walk out of this mock taverna with its sunset murals and into a new life together. Riding away on our magic carpet.

The only problem is: it would be a lie. And, within time, this piece of information would set itself free. Like it always does. Like it did with Luke. Like it did with Siraj. Like it did with Desdemona. Like it did with Fiona. You see, I don't know Alex. Or rather, what I do know isn't enough. I know he is a good cook. I know he likes Björk. I know he used to like Ice T. I know he never deliberately wants to hurt anyone. I know he has a high and well-deserved IFR. I know he always tried to defend me when Desdemona was on the attack. I know he can't be trusted.

And, deep down, he must also realize that neither can I.

"You know," he says after a very long time, looking strangely relieved, "you are right. I like you one hell of a lot, Martha Seymore, I really do. I fancy the knickers off you. You are a great friend and good company. But it is true. I don't love you. Not in the way that matters. I'm sorry."

"Don't be," I tell him, placing a supportive hand on his. "I don't love you either. But let's not go telling Luke and Desdemona."

"No. Let's not."

We burst into giggles, remembering their faces as they watched us seal our "love" for each other with that scene-stealing Hollywood kiss, and then call the waiter over.

"We'd like to order a bottle of red wine," Alex informs him.

"The house red?"

"Yes. That's fine . . ." Alex looks at me and remembers something. "No. Sorry, wait. I think I've changed my mind. Could we have the Merlot instead?"

"*Si señor*," says the waiter, in a very dodgy Spanish accent.

The wine arrives. We drink it. We talk bollocks. And, as the conversation becomes ever more testicular, I can't help noticing that Alex is becoming ever more good-looking. Not Guy Longhurst good-looking, but good-looking in an honest way.

The slightly podgy cheeks and tired loops under his eyes are uniquely attractive, I decide, framed as they are by those soft cherub curls. And his voice, with its positive inflection at the end of every sentence, is doing something to me inside. Something rude.

So when we have said good-bye to the last of the Merlot we pay the bill and leave. And as we stagger onto the pavement, raising our arms at the sight of a black cab, we know where we are going.

We are going back to his place.

We do not know whether this is to be the last time.

What we do know is that it will not matter either way. This is because, for the first time since we met, we are being honest with each other.

No love lies. No guilt.

In the taxi I hold Alex's hand and look outside the window. Everything looks beautiful. The buildings we are driving past are bathed in a warm orange glow as night moves closer. Alex presses his fingers gently into my palm, I lower my gaze to see the people walking on the pavement. Suits, skateboarders, a few remaining shoppers. We pass a group of teenage girls crowded around a wooden bench, laughing and playing with their mobile phones. All of a sudden London feels like the best place on earth. The whole of human life is here, bathed in the same soft sunlight.

I catch our reflection, speeding across a shop window. We could be anyone. Two sexed-up singletons in the back of a taxi. Two friends. A Couple in Love. Just another one of those million London love stories which keep this city moving. I look back and smile at Alex. He smiles in return, then kisses me on the side of my head.

As we turn the last corner everything seems clear. I know

that, whatever happens next, it will be on my own terms. It may not be the secret key to the universe, but right now, on the backseat of this taxi, it is working for me.

"Tell me where you want to stop." The taxi driver breaks my train of thought. Alex looks out of the window and realizes we are only a few doors away.

"Here. Here's fine."

He hunches forward to pay the driver and, as he does so, I get an irresistible urge to pinch his bum. And so I do. But the problem is, I think I pinch it a little too hard. This is confirmed when Alex's head jerks up in shock and bangs against the roof of the taxi. His hand, holding his wallet, shoots towards his head causing a shower of coins to fall all over the taxi floor.

The driver releases an exasperated sigh which lasts so long we have nearly picked up all the coins by the time it has finished.

"We're sorry," we tell the driver, as we climb out onto the street. And then, as he drives off, we burst out laughing.

"You've really done it this time, Martha Seymore," Alex tells me, trying to sound cross.

"No! What are you doing?" But it's too late—he's already doing it. Picking me up and carrying me over his shoulder while he walks down the street.

"Alex!" I scream, still laughing. "Put me down! I mean it, put me down now!"

But somehow he translates this as, "Slap me on the bottom so that the old man walking his dog on the other side of the road can look on in disgrace."

"Put me down, you stupid caveman!"

This time he does.

"Caveman?" he says, with a cheeky smile. "I like the sound of that." And then I laugh some more, until I see something in Alex's eyes which suggests he is about to be serious.

"Luke must have been mad to let you slip away." I don't know if he means it or not but right now I don't care. He sounds like he means it, that's the main thing. He leans forward and kisses me, on the lips this time. A real, grown-up kiss. And as we kiss I start to feel dizzy, as if the whole street is swirling around us. As if the space of nine lost years has been packed into a single moment.

The kiss ends and he looks at me again, as if he is about to be even more serious. "We're farther away than I thought."

"Sorry?"

"From the house. We're farther away than I thought. The taxi's dropped us off at the wrong end of the street. I must be a bit drunk."

"Oh," I say, relieved. "Well, we'd better get going."

And then he smiles that sixteen-year-old boy smile I have almost forgotten. "Race you," he says.

"What?"

"I'll race you. First one to the door wins."

I sigh and give him my "that-is-so-immature" face.

"OK, sorry Martha. Bad id—" But before he has time to finish his sentence I am off like a whippet, running faster than when I was up against Desdemona on sports day in the fifth year. I dodge past lampposts and a misplaced traffic cone with athletic ease, and my head cranes back towards the sky.

"MARTHA! THAT'S CHEATING!" I can hear Alex call after me as he too starts to sprint. I smile, still traveling at what must be nearly forty miles an hour, and don't look back until I reach the invisible finishing line. Until I have made certain my hand is the first to reach the turquoise door.

"All right," pants Alex, placing his keys in the lock. "You won."

"I know," I tell him, and follow him inside to claim my prize.